UNDER THE LINDEN TREE

KARI H. SAYERS

UNDER THE LINDEN TREE
Copyright © 2020 by Kari H. Sayers

ISBN: 978-1-68046-848-9

Published by Satin Romance
An Imprint of Melange Books, LLC
White Bear Lake, MN 55110
www.satinromance.com

Published in the United States of America.

Cover Design by Ashley Redbird Designs

1

MAN OVERBOARD

Nestled deep in the San Bernardino Mountains, about five thousand feet above sea level, lies an expansive lake, still and dark. It is bordered by a string of large, lake-front homes like a giant's necklace. Sloping upward behind these mansions are majestic sugar pines, noble firs, and tall cedars that hide clusters of rustic cabins. Even without binoculars, I can see it all clearly from the deck of our home that overlooks the lake, only a few feet from the water.

My favorite time of the day is before dawn when everyone is still asleep. I take my coffee out on the deck to work on my novel or to simply enjoy the solitude. It's very dark up here at night. The city lights from the megalopolis of LA do not reach this altitude. Yet if the moon is out, there's a glimmer and sheen on the lake below and even the smallest ripple becomes visible.

It was such a night in late spring that I sat huddled in a blanket with my laptop under the soft glow of the outdoor gas heater, a steaming cup of hot coffee on the side table next to me. Clouds were scuttling across the sky, now and then obliterating the moon so that darkness alternated with bright moonlight.

I was trying to work out the plot of my sixth mystery novel: Mrs. Luella Jones, a black middle-aged principal of an elementary school in Los Angeles, had been found lying face down in a pool of her own blood, brutally stabbed to death in her school office. My sleuth, Jule McCormick, an ex-nun turned psychology professor, had visited the school the day before. She returned the next day to retrieve a folder she had left behind. Police officers were everywhere, and when she heard about the gruesome murder, she offered her assistance. It was not the first time she had helped the LAPD.

I was deep in thought when the moon once again showed her face from behind a vanishing cloud, flooding the lake with light. Suddenly I noticed ripples on the water and heard the low purring of an engine. "What on earth was a boat doing out on the lake at this hour?" I wondered. It was too early for even the most avid of fishermen to be out. The boat slowed and then came to a virtual standstill. I heard a muffled splash as if something heavy had been thrown overboard; it was not an anchor, for the boat turned around and glided back from where it came.

The residents around here take pride in keeping the lake clean, and the authorities deal severely with people who dare dump trash and garbage into the water. I put my laptop down and walked over to the front edge of the deck. Leaning over the rail, I peered through the dark to see where the boat had stopped. I felt certain it was docked at one of the mansions not too far away. The lake is relatively shallow at this end, and the water was crystal clear after the winter's rain and snow. It should be easy to discover if something was tossed overboard.

A sudden gust of wind rustled through the trees, tossing some old leaves around on the ground before it swept across the lake like a ghostly witch on a broom. I shivered a little, half expecting to see the water sprite stick its ugly head up from the water. I was reminded of an old painting on my Norwegian grandmother's wall of a forest tarn with reflections of the moon and the water sprite emerging from the water in the form of a white horse.

I shook the eerie feeling off and went inside, checking on John Patrick, or JP for short, who slept in his crib in the far corner of our bedroom. I stroked his brown hair that was growing blonder by the day. It was hard to believe that he was over two years old. I looked at my husband, Chris, lying there so peacefully. It was almost impossible to imagine that he was paralyzed from the waist down. The terrible accident when a burning beam fell on him seemed so long ago.

I lay down beside him, and when I kissed his forehead, he stirred and mumbled something.

The next morning, the physical therapist came and massaged Chris's legs while I was in the kitchen making coffee. When the therapist left, Chris came into the kitchen with JP right behind.

"I told Emilio that I'd work out on my own for a while," he said in a matter-of-fact tone as I came over to give him a good-morning hug.

"Is that a good idea, Chris?" I said.

He didn't answer me.

"Hello, *mamacita*," Chris greeted Maria, our combination nanny, caregiver, and housekeeper, who was just coming through the side door.

Maria had been like a mother to Chris and his brother, Ed, since their own mother died when they were quite young.

"*El desayuno esta listo para mis niños*," she said.

I was constantly reminded how devoted this short, stout woman with a pretty round face was to Chris's family. Although she had three grown sons at home, she had now also "adopted" JP.

"Thank you, Maria," I said approvingly. "I don't know how I would manage without you."

"Oh, you're fine," she said and smiled.

"Did you hear me get up last night?" I asked Chris as we sat down for breakfast.

"No. What were you doing up so early again?"

I ignored the question. "Someone threw a heavy garbage sack into the lake in the middle of the night," I said.

"Where? How far out?"

"About 1500 feet or so. I was out on the deck when a small boat came out from the shadows, maybe from one of the big mansions on the north shore. It stopped, and someone dropped a big load of something overboard."

"Load of what?"

"I don't know. The boat turned around and went back."

"Damn these people. They come here and think they own the place."

"But I've no idea who they were."

"I do. A bunch of people from the East Coast or somewhere go in and out of the big Lundgren estate, you know the real estate developer who died a couple of years ago. The house has either been sold or leased."

"I wonder if I've met them."

"I don't think so. They're not around much. They come and go."

"There's a middle-aged couple with a little white dog that I see on my walks sometimes," I said. "They're not very friendly, but from the little they've said, I can detect a New York accent."

"Maybe. I guess it could be them."

"What's on your agenda today, Chris?" I asked.

"Not a whole lot," he said between bites. "I'll go out to the hospital and talk over a bid on a couple of jobs for them." Despite his injuries, Chris still ran his father's construction company.

"The doctor sounded pretty optimistic yesterday," I said. We had just been to see the orthopedic surgeon at USC the day before.

"Oh, I'll walk again. You can bet your life on that, but it's almost killing me to have to wait so long."

"Be patient," I said in a comforting tone. "The doctor said something about getting all your functions back when you can wiggle your toes. That was really funny."

"Yeah, who knew it was so important to wiggle your toes," he said with a short laugh.

He ate in silence for a few minutes while I got up to help JP finish his breakfast. Maria helped him down from the high chair and cleaned him up.

"Do you think I should call your brother and tell him what I saw last night?" I asked casually as I sat down again to finish my coffee. "Do you think he'd have time to investigate?"

"Maybe. He has a lot on his mind."

"True." I cocked my head and looked at him. "He has a lot of women throwing themselves at him these days."

"Yeah, he's a good catch, being the town sheriff and all."

My thoughts went to our nephew James, Ed's only son, who had lost his mother last year. His mother, Elizabeth, had been a math teacher at the high school when she developed a particularly aggressive form of breast cancer. James was a senior in high school, a vulnerable age. He often came over after school to do his homework and play with John Patrick.

"James can't stand any of them," I said.

"I know how he feels. Ed and I couldn't stand the floozies my father dated after my mother died. We always feared he would marry one of them."

"Who took Elizabeth's job after she died? Do you know?"

"I have no idea. Are you interested?"

"No, not really. She taught math. I teach composition and literature, and that's different."

After breakfast, I took Chris in his wheelchair and our German shepherd, Duchess, on a leash for a walk on the path along the shorefront while Maria took JP to nursery school. To my surprise, we met the very same couple we had just talked about and their little white poodle mix. Duchess and the little poodle—or whatever it was—started to sniff each other, but the wife pulled her dog back, and Chris barked out an order for Duchess to heel.

The couple looked innocent enough. The wife's gray coat was of good quality, and her short hair was blonde with a few fashionable streaks of brown, clearly not styled by our local hairdresser. She smiled and seemed friendly enough. The man's blue baseball cap and sunglasses, however, didn't exactly invite conversation, but to each his own. They didn't strike me as people who would illegally dump garbage in the lake.

"What a couple of snobs," Chris commented disapprovingly. Like everyone around here, Chris likes to talk to everyone. He was so completely different from my first husband, a taciturn bush pilot who was killed when he crashed his plane in a severe sandstorm in North Africa.

"Not everyone is a talker like you, Chris," I said. "And this couple didn't appear to want to carry on a conversation."

We turned around and strolled home at a leisurely pace. Pushing the wheelchair in silence, I wondered who was on that boat and what had been thrown in the lake.

2

CLUES

E d stopped by at lunchtime. The roar of his motorcycle and the short chirp of his siren announced his arrival. He cut an imposing figure in his brown uniform and high black boots, but he was really a mild-mannered man and looked very much like his brother—over six feet tall with short dark brown hair, glittering blue-green eyes, and straight white teeth. I told him about last night's incident.

"What time was it?" he asked.

"I don't know exactly…a little after three or maybe closer to four in the morning."

"Can you pinpoint the place?"

"I was standing on the deck, and it was straight out about 1500 feet, a quarter mile or so."

"Was it a big load?"

"Yes. It must have been since I could hear the splash. It looked like a big garbage sack of something."

"It might not have been that big. The acoustics are pretty good around here. With the mountains all around it, the lake is like the bottom of a cauldron."

"You mean like theater-in-the-round?"

"Something like that," he said in a matter-of-fact tone, and after a moment's pause he continued, "but it does seem strange. I'll put a couple of deputies on it and check it out. It's pretty quiet at the station today anyway."

He ate a sandwich with us before he left.

After we had worked out in Chris's gym and Chris left, I went out on the deck just as a small blue and white speed boat slowly circled around on the water at some distance. Leaning over the railing, I waved, but they probably couldn't see me. A few minutes later, the boat came racing toward our dock and two uniformed deputies that I knew only slightly by sight stepped out. I went back inside and grabbed my coat and hurried down the gravel path to meet them.

"Hi. I'm Megan Viets," I said. "Chris Cronin's wife."

"Yeah, I think we've met before," the older one said and introduced himself as Officer Kyle Wilson. He pointed to his younger partner. "And this is Deputy Richard Madden."

"Nice to meet you," I said a little breathlessly. "Did you see anything?"

"No, sorry, Mrs. Cronin. There's lot of kelp on the bottom, and the lake is deeper than people realize."

"I know," I said and sighed. I told them exactly what I had seen.

"Well, it couldn't be a body since no one has been reported missing," the younger of the two said jokingly.

"No, but it was something big and heavy," I persisted. "So, it's not exactly a needle in a haystack."

"Okay," Officer Wilson said. "You come out with us then and see for yourself."

We went straight out, and I kept looking back at the house to gauge the distance. We circled around but found nothing.

"Maybe if I brought my bathing suit and goggles and did some snorkeling around here for a while," I proposed.

"Feel the water, ma'am. It's still pretty damn cold," Wilson said, shaking his head.

I leaned over and put my hand in the water. It was freezing.

"I'll ask Mr. Cronin if we can take a couple of divers out," he suggested.

We headed back in, and the two deputies dropped me off and left. Chris was back and was working in his office.

On Saturday, many boat owners had taken their cruisers out on the water, some probably for the first time this year. I was tempted to take our own cruiser out and do some skin diving, but I had never taken the boat out by myself. People fell overboard all the time. It was often windy, and other crafts raced by too close and created unexpected waves. Some also drove their boats while drunk and created hazards not only for themselves but also for others.

Later in the day, Ed came by and told me a fisherman, a doctor of psychology no less, had caught a shoe on his line and turned it in for some reason.

"Can I see it?" I asked hopefully.

"You can come over to the station if you wish, but I don't know what for."

"Well, you never know. When will you be back in your office?"

"I'm going over there right now."

"I'll take my own car," I said. I grabbed my purse and jumped into my faithful Subaru.

Ed was already at his desk when I arrived but got up to show me the shoe. It was a new black men's shoe in the latest Italian style.

"The doctor thought someone might have lost it when he accidentally fell overboard while partying last night," Ed explained. "He said he had heard boats go out, but he thought that was before midnight."

"Did he find it in the same place?" I asked excitedly.

"It was in the same general area, yes," Ed said.

It couldn't be from a body, I told myself. It would be too much of a coincidence. This was not a mystery novel but real life. But, then again, it had to be from a body. Why would someone willingly go out on the lake wearing new leather shoes?

"I'm going to send out a couple of divers on Monday," Ed said in a business-like tone. "It's a good idea anyhow after the winter storms. Who knows what's down there?"

We slept late the next day, and I took my time helping both John Patrick and Chris get dressed before we had a light breakfast as Chris and Ed had agreed that we were all going out for brunch at the Wagon Wheel Inn since Maria had the day off.

Ed arrived with a new girlfriend, Vee, a pushy red-haired realtor in a flowery tight-fitting skirt with a matching jacket and black high heels. She breezed in exuding arrogance and immediately fluttered over to our fireplace that I had always thought looked pretty grand.

"It's nice," she conceded. "A large stone fireplace always adds to a living room, but it needs to be cleaned."

"There's a little soot left from a fire last year," I explained apologetically, without really knowing what I was apologizing for. "But we're not selling the place."

"The furniture is a bit too heavy and outdated, but the room is staged pretty well, particularly with the well-placed grand piano in the corner. It should sell quickly."

"Thank you," I said coldly. "And it's a Steinway by the way. Do you know anything about pianos?"

"Oh, no, but I think a grand piano adds to a room." She looked around. "It's a shame the windows are so small. It makes the room too dark."

I didn't answer, and she continued to prance around like a show horse in an arena, scrutinizing everything as if she were appraising the place and getting it ready for sale. JP and I followed behind her.

"We're not selling the place yet," I repeated, but she didn't seem to pay any attention.

"The gym and the little office are good selling points," she went on authoritatively as she swept past us and into the kitchen.

"And the kitchen is fairly up to date with high-end steel appliances. The bedrooms are upstairs, I presume?"

"Yes, and there's a master bedroom and bathroom behind the kitchen and the dining room," I said irritably. "You're welcome to take a look, but what has given you the idea that we're selling the place?"

I followed her out on the deck, where she surveyed the view of the lake as I tried to accommodate her the best I could for Ed's sake, but my cheeks were starting to burn. What was Ed doing bringing this odious woman over here? Had he and Chris talked about selling this place?

The front door slammed as Ed's son, James, came in. He went straight for JP and started playing peek-a-boo with him, walking right past Vee, treating her as if she was just air. He had grown tall and thin, with the same brown hair, but a little longer, and the same glittering eyes as his father and uncle.

"Hi, Megan," he said cheerfully when he saw me. "I brought my math book."

"Great," I said. "Let's go upstairs then."

We took JP with us and went up to the media room, where we sat down at a small table while JP tried to climb up on the couch and chairs in front of the big television screen. Finally, he dropped down on the floor next to his alphabet blocks.

No sooner had James opened his book than Ed came in. He was in civilian clothes today, but, as was his custom, he wore a voluminous beige sports coat that concealed his gun.

"We're ready to go to brunch," he said jovially. "Wanna come?"

James looked down and fumbled with his math book.

"Okay," I said. "We'll be down shortly."

Ed left us alone. "Do we have to go?" James asked pleadingly.

"Come on, James. They have good food over there."

He rose reluctantly and picked up JP, dragging his feet demonstratively as we made our way down the stairs.

Ed helped Chris into the front seat of the Odyssey van with ease. James strapped JP into his car seat in the middle section. James and I went all the way back, and Vee slid into the seat next to JP.

"I thought the weekends were busy times for realtors," I said to Vee, trying my best to sound friendly.

"Yes, I'm meeting some clients afterwards," she answered without turning around to look at me.

Wagon Wheel Inn is a popular restaurant located in the next hamlet. Not surprisingly, a large wagon wheel was prominently placed next to the door. The inside was dark and noisy, decorated in a rustic mountain style with thick brown beams across the ceiling, small windows, and wood-paneled walls from where the requisite deer heads leered down at us. The hostess guided us to a big round table with a red and white checkered tablecloth and brought a highchair for JP that we placed between James and me. We ordered grilled salmon, and I broke off pieces for JP, making sure there were no bones. Of course, rather than eating, he insisted on continuing his game of peek-a-boo with James. Chris was on the other side of me, handsome as ever, bantering shamelessly with the young, scantily-dressed waitress. I ignored him and asked James about school.

"If James wasn't my favorite nephew, I'd be jealous," Chris said good-humoredly as he turned toward us and put his arm around my shoulders.

"I'm your *only* nephew," James quickly shot back without looking at him.

"I know," Chris said. "And a handsome one too," he added more wistfully.

I pinched Chris's cheek and smiled encouragingly. It made me happy to see him have a good time. There were times when we were home by ourselves that he was quiet for long periods of time, with the glitter vanishing from his eyes.

Ed and Vee appeared to carry on an animated conversation. That is, Vee talked, and Ed mostly listened, or at least tried to. As we finished our meal, I pondered what the divers might find in the lake.

3

WHAT THE DEAD MAN SAID

The following day at lunchtime I saw a patrol boat on the lake again. I had been out on the deck to check several times but I didn't stay outside long because it was a chilly day. Other boats had motored over, out of curiosity perhaps, or maybe they were offering to help. The more the merrier, I thought.

I kept checking, but I was in the middle of trying to make lasagna while Maria was cleaning upstairs and Chris was reading a story to JP about a little girl who was so good that she had received medals for her goodness and was allowed to play in the prince's garden, which had no flowers because they had been eaten by the pigs. The good little girl was hiding from the hungry wolf, but the clanking of her medals gave her away, and she was eaten by the big bad wolf.

"Hey, what kind of story is that to read to a little boy?" I asked. I wasn't too pleased but realized that JP wouldn't be able to understand it anyway.

"It's from one of your books that I found on the bookshelf in my office," Chris said righteously.

"Stick to nursery rhymes for now, will you?" I suggested and picked up my old *Mother Goose* book from the floor and gave it to him. Then I went out on the deck again as the patrol boat was leaving.

James came over in Chris's old Range Rover that Chris had given him when he got his driver's license. Ed joined us a little later, and we all sat down to dinner together.

"I guess they didn't find anything today," I said to Ed.

"No, but we're going out again tomorrow."

"Were you out there too?"

"No, I had to go down the hill for a meeting."

"Maybe they'll have better luck tomorrow," I said hopefully.

"Maybe. They're evidently finding all kinds of curious items—shoes, jackets, broken cups and plates."

The next day, the divers started early. It was sunny and warmer, and by midday I saw them haul up something big and heavy. As soon as they had the load in the boat, they took off and left.

I grabbed a light jacket, got in my old Subaru, and drove over to the station, where I was ushered right in. Officer Wilson was sitting at his desk, but he got up and came over to greet me.

"You found something," I said eagerly.

"Yes, and it is a body," he said solemnly. "The coroner is on his way over. It's a male Caucasian, middle-aged, not too badly decomposed but bloated, which caused the body to break loose from the kelp, but the partially ripped sack also got tangled in the kelp, which prevented it from rising all the way to the surface." He paused and looked at me as if to check how I was taking all this in before he continued, "He was wearing gray slacks and a navy blue sports coat. We'll probably have to cut the clothing off because of the bloating, but we can't remove anything until the coroner has examined him."

"I'll come back tomorrow, if that's okay."

"Why don't you call first," he said as he turned and walked back to his desk.

"Thank you," I said. "And good work."

I told Chris as soon as I walked in the front door.

"Good for you," he said simply, although I detected a little condescending tone when he continued. "Now you have a real mystery to solve."

"I wonder who it could be?"

"That's for you to find out, not me," he answered coldly as he rolled himself into his office.

"Chris, don't take that tone with me. I would think you'd want to find out who it is too." I followed right behind him.

"Sorry, honey, but I don't have time for all of this. I have a lot to do, and this is really a case for Ed and his people."

I sighed and turned away. "I guess you're right."

JP and Maria were in the kitchen, where I joined them, and we set the table for supper. Maria had made Mexican casserole, her specialty. And Chris's favorite. After dinner and the regular routine of singing and reading to JP before putting him to sleep, I sat down at the piano and played some old folk tunes. I made a mental note of the fact that the piano needed another tuning again. Chris wheeled himself over to the fireplace and hoisted himself out of the wheelchair and onto the couch as he often did. He was remarkably agile despite his handicap.

"Are you happy, Megan?" he said out of the blue.

I stopped playing and looked at him curiously. "Yes, why?"

"I don't know. I don't provide you with any excitement."

"I have plenty of excitement. And what's all this about all of a sudden?" I walked over to the couch, sat down on his lap, and gave him a hug. "I love you, and I have a son. What more could I want?"

"I don't know."

I kissed him on the forehead. "Do you know how long I waited for this child?" I looked away. "I was married for eight years and couldn't conceive, remember?"

"Yeah, I remember." He looked at me. "Do you miss Robert?"

"No, he's dead and gone. We had some good times, and it was exciting to live in Africa and the Middle East, but that period of my life is over."

"We may not have any more children the way it's going with me."

"Chris, what kind of talk is this? Remember the doctor said that when you can wiggle your toes, all your functions will be back."

"Maybe you should have an affair." He looked down as if he were studying his hands.

"Chris, this conversation is ridiculous. Sex is not that important to me right now. Actually, I just read a study of women in their thirties who were raising children, and for the overwhelming majority their libido was low, sometimes embarrassingly low, for some who had a loving husband."

"I don't believe you."

"Believe what you will, but it's true." I paused. "If the tables were turned, I suppose you would have left me then?" I said accusingly. "That's not a very comforting thought."

"I don't know. You're a good girl. Too good for me." He looked at me earnestly.

"Like the girl in the story who was so good she was eaten by the wolf."

That put a smile on his face.

"Look. I'm not cut out to be a mother hen with a lot of chicks around her," I said conclusively and gave him another squeeze. "Ed has only one son and that seems enough for him. I know you miss your own little girl, and I wish she could be with us, but now you have JP and me. My friend Susie has only one daughter and is doing a great job with her but doesn't want any more. Cindy and Chad have no children, and neither do Jonathan and Cheryl." I thought for a moment. "What is Cheryl to you again?"

"She's my sister-in-law's sister."

"Yes, and a great nurse too. Jonathan and Chad have their investment businesses, and Cindy has her art. People today don't depend on children for their happiness." I was on my soapbox now. "Anyway, I have plenty to do with JP, and I think it's an advantage to having only one child, and JP has James too. And look at how advanced he is. He's already talking, not only in English but in Spanish too. And he's eating by himself, such as it is, and all of this because we have time to sing and read to him and play with him."

"And he'll be a good singer too," Chris said finally in a more upbeat tone.

The next day, I drove over to the station again. Ed was in his office and told me what the coroner had reported. "The victim was shot in the back of the head, execution style. We removed his clothing, but there was no identification. The body has been taken to the forensic lab in San Bernardino for pictures and further examination."

"Did he wear shoes?"

"No, just socks."

"That sounds strange. Do you mind if I go down to the forensic lab?" I asked.

Ed looked at me earnestly. "Okay, I'll go with you," he said finally.

I rode next to him in his black and white sheriff's car down the winding mountain highway. "Do you think we'll find out who that person is?" I asked. "There will at least be fingerprints if the body is not that decomposed."

"Maybe," he said thoughtfully. "There may be clues in his clothing, and we'll send out his picture."

Ed drove fast, and I kept swallowing to try to make my ears pop. I could barely hear him over the constantly crackling radio, and he finally turned it off.

"Maybe you can figure it all out," he said and shot me a quick glance.

"Well, you never know," I said.

I remained silent for a few moments. "Do you miss Elizabeth?" I asked in an effort to change the subject.

"What do you think?" he snapped back.

"Sorry, that was a dumb question. Sorry."

"It's okay," he said more consolingly. "James has sure taken to you."

"I'm glad," I said. "He's a good kid. I guess he wants to take a gap year and apply to USC or UCLA next year."

"That's what he says. Is that maybe one of your ideas?" He shot me another quick glance.

"No, but it's not a bad plan. He could travel and take some time to figure out what he wants to do with himself. He's still young, and an extra year is good for most students."

"What are your plans for the future?" he asked after a while.

"I don't know. I guess I'll go back to teaching. What about you?"

"I'll probably go back to school to get a PhD in criminal justice and teach at a college somewhere. That's what Elizabeth wanted me to do."

"That sounds like a really good plan. You have your master's degree then?"

"Yes, in criminal justice from USC."

"Criminal justice is a popular major today."

He concentrated on the traffic for a few moments before he continued.

"I majored in criminal justice because I guess I always wanted to be a police officer. I took drafting in high school and knew I didn't want to sit at a desk all day. But law enforcement today is a dangerous racket. We just hired a Russian deputy, maybe it was a year or so ago. He seemed like such a good candidate, and he speaks very good English. But I'm worried about him. He's trigger-happy. I was over at his house one day, and on a white stucco wall in his garage he had written down a detailed list of all his favorite weapons. 'That's quite a list you have there,' I told him. 'Yeah,' he said. 'And I own them all. Wanna come in and see my collection?' So, we went into his study."

"Oh, you mean his man cave?" I said teasingly.

"Yeah, I guess that's what you call it now." He smiled. "Anyway, he had quite a collection, and some of the guns were loaded and ready to fire. Crazy."

"Do you think he could be a spy then?"

"Why do you say that?"

"Isn't Russia still our enemy?"

"Who knows who our enemies are or what they look like these days? Anyway, it's not a question you can ask somebody, but I don't think so. I met his wife, an attractive woman. They have two children, and they all seem so Americanized."

"Then he's probably fine. I'm from the Midwest, remember? I grew up on a dairy farm in Wisconsin. And out there everyone, men and women both, owns a lot of guns, and they know how to use them too. I remember many of our neighbors out there, even older women, slept with loaded guns under their pillows."

It took us only about half an hour before we reached the town of San Bernardino, and Ed swung into headquarters, where he parked in a reserved spot.

Coming with Ed made it easy for me to go through security. The body was in the freezer, but an assistant rolled it out on a gurney and removed the sheet so we could see his face. He had dark, short hair and olive complexion.

"He appears to be in his forties," I said. "But I've certainly never seen him before. Where are his clothes?"

We were shown into another storage room where clothing was neatly folded and stacked on large tables. Both his slacks and his coat were of good quality, well made, and did not appear to be off the rack at JCPenney. They had simple labels with the name Franco on them.

"Does that mean anything to you?" Ed asked.

"Well, the clothes are tailor-made," I said. "And I remember a tailor in London by the name of Franco."

"That's a start," Ed conceded.

"That would be too much of a coincidence," I said, "but let me look online and see if there are other tailors by the name of Franco somewhere."

"The detectives have already done that," the assistant said. "And there is a tailor by that name in London as you say."

"What street?"

"Kingston Street or something like that I think they said."

"Oh my God. That might be him. As I recall, his shop was not on Saville Row, the street famous for the best tailors in the world. His shop was on a side street."

Ed whistled. "Now we're getting somewhere."

"Well, what do we do now?" I said.

Ed contemplated for a moment. "We have to call in the FBI," he said after a while.

"How long can you hold off?"

"Not long. It's procedure. This case smells of international intrigue."

"What would you say to me taking a trip to London?"

"You mean London, England?"

"I've been itching to go back to Europe anyway now that John Patrick is getting more independent. Maria is really a great nanny, and you and James will help out, won't you?"

"What will Chris say?"

"Nothing, I think. But I'll go home and find out. He doesn't think I'm getting enough excitement these days, so I'll tell him I've taken his advice." I paused. "Can you release his clothes to me then?"

"I am taking a big risk. How long would you be gone?"

"Oh, less than a week."

"What about taking pictures instead?"

"No, that won't do, Ed."

"You'll take the clothes to the famous tailor then? But how do you know this guy will cooperate?"

"Well, I'll figure out a way. I never had him make any clothes for me because he's very expensive, but I have some influential friends who use him regularly. I'll do my name-dropping trick, and maybe I'll have him make me a new dress or suit as well. I never really felt I could spend that kind of money before, but now my finances have improved."

Ed chuckled. "The department will reimburse you," he said.

"I'm not worried about that. I'll check my phone for flights tomorrow right now and let you know after I get home and talk to Chris."

I found several seats in business class on a nonstop flight to London on American Airlines leaving the next afternoon, a flight I'd actually taken many times before. I selected a window seat and emailed my friend Caroline to see if she could put me up for a couple of days until I found a suitable hotel. I felt certain that Chris would have no objections.

Ed checked out the dead man's clothing and gave them to me.

"What about the shoe?" I asked.

"The shoe appears to be too big for this man's feet," Ed said. "But then again, his feet are swollen, and it's hard to say."

"Somehow, I feel the shoe is connected to this whole thing too," I said. "Although I don't really believe in coincidences."

"But what about the tailor? Isn't that a coincidence?"

"Actually, I know a lot of famous tailors in Europe," I said with my nose in the air. "Remember, my first husband flew around with sheikhs from the Middle East, and I had to locate fine stores including tailors for several of them. There's a lot of snobbery over there."

"I guess JCPenney wouldn't do for them then," Ed said and smiled.

"No. Not even Nordstrom or Saks Fifth Avenue, although Saks in New York is up there as is Harrods in London and some other fine stores in Geneva and Paris."

"Strange people."

"True, but don't you think you find the same snobbery among the upper classes here too."

"Upper classes?"

"Yes. Don't tell me you believe we live in a classless society here in the United States."

"Not entirely, I suppose. But we arrest them the same, no matter what class they think they belong to."

"Not always."

"What do you mean 'not always'?"

I remained silent. I needed to go home and talk to Chris.

4

LONDON

I took a Lyft to the international terminal at LAX. "Why don't you use Ontario or John Wayne Airports? They have international flights now too," the driver suggested, perhaps dreading the mess at the busy Los Angeles Airport.

"I guess I'm used to the terminals at LAX," I tried to explain as I continued to braid my hair while checking that I had my passport and boarding pass. "I'm going to London, and it won't be that bad this late in the day." I had flown in and out of there with or without Robert many times when we lived in Africa. That is, when I couldn't get an empty seat on Robert's plane when he flew dignitaries to the States.

My TSA clearance was still valid, so I quickly breezed through security and had time for a drink and a snack before boarding. I texted Chris when I arrived at the gate.

Ready to board. All well. Love you.

He had been surprisingly encouraging when I told him about the trip. "Yes, that's a good idea," he had said. "It's time for you to get away." He had looked at me and held out his arms to embrace me. "How long will you be gone?"

"About a week. I'll stay with a friend the first few days. I'll email you when I get there. Texting is expensive internationally, and I'll also give you my friend's phone number in case you cannot reach me on my cell."

I boarded early. Business class provided more leg room and comfort, and as soon as I sat down in my window seat, a model-like blond male flight attendant came over with a tray of drinks. A dark-haired woman in her fifties came in right afterward. She took off her black suit jacket and handed it to the attendant to hang up before she sat down next to me. She wore a white shirt with leopard print on the collar and cuffs, her black hair pulled back in a ponytail. She looked at me appraisingly as if trying to figure out what this woman in teal sweats and a blonde braid was doing in business class, but she smiled encouragingly.

"I'm Megan," I said with a smile. "I'm going to visit a friend in London on short notice. And this was one of the few seats left."

"I'm Mary Jane," she said. "What a lovely ruby ring you're wearing."

"Thank you. It's a gift from my husband."

"How nice! I hope your friend is okay."

"Oh, she's fine. I'm actually trying to locate someone, or rather I'm trying to learn the identity of a man found drowned in a lake in the San Bernardino Mountains."

"Oh my goodness. Are you with the police?"

"No, not exactly, but I'm acting on behalf of the police. My brother-in-law is our town sheriff."

Her eyebrows rose, and she looked puzzled.

"And how about you?" I said before she had time to respond. "Business trip?"

"I work for the United Nations, and I'm going to a few countries in Africa to set up schools, or more specifically, ESL programs, that is English as a Second Language."

"Yes, I know. I teach too, and I used to live in Africa," I said.

Her eyebrows rose even higher.

"My first husband was a bush pilot and flew all over the continent and the Middle East. He died when he crashed his plane in a severe sandstorm in North Africa about five years ago."

"Oh, I'm so sorry."

"It's okay. It's a long time ago, and now I'm remarried and have a two-year-old son."

"I have a son too, but he's grown and is getting married, and I'm looking forward to becoming a grandmother." She paused. "Where in Africa did you live?"

"Nigeria. Lagos," I said.

"That must have been an adventure," she continued. "The Nigerians speak good English, but many Africans speak French as their primary language, as you probably know. And there are also many who speak only their tribal languages, so English seems to be the logical language to concentrate on now, and that's really what the Africans themselves want."

I agreed. "Actually, I'm not teaching right now. My husband, Chris, is a contractor, but he was paralyzed two years ago when a burning beam fell on him and damaged his spine. And so, I stay home and take care of him and our son."

"Oh, I'm so sorry about your husband's accident. What did you use to teach?"

"Literature and writing at Pacifica Community College. Now, I'm actually concentrating on writing mystery novels."

"How interesting. What's your pen name? Maybe I've read some of your books. I love mystery novels."

"Megan Viets." I took my purse from under the seat in front of me and pulled out a card with a list of my novels on the back.

"I used to be the academic dean at Temecula College, not that far from you," she said and handed me her business card: Mary Jane Goodwin, PhD.

"I think I've heard your name." I paused. "The murder victim in my current book is or was I guess, a principal, but an unpopular one, a mean one really, hated by most, and many truly had cause to pick up a knife and kill her."

My seatmate busied herself with her pillow and a blanket as if she were afraid I was going to tell her the whole plot.

"What countries in Africa will you be visiting?" I asked in an effort to allay her fears.

"Togo and Chad to start with and perhaps Mali," she said. "And you probably even know where they are."

"Yes, I do. I haven't been there, but I know they are very poor countries." I looked at her. "A good friend of mine is in the Democratic Republic of Congo. His name is Dr. Frederic Pagel, and he's in the carbon offset trade business. You know, where countries like Germany pay people not to cut down valuable trees. He used to teach global studies at our school. Maybe you'll run into him," I said and chuckled. "It's a small world."

More drinks came and then supper was served. We commiserated on the state of education, college students' inability to write, their absenteeism, the proliferation of gun violence and terrorism, until the flight attendants turned off the cabin lights, and we decided to go to sleep.

Immigration at Heathrow Airport was efficient and quick. I called Caroline and told her I'd take the "tube" and a taxi to her house and probably be there a little before noon.

The underground goes right into the airport at Heathrow. I got some English pounds from the ATM machine and took the train to Paddington and from there a black London taxi. It was raining, and I realized that I had forgotten to bring an umbrella.

The traffic was horrendous as usual, but the cab driver skillfully maneuvered through the busy streets lined with monotonous row houses only separated from the traffic by the sidewalk.

Caroline came down the front steps of her brick house in a raincoat and boots, carrying an umbrella. She came all the way out to the curb, opened the cab door, and handed me a second umbrella. "Hi, Megan," she said quickly. "Sorry about the awful weather we're having this spring. Not like the sunny shores of Nigeria." She smiled and gave me a kiss on the cheek.

I had met Caroline in Lagos at another expatriate's house, and we had kept in touch. She had even come to see me right after my first husband, Robert, died. A couple of years older than me, she was a good-looking woman even in the rain—tall, with short brown hair, a beautiful complexion, and sharp, intelligent eyes, the kind of woman people instantly admired and were drawn to because she was personable and easygoing and never took herself too seriously, always game for fun and adventure.

I gave the driver a bill, hoping he would give me correct change while Caroline said something flippant that I didn't quite catch to the cab driver. He laughed, and she grabbed my suitcase off the cab floor. I took my carry-on, and we climbed the few stairs to the solid dark blue front door with a shiny brass knocker. Although the outside looked dreary, the inside was elegant. Caroline stored our umbrellas in the umbrella receptacle and set my bags down in the hallway. On the right was a formal sitting room furnished in expensive-looking Queen Anne furniture. On the left was a spacious office.

"We'll take your things upstairs later," Caroline suggested. "Come downstairs and have a hot cup of tea first."

Downstairs was a modern kitchen, a spacious dining room, and a cozy sitting room with a glass door leading out to a small garden. Her big long-haired gray cat, Basil, met us. "Oh, you still have your cat, I see," I said.

"Yes, but he's getting old, and he is half blind."

"I'm sorry."

"Oh, he's okay," she said unsentimentally. She was a practical woman. "Richard is in the country, so we have the whole house to ourselves."

Richard was her husband. He had the honorable title of peer. "He's in the book," as Caroline would say, the titled, privileged class. He was also an antiquarian bookseller and was involved in some way with the British Museum. It was in that capacity that he'd been in Nigeria when Robert and I lived there.

"So, what's all this about a murder case?" Caroline inquired. "Does it have something to do with your next book?"

"Well, actually, I thought I should try to be the investigator myself this time and solve a real case instead of inventing one for my sleuth, Jule McCormick."

Caroline looked at me and smiled indulgently as she handed me a cup of steaming tea and what the English call a biscuit.

"You've used the tailor Franco, right?" I asked.

"Yes. Why?"

"The clothes the murder victim was wearing were made by Franco according to their labels. I need to take the clothes to him and see if he remembers the murdered man. I have a photograph of him in my carry-on too."

"Splendid. Do you want to go right now?"

"No, can we wait till tomorrow?"

"Fine, but we should take a walk to keep you awake. I need to take some flowers to a sick friend at St. Thomas' Hospital. Are you up for a walk down to the river?"

"That's a great idea," I agreed.

We finished our tea, and Caroline helped carry my suitcase upstairs to the guestroom, decorated in a cat motif with a big cat in the center of the bedspread, two cat bed-stand lamps on either side of the bed, and a cat rug.

"I better not look at that comfortable bed too long, or I'll fall asleep," I said jokingly.

"So, you have a new husband and a son now," Caroline said. "Do you have recent pictures?"

I took out my phone and showed her a few.

"They're a handsome pair," was her quiet response. "The little one has grown since the last pictures you sent."

Richard was more than ten years older than she was, and they had no children, probably by choice.

We grabbed our umbrellas and walked outside. The rain had stopped, but it was still cloudy and foggy.

"And how did you get permission to take the clothes off the drowned man's body and bring them all the way to London?"

"Chris's brother is the town sheriff, and since no one had been reported missing, and there was no identification of any kind, he gave me a week to come up with something. I'd better come through."

We talked about our time in Africa, common acquaintances, and how we longed to go back.

The long walk did me good. When we returned to the house, I called Chris. He picked up after only a few rings. "Hi, Chris. I'm safely at my friend's house in London. How's everything back there?"

"Great. We have just gotten up and are getting ready for breakfast."

"It's evening here, and we just returned from a walk, and I'm dead tired. I slept a little on the flight, but not much."

"I'll put the speakerphone on. Here's JP."

"Mommy in London," he said clearly and giggled.

"I told him where you were," Chris explained, "and he evidently thinks it's important because he keeps repeating it." He paused, and I heard JP in the background. "Anyway, get some rest, and we'll talk tomorrow. I love you."

"Love you too," I said.

As soon as my head hit the pillow, I fell fast asleep.

5

VISIT TO THE TAILOR

When I finally woke up, the sun was peeking through cracks in the window shades. Caroline was already up, and after a quick breakfast of toast and tea, I put the dead man's clothing in a plastic sack. We made our way to the tube station and took the underground to a station close to Kingston Street. Caroline took it as a matter of course that she should come along. I was very happy for the company because I knew she had used Franco the tailor in the past, and he might be more willing to talk to her.

Franco's shop was on the second floor, which the British call the first floor, of an old building. There was no lift, so we climbed the worn wooden staircase and entered an expansive room with large wooden tables covered with heavy bolts of material. Along the back wall sat men and women at their industrial sewing machines.

A small gray-haired man with gold-rimmed glasses and a worn tape measure around his neck approached us.

"Good morning, ladies. How can I be of service today?" he said in a charming Italian accent.

"How do you do, Franco," Caroline answered. "You probably don't remember me, but you've made some things for me in the past." She looked at me. "This my American friend Megan Viets from California. She's writing a book." She paused and then added, "I'm Caroline Styles."

"Oh, yes, I remember. Lady Caroline, isn't it?"

Caroline smiled benevolently. "I had a dress made here a couple of years ago."

Before she could continue, Franco interrupted her, "I remember. A silk dress with cats."

"Brilliant," Caroline said, and we all laughed.

"You have a good memory," I said as I placed the plastic bag on the table nearest me and retrieved the picture from my purse.

"What kind of books do you write?" Franco asked politely.

"Mysteries," I said. "And I was hoping you could make a nice business suit for me to wear to my book signings."

"My pleasure, madam. Do you have any particular color or material in mind?"

"Yes, I do," I said and paused. "But before we get to that, I'd like to show you some clothes you made for this man." I showed him the picture. "Do you remember him?"

His jaw dropped, and he looked straight at me.

Caroline came to the rescue. "Franco, Miss Viets is trying to solve a real-life mystery that she will use as a springboard for her next novel."

I carefully removed the sports coat and trousers from the bag. "Do you remember making these?" I asked hopefully.

He shook his head slowly. "Why do you want to know?"

"The man is dead," I said and bowed my head.

"What happened to him?"

"He was murdered and dropped into a lake one night, and I happened to witness it. The sheriff fished him out of the lake the next day, but he had no identification other than the label on his clothes."

"*Gesù santo, Maria, e Giuseppe.* Son of God Almighty," he muttered under his breath in half Italian and half English and crossed himself quickly. "I'm just a simple tailor. I don't want to get involved with the police. I make clothes for anybody who pays, and he and his friends pay me well. They also pay me to shut my mouth." His words poured out as he looked down and twisted the well-worn measuring tape.

"I'm not from the police," I said calmly. "And you will not be involved with any police department. I'm working with a sheriff in San Bernardino, California, as a private citizen." I tried to sound reassuring. "This man has not committed a crime as far as I know. He's a victim of a crime, and I'd like to find out who his killer is. Do you remember his name?"

27

"I think it was Bandini, but that may not be his real name," he said more calmly. "I can look him up."

He walked over to his cluttered desk and opened an old-fashioned accounting ledger. Caroline was examining some big rolls of material.

"His name was Aldo Bandini," he said as he turned toward me.

"Did he give you an address?'

"No, but my assistant sent two suits, some shirts that my daughter makes, and several coats and pairs of slacks to this address in New York."

I quickly got out my phone and entered the address in my notes. "Thanks a million, Franco." I was ready to give him a hug.

"You look like a nice lady," he said thoughtfully. "Maybe this is something you don't want to get involved in."

"I'm not getting involved. The guy is dead, and I'd just like to find out who he is, or I guess was, and who killed him." I paused and smiled. "And now, how about making a nice suit for me?"

He showed me some bolts of fine wool gabardine in plain black and navy blue with faint stripes. I chose the navy, and Franco showed me a variety of styles. Caroline came over and helped me choose, and Franco started taking my measurements. I offered him a deposit, but he declined.

"I'll call you at Lady Caroline's for the first fitting tomorrow or the next day."

I gave him my cell phone number and email address as well. Before we said good-bye, I made sure I had the clothes in the bag and the picture in my purse once more. Then we made our way down the stairs.

"Unbelievable," Caroline said excitedly as we walked down the sidewalk toward the underground. "What will you do next?"

"I don't know. I guess I'll go to New York and look up the address Franco gave me and ask for Aldo Bandini."

"But Franco said that may not be his real name."

"I know, but it's a start. And who knows? Something else may crop up."

"Do you want to stop by Scotland Yard?"

I shot her a quick glance to see if she was serious. "You mean *the* Scotland Yard?" I said incredulously.

"Yes, I know a couple of policemen there. Do you remember Percy Simmons who was out in Nigeria training the local police force when we were out there?"

"Vaguely. Is he with Scotland Yard now?"

"Yes. We can just walk down Whitehall and toward the Embankment. It's only a few blocks."

"Do you think he will take us seriously?" I said doubtfully.

"Why not?"

"Well, I guess it can't hurt."

Lady Caroline was not one to be intimidated by names and fancy titles.

"We'll tell him that we just wanted to stop by and say hello since you remember him from your time in Africa."

The venerable, large and imposing brick complex soon appeared in front of us. "It's quite an impressive building," I said admiringly.

At the gate, Caroline announced her name to a female officer and told her we had come to see Commissioner Percy Simmons. The officer ushered us through security and gave us directions to his office. We walked through a maze of endless corridors and climbed stone stairs to the third floor and more winding corridors. I wasn't sure we'd be able to find our way out again.

Commissioner Simmons was in a meeting, the meticulously dressed receptionist told us. Not a hair was out of place. "Would you care to wait?" she said, and without waiting for a reply, showed us into a waiting room. A large portrait of Queen Elizabeth II peered down at us from the wall facing the entrance. Smaller portraits of other members of the royal family decorated the other walls. Otherwise, the room looked rather plain, and no one else was waiting. As we sat down on the plain aluminum tube chairs, I looked at Caroline, and she looked at me.

"What are we doing here, Caroline?" I asked. "This is the famous Scotland Yard."

We both started laughing hysterically.

"Let me tell you, Megan, that after attending a tea with the Queen at Buckingham Palace a couple of times with a bunch of old women from who knows where, nothing impresses me any longer."

The receptionist peeked in and told us that the commissioner would see us now. She led the way into a spacious office with dark paneled walls and an enormous mahogany desk, behind which sat Commissioner Simmons, a large, middle-aged man with a fleshy face and bushy eyebrows. Behind him was another portrait of the Queen. He rose as we entered and came around his desk to greet us. "Hello, Caroline," he said simply as he gave her a quick peck on the cheek. "What brings you here today?"

"Hello, Percy. Sorry to disturb you, but do you remember Megan Viets from Lagos? She and her husband were living in Nigeria at the time we were there. He was a bush pilot who unfortunately was killed when his small plane crashed."

"Yes, I remember," he said, untruthfully I presumed.

"Good to see you again," he said in a surprisingly soft voice. "Are you still living in Africa?"

"No, I'm back in California now. My husband's plane crashed during one of those terrible sandstorms in the Sahara Desert. After he died, I moved back to the States."

"Yes, I do remember that now. I'm sorry."

"It's a long time ago now, almost five years, and I have remarried."

"Megan is a mystery writer who's working on a real murder case," Caroline explained.

Commissioner Simmons' eyebrows rose as he looked at Caroline and then at me. I gave him a summary of the case as best I could and described how we had taken the clothes the murder victim had worn to Franco the tailor, whose labels were on the sports coat and slacks. "Here's a picture," I said and showed it to him. "Franco identified the man as Aldo Bandini, but I understood that might not be his real name. Any clues?"

"No, but I can scan it and see what comes up." He took the picture and called his secretary. He gave her instructions on what to do, and she left. "And what is your connection to all of this?"

"My brother-in-law is a sheriff in San Bernardino, and I'm working with him unofficially. I witnessed the crime, or at least the dumping of the body, and identified the tailor who had made the clothes."

"Good detective work," he said and smiled.

"Franco reported that he had shipped the clothes to this address in New York." I showed him the address on my phone. "I thought I'd stop there on my way home to see who lives there and if they knew the victim."

"We can look it up on the computer," he suggested, and he sounded interested. He punched in the address, and a big house on Long Island came up.

"Wow!" I exclaimed. "Whoever lives there is no pauper."

"It's also an area where some known Mafia bosses live, although that doesn't mean anything. Franco is not a tailor for the poor, is he?" He paused and looked more closely at the computer screen. "The registered owner is listed as Giovanni Moravia."

I wrote down the name. It sounded familiar, so I quickly googled it. "That's the birth name of the famous Italian novelist Alberto Moravia," I said. "I wonder if they're related." But my comment was met with blank stares.

"Megan teaches literature," Caroline said apologetically.

We thanked the commissioner for his help, and I gave him my phone number, email, as well as Ed's contact information.

"I'll let you know if I hear anything," he said encouragingly.

All three of us talked some more about Africa and how we missed the expatriate lifestyle. We finally said good-bye, and after a few wrong turns we found our way out again.

"That was an impressive visit," I said. "How about we grab a bite to eat? My treat." I looked around to orient myself as to where we were exactly. "Do you remember that Thai restaurant that I seem to recall was located right around the corner from Leicester Square? That's not too far from here, is it?"

"No, I believe it's still there, and it's not too far. Then I think you might want to see a play. Am I right?"

"Yes. What a great idea! Let's check out what's playing while we eat."

Thirty-Nine Steps was still on, and neither of us had seen it. The matinee started at 3:00 p.m. Perfect timing. Not surprisingly, it was well done and entertaining—a zany, fast-paced mix of a Hitchcock mystery and a spy novel with a dash of Monty Python and some old-fashioned romance.

6
_____

GOOD-BYE TO LONDON

After we returned home later that evening, I went up to my bedroom and called Chris. It was still morning in California, a perfect day, of course—cool but not cold. I told him about my day, how I enjoyed London, except for the weather, and that we'd have to come here together one day. JP was too busy playing a game with Maria to talk to me. Out of sight, out of mind, I guess.

Then I called Ed. He was in a meeting, but evidently my call was important enough for him to leave and call me back.

"How's it going over there?" he said a little breathlessly. "Are you okay?"

"Of course, I'm okay, and I have some information for you. Are you ready?"

"Go ahead."

"Well, according to the tailor, the victim's name is Aldo Bandini. Does that ring a bell?"

"No. I doubt that he could be a resident up here, although he could be a weekender."

"It may not be his real name," I said. "But there's more. Franco remembered that he had sent suits, shirts, and jackets to an address in New York. My friend Caroline whom I'm staying with knows some people at Scotland Yard, so we paid a visit to Commissioner Percy

Simmons. He used to train police forces in Africa when Caroline and I lived out there. Are you still there?"

"Yes, I'm listening."

"He scanned the photo and looked up the address, a lovely estate in a ritzy part of New York, which should not be a surprise as Franco is an expensive tailor." I took a deep breath and cleared my throat. "He's making a suit for me too. I dread seeing the bill, but I thought I should give him some business for his willingness to cooperate."

"I'll run the name and address through here. Email it to me."

"Okay, I will. The owner of the estate, by the way, is listed as Giovanni Moravia. I gave Commissioner Simmons your number and contact information in case he learns something at this end. He actually seemed quite interested."

"When are you planning to return?"

"Well, I'll stay and pick up my suit. Then I thought I'd stop in New York and see if anyone is home at the Moravias."

"No, Megan. This business is for the big boys. I have to call in the FBI."

"Ed, I am a big girl. This is not the last millennium. Give me just a couple of days."

"Megan, this is more than our small department can handle. We may have stepped into a hornet's nest here."

"Okay, I agree, but a couple of days are not going to make a difference to them."

"I know people in the New York Police Department. They can send someone to check out these people."

"I bet you they won't get any good information with all their procedures, policies, and strong-arm techniques."

"This is crazy. I don't know why I'm allowing this," he grumbled.

"Because you're a smart guy, Ed."

"I could get us in trouble over this. This is not a plot in one of your books." I could hear a sigh of protest.

"I know, but I'm pretty good at getting people to talk."

"You probably are, but this kind of detective work is dangerous stuff and best left to the professionals. We don't know what kind of people we're dealing with here."

"Ed, you have a skewed perception of women. Do you have any women working in your department at all?"

"In the office, yes."

"You need some female officers."

"We're doing just fine, Megan. Or are you fishing for a job?"

"Women sometimes have a more fine-tuned intuition."

"We're dealing in facts here, ma'am."

"Good, but sometimes you may need to act on a hunch."

"We do that too."

"Oh, Ed, you're impossible." I was about to hang up on him but thought better of it. "How's your brother doing?" I asked in effort to change the subject. "I just talked to him. He seemed fine to me, but how does he seem to you?"

"He was in good spirits yesterday. My father landed a big job in Fontana that will provide work for many of his men."

"Yes, Chris told me. I wonder if Joe is working too hard. He may need more help. What do you think?"

"Oh, he'll figure it out."

"I guess you're right. How's James?"

"Fine, but I think he misses you too."

"And how about your realtor bimbo?"

"You don't like her much, do you?"

"You're correct there, but more importantly, James hates her."

"Oh, I don't think he cares."

"See what I mean? You don't see the clues."

"What clues?"

"She's a gold digger. She has her eyes on your properties and money."

"I don't think so. She's an old friend that I've known for years."

"I just want you to remember James. He's your only son and is at a vulnerable age."

"I know, and I appreciate your concern, but I'm still a healthy male." He paused for a moment before he continued jokingly, "And you're not available."

"Okay, Ed. I think we'd better hang up. I'll call you tomorrow or the next day. Is this a good time?"

"Yes, this is fine, but any time really. Enjoy London. I see the weather is still pretty cold over there."

"Yes, but it's just a matter of putting on the right clothing. And it sure is easy to get around here."

He said good-bye, and we hung up. I could hear Caroline rummaging around in the kitchen so I went downstairs to join her.

"Caroline, do you think Franco can be ready for my first fitting tomorrow sometime?" I asked.

She was busy preparing a pot of tea but turned around to face me. "I'll call him in the morning."

What a great friend Caroline was, always so accommodating. "Then I'll wait until tomorrow to book a flight to New York for Thursday afternoon. Is that okay?"

"Of course." She poured milk in a cup, filled it with the hot brew, and handed it to me. "I was actually planning to go down to see Richard in the country on Thursday or Friday. You could come too if you can stay the weekend. I'm sure Richard would love to see you."

"Can I take a rain check on that?"

"Sure." She took a sip of tea before she continued, "Tomorrow I have an obligation at the Temple Church. You remember that place, right? We were there together once."

"Of course, I remember. It's the one mentioned in Dan Brown's *The Da Vinci Code.*"

"You're welcome to come along."

"Let me see when Franco can fit me in first," I said.

We finished our tea and talked about all the good sales in London at this time. I decided to do a little shopping rather than spend time in a dusty old church.

When Caroline called Franco the next day, he agreed to have my suit ready for the first fitting at four o'clock. I booked a seat to New York on American Airlines again for the following day.

I left Caroline at the tube station and continued walking toward Oxford Street. It was cloudy and cool, perfect walking weather. My thoughts went to the times Robert and I had flown up here from Africa to shop, relax, and have fun; how we'd gone pub crawling with Caroline and Richard from one famous pub to the next around Fleet Street, pubs where Charles Dickens, Lord Tennyson, and Samuel Johnson used to hang out; how we'd bantered and laughed. It didn't seem that long ago although it must have been over five years. Once Robert had flown all of us up in his plane. Richard had paid for the fuel and the various landing and parking fees at Stansted Airport. Now I was exploring London on my own. Maybe Chris and I would come to London one day, but it would be a while. On Oxford Street, I browsed the shelves in my favorite book store before I checked out the sale at Debenham, my favorite department store. A couple of blocks down the street I had coffee at Starbucks. People of all colors and nationalities hurried to and fro with their shopping bags. People everywhere like to shop. On my way to Franco the tailor I made a short detour to Regent Street and stopped by Hamleys Toy Shop and bought a little stuffed rabbit for JP.

Franco was ready for me as soon as I arrived, and the suit looked fabulous even if it wasn't completely finished. He would send it when it was all done. He did it all the time, he said, and charged an even one thousand pounds to my credit card. He was certainly not a tailor for the have-nots.

I hopped on a double-decker bus that took me up to Oxford Street again, where I bought a colorful scarf from one of the street vendors before I met Caroline at Victoria Station.

"You should have come with me to the Temple Church, Megan," Caroline said as soon as I was within earshot.

"Why? You know I've been there before and marveled at its eight-hundred-year-plus history." I stopped and looked at her. "Do you like my new scarf?" I said in an effort to change the subject.

"Yes, it's nice," she said and smiled curiously. "I know you've been all over London and know everything about the city, but this time you would have met Princess Anne."

"Princess Anne who?"

"The daughter of our beloved Queen. You surely know who she is, don't you?"

"*The* Princess Anne?" I said, my eyebrows slightly raised.

"The one and only."

"Wow, Caroline! You certainly hobnob with a motley bunch of people."

We decided to buy last-minute tickets to a new production of *King Lear* at the Old Globe. We had just enough time to take a taxi to a Sherlock Holmes-themed pub we had visited before to indulge in a big plate of fish and chips, which was not quite as good as we remembered it. The production of Shakespeare's play about the old king who decides to give up his crown to his not-so-loving daughters was, however, excellent. No surprise there.

"So, tomorrow you'll be in New York," Caroline commented on our way home. "You've got to let me know what you find out there."

"I will. The whole case will probably turn out to be a modern version of a Shakespearean tragedy. What do you think of that?"

Caroline laughed. "The old bard didn't leave much untouched, did he?"

7

NEW YORK

Heathrow Airport was even more crowded than usual, with long lines everywhere, but I finally made it to the counter. I checked my bag, showed my passport, and got my boarding card. I adjusted my new scarf that I was wearing because it was a chilly day. Then it was on to the myriad of security checkpoints.

"Can I feel your scarf?" a security agent asked me.

I thought he was trying to flirt with me, so I smiled but said obligingly, "Here, I'll take it off."

He looked at me seriously. "We have been instructed to check all women with scarves," he said.

"What for?" I asked curiously.

He didn't answer but just ushered me on.

Several security agents stood on either side of the doorway. I tried to upgrade to business class, but it was full. However, the agent gave me what they called a premium seat next to an older Italian woman who spoke no English, which didn't prevent her from trying to carry on a conversation with me. As our conversation continued, however, I started to get the gist of what she was saying as her Italian seemed to fall somewhere between the French and Latin that I had studied both in high school and college. Her daughter had put her on the flight, which originated in Rome, she told me. Another daughter would pick her up in New York. She asked if I could help her through immigration and customs. I assured her it would be no problem. We ate, slept, and talked. Unfortunately, as we passed through customs, I lost her. I looked around for her but figured she would find her way after coming this far. No sooner had I exited the door of no return than an agent ran up behind me and asked me to come with him. To my surprise, he took me back to the customs area, where the poor woman had had an anxiety attack. She grabbed me and hugged me and babbled on in Italian, blessing me profusely. We walked out together, and I delivered her safely to her daughter, who after hearing her mother's story, insisted on giving me a ride into town.

"That's very kind of you, but that's not at all necessary," I said. "I'm familiar with New York, and I'm going all the way in to Time Square."

"No problem," she persisted. "I have a driver waiting outside."

And so I rode with them through the busy streets of New York, listening to the animated conversation between mother and daughter.

I had booked a room at the Hyatt, and as we stopped in front of the guarded entrance, the daughter gave me her business card with an offer of help if I needed anything in New York.

Well ensconced in my hotel room, I called Chris on FaceTime to tell him where I was. Although it was a little distorted, his face was as handsome as ever, and I ached to touch him.

"Do you miss me?" I asked him teasingly.

"Yes, I miss you. When are you coming home? Tomorrow?"

"Saturday," I said. "I'll follow up on a lead tomorrow. If you don't hear from me by tomorrow night, I've been kidnapped. I almost was this afternoon."

"What happened?"

"Well, I sat next to an Italian woman on the plane and helped her through immigration and customs. The agents even let me back into the customs area after she had a medical emergency. I helped her find her daughter, who then insisted on giving me a ride to the hotel."

"But you didn't accept, I hope."

"Of course I accepted. She had hired a chauffeured limousine, and they took me straight to the door of the Hyatt."

"You're crazy. Be careful. There are a lot of strange people in New York. I lived there for a whole year, remember, trying to stay out of trouble."

"Well, you didn't try very hard, did you?" I said teasingly and paused. "Are you still feeling tired? Maybe it's time to see a doctor again."

"I'll be all right, and you be careful."

"I will."

After I undid my braid and put my hair up in a bun, I went outside. If I was lucky, I would take in another show. The theater district is not far from the Hyatt, and it was early in the evening, so I felt safe. On 49th Street, I caught a glimpse of the marquis above the Ambassador Theatre. It was still featuring the razzle-dazzle show *Chicago*, so I purchased a ticket in the third row and had just enough time for a snack and a cup of coffee.

The Ambassador is a spectacular theater in art deco décor with plush red carpets and seats. In college, I had thought of auditioning for shows in Los Angeles, but all I could probably have hoped for would have been a place in the chorus somewhere. In graduate school I met Robert, and then we got married and moved to Africa.

Chicago was fabulous, a truly sizzling show, with innovative choreography and great singing. No, I would not have made it in this genre.

I started to walk back to the hotel afterward, and I was only a block away from the theater when a man in his fifties, bald and shorter than me, with metal-rimmed glasses came up beside me.

"You're alone this evening, ma'am?" he asked seductively.

"No," I said. "My husband is waiting for me over there." But I realized immediately that I should not have dignified him with an answer.

"I'll take you home and give you a good time too," he persisted.

I tried to ignore him, but walking by myself all the way back to the hotel was not going to work. I stopped and tried to hail a taxi, but they were all taken. All the theaters let out at the same time, of course. The man was still there. I gave him a stern look, but he just pulled his lips back into a grotesque grin. Where were the police when you needed them?

I thought about my mission the next day. Maybe this was a little warning that I might be a bit naïve. Maybe I should have asked Ed to come out here and help me investigate. This was not my job. Why should I care who this man Bandini was? Maybe he deserved to die. But I was born nosy and had to find out.

The creepy guy was still there, but a couple with two teenage children were walking down the street toward Times Square, and I decided to follow them as closely as I could. Fortunately, they stopped and turned around to face me. I must have looked innocent because the wife immediately asked in a friendly voice if I was alone.

"Well, yes," I said apologetically. "I thought I could walk in peace down to the Hyatt Hotel after the show, but I guess I had forgotten about all the unsavory characters that still come out at night around here."

"You can walk with us," she said. "We're staying at the DoubleTree. It's not too far."

"Thank you." We started walking. "Where are you from?" I asked, not knowing what else to say.

"Des Moines, Iowa," the wife answered. "I'm Erica." She held out her hand to shake mine and then pointed toward her husband. "This is my husband, Greg, and these are our children, Emily and Greg Junior."

I told them I was from the Los Angeles area and that I had just come from London that afternoon. "I thought I'd take in a show before going to bed," I continued. "I have a meeting tomorrow, and then I'm heading back to LA on Saturday."

They had seen *Chicago* too. Their children had been in musicals back home in Des Moines and had been bitten by the acting bug.

I had planned to call Ed but the evening's encounter had left me unsettled and I went straight to bed.

8

NEW LEADS

New York, and especially Times Square, is a bustling place at any time of day, but on Friday mornings, the constantly blinking lights are even brighter as the whole world seems to congregate here, people of all ages in all types of clothing scurrying aimlessly back and forth with no discernible sense of direction, darting between honking taxis, delivery vans, and other motor vehicles, or just hanging around on street corners.

I clutched my voluminous purse with the dead man's picture and held the plastic bag with the carefully folded jacket and slacks firmly in my hand. Since yellow cabs were everywhere, I decided to take a taxi rather than wait for a Lyft or Uber driver. I hopped into one, and he took off before I had even closed the door. The driver's name was Ade, he told me, and he was from Nigeria. I told him I had lived there and knew it well, and we struck up a conversation. He was working day and night, he said, in order to pay for his daughter to come to the United States to study nursing. He spoke good English and was an excellent driver, gliding seamlessly in and out of lanes. I might not have found the place by myself because the street was closed to traffic before we had reached the house number. A new thoroughfare that was still under construction blocked the whole area. But Ade was undeterred, and while the meter was running merrily, he backtracked to find a way through to the other side. In the midst of all this, he managed to give me his card and told me to call him directly when I wanted to return to the hotel.

He finally stopped in front of a palatial light-gray home with arches and columns, and after paying the fare and adding a generous tip, I walked up to a solid oak door. As I pushed the doorbell, I heard chimes and light running footsteps inside. Soon a smiling teenage girl with bright blue hair, dressed in a black shirt over black stretch pants opened the door. Her eyebrows rose, and her soft brown eyes widened as she saw me. "Oh," she said breathlessly, "I was expecting a friend."

"Hi," I said, trying to sound friendly. "Is your mother or father home?"

"No, but my grandmother is here. Come in."

I followed her into an expansive hall with Persian carpets, a big crystal chandelier, and a curved staircase that led up to a railed landing.

"Grandma!" she shouted as she darted up the staircase. "Someone is here to see you."

She disappeared through a door, and immediately afterward, an older woman, in her sixties perhaps, appeared. Her short, dark wavy hair was streaked with gray, but her smooth olive skin showed few wrinkles, and her big brown eyes sparkled. Her shirt-dress and slip-on shoes matched her eyes. "Hello!" she called down. "Are you the realtor? You're early." She started down the stairs, holding on to the well-polished rail.

"No, I'm afraid not," I said and looked straight into her face. I'm looking for Aldo Bandini. I was hoping he was here."

"Are you from the police?"

"No. I've just come from London. He ordered some clothes from a tailor, and he gave this address. I have his sports coat and slacks here."

She frowned "No, I don't know anyone by that name," she said flatly. But her eyes had lost their luster, and she started to fidget with her hands. "I'm sorry I can't help you." She turned and started to walk upstairs again. "And I'm expecting a realtor. That's why I came down. If you'll excuse me…"

"I have a picture of him with me," I said boldly and followed her upstairs. "It may be that he uses another name."

She turned toward me as I held the picture in front of her. Blood seemed to drain from her face, and she turned white. I quickly pulled the jacket and slacks from the bag and showed them to her.

"As I told you, I don't know this man," she said, trying to regain her composure.

"I think you do," I said sternly.

"Has anything happened to him?" she asked quietly.

"He's dead. Killed and dumped from a boat into a lake," I said mercilessly, without showing any emotion.

"No." She put her hands in front of her face. "Holy Jesus. Son of Mary," she said frantically.

"So, you do know him."

"Yes, he's my nephew, my brother's son." She started to sob quietly. "Are you from the police?"

"No," I said, but I'm not sure she heard me.

"He often stayed here with me because he didn't always get along with his father after his parents divorced. My own husband died over ten years ago. My granddaughter is staying with me now. Did you know Aldo? You're not his girlfriend, are you?"

"No, I didn't know him. Did he have a girlfriend?"

"Yes, I think so. At least he told me he was going over to see his girlfriend sometimes. He was never married."

"Any idea where she might be?"

"I think here in New York."

"So his name was Aldo Bandini?"

"Yes, he took his mother's name after she and my brother got divorced. He was a lawyer, just like my brother, but I think he had some nasty clients."

"What's your brother's name?"

"Frank Artusio. I'll call him. Maybe he can come over for lunch. Can you stay for lunch?"

"That's very gracious of you, especially since I just barged in on you like this. I am really sorry to intrude."

"Come on up to my sitting room."

We entered a cozy room with a fireplace and two plush red couches on either side of it, a small table between them. On the other wall, a large window overlooked a well-manicured garden.

"But now you have to tell me how you are involved in all of this. You said you were not from the police."

"I witnessed the crime. Or at least partially. I saw the boat, but it was in the middle of the night, and I couldn't see the people who tossed the victim overboard. My brother-in-law is the sheriff in our small town. I'm working with him as a sort of private investigator."

We sat down on opposite couches.

"Aldo was a good kid until his mother and father broke up. He studied law at New York University, but I always had a feeling he got involved with the wrong people."

Her cell phone was on the table. She picked it up and punched in a number. "Hello, Frank. It's Rosemary. You'd better come over. It's about Aldo. A young woman is here with his clothes and a picture she'd like you to see."

She held her hand over the phone as she looked at me. "What's your name?" she said.

"Megan Viets."

She repeated my name into the phone and handed the phone over to me.

"I'm sorry, sir," I said, trying to be polite. "But I'm afraid I have some bad news for you."

"Is he dead?"

"I'm afraid so. I have his picture and some clothes. I guess you may have to come out to California to make a positive identification."

"I'll be over in an hour. Can you wait?"

I said I could, and he hung up.

"I'm sorry," I said and gave the phone back to her. "And you're Rosemary, I understand, then."

She said that she was.

"So where did Aldo Bandini work? Did he work for a firm?" I asked.

"I don't know exactly. He was a defense lawyer and worked mostly here in New York, but he often traveled to Chicago and the West Coast. He made a lot of money, but being a lawyer, he never talked much about his work."

The sound of chimes came from downstairs, and Rosemary got up and walked toward the door. "That's the realtor. I'm planning on selling this house. My husband is not coming back. He was a commercial real-estate developer and actually built this house many years ago. His business prospered so I'm well taken care of, but I want a smaller place now, somewhere more quiet. I'll tell her to come back another time."

We walked downstairs together, and after she apologized to the realtor, a smart-looking woman in her forties, we went into a bright commercial-size kitchen with a large island in the middle and two forty-eight-inch Viking stoves and a Subzero refrigerator along the wall. A cook in a white cotton coat was walking back and forth between the island and one of the stoves, preparing lunch.

"What a wonderful kitchen!" I exclaimed. "You could cook for a whole army here."

"We have a large family, and all of us get together and invite friends and business associates for dinner every Sunday."

I walked around, and the cook lifted the lid of a pot to show what she was preparing—chicken Alfredo.

"My granddaughter has invited a friend over for lunch, and they requested it," Rosemary said as we walked into the adjacent dining room, where another crystal chandelier hung from the ceiling and a shiny cherrywood table that could seat sixteen occupied most of the space. The table was set for four, but Rosemary added another place setting that she took from the matching cherrywood buffet.

"I'll tell Annie that we'll have lunch as soon as my brother arrives," she said and walked back into the kitchen.

I wondered what this lawyer would have to say about Aldo Bandini.

9

THE VICTIM'S DESTINY

Rosemary's brother arrived promptly, dressed formally in a dark-blue suit. His gray, wavy hair was carefully brushed back, and his big brown eyes and smooth olive skin matched his sister's.

He greeted his sister and great niece with effusive hugs and kisses, and I was properly introduced before we sat down at the table. The granddaughter's friend also had blue hair and was dressed in all black. It was hard to tell them apart.

While the children were present, we did not talk about the deceased relative, although it's doubtful they would have paid any attention.

"What are you girls up to this afternoon?" I asked in an effort to include them in the conversation.

"We're going to see a movie at the mall," the granddaughter said, and they both giggled.

"And what are you going to see?" I continued.

"Maybe *Wonder Woman 2*. We're just waiting for Grandma's driver to take us." They giggled some more.

The chicken Alfredo was excellent. The two girls finished quickly and disappeared.

While Rosemary served coffee from a pot the cook had brought in, I turned to the man who had been introduced as Frank Artusio, Rosemary's brother. "I guess you would like to see the picture of the victim and his clothes," I said.

"Yes, that's what I'm here for, isn't it?"

"Right." I gave him the picture first, and he studied it carefully.

"It looks like Aldo, yes," he said uncertainly. "Although it's hard to tell exactly."

"I think I can see the scar over his left eye," his sister said. "Do you remember, Frank? From when he fell off the horse we had and he cut himself on a sharp stone. Remember how he bled?"

"Yes, but it could be an imperfection in the picture."

I took out the clothes and showed him.

"I don't particularly recognize these," he said.

"They were made by a tailor in London. The victim, possibly your son, was wearing them when he was found in the lake." I looked straight at him, but he showed no emotion. "We recognized the name of the tailor from the labels, and I traveled over to London to see if he could remember the poor guy. He did, because your son was evidently a good client. The tailor said his records showed that he sent these two items and several suits and shirts to this address."

Artusio remained silent for a few moments before he responded, "So you took possession of these clothes, traveled to London by yourself, I presume, and found the tailor who had made these clothes belonging to a drowning victim you claim to be my son."

He paused, but I remained silent. I didn't want to interrupt his thought process.

"Forgive me if I'm a bit skeptical," he continued. "But your story is full of conjecture and innuendos. Who are you working for? It's not the FBI, because they do not operate like this."

Blood rose to my cheeks, but I cleared my throat and looked straight at his face. "The FBI has, of course, been notified," I said untruthfully. "But they work slowly, and since no one has been reported missing, the case may not have high priority."

"So, why are you so interested in all of this? And what do you want from us?"

"Nothing. Why would I want something from you?" I didn't wait for an answer but continued without pause. "My brother-in-law is the sheriff in our town, and since I witnessed the crime…"

"You saw this man get killed?"

"Not exactly," I said and told him what I had witnessed. I talked to him as I would talk to a recalcitrant student. "Both the sheriff and I want to find out who the killer or killers are. If this is your son, I would think you would want to find out too."

He shook his head and pulled his lips back slowly into an unsympathetic grin. "You and your country sheriff are in way over your heads, young lady," he said condescendingly.

I clenched my teeth in an effort to stay calm. "You don't want to find your son's killer?" I asked incredulously.

"I know who they are, and the faster you remove yourself from all of this, the better. Who are you anyway? The sheriff's girlfriend?"

"I am married to his brother," I said indignantly. "I'm a teacher at a small college in Los Angeles, and before I took a job as a teacher, I lived in Africa with my first husband, who's deceased."

"I'm sorry," he said in a conciliatory tone. "But you're still naïve. The people my son was working for don't mess around."

"Aldo wanted to drop those nasty clients," Rosemary interjected.

The lawyer looked at her. "You don't leave the mob, Rosemary, except in a coffin. You should know that. Your crooked husband had plenty of dealings with them. Or have you forgotten?"

He turned to me. "I told Aldo time and time again, but he never did listen to me."

I looked at a big clock on the wall. It was already five minutes after 2:00 p.m. I needed to get out of there. The lawyer was right. I was in over my head, and I needed to talk to Ed. He'd better let the FBI take over the whole case.

"So you don't want to come out to California and make a positive identification then?"

"No."

"How about you, Rosemary? How about taking your granddaughter to Los Angeles? Go to Disneyland? From what I know, these people have a code of honor and will not harm a grandmother who wants to say good-bye to her favorite nephew."

Frank Artusio nixed this idea with a disdainful laugh.

I rose and thanked Rosemary for a delicious meal.

"I'll call a cab for you," Artusio offered, and I accepted. Ade was probably in another part of town already, and I didn't want to wait.

The taxi came quickly. We said good-bye, and this time I took my time getting into the car. While the taxi driver skillfully maneuvered his way back to the hotel, I just sat there in a total daze. I needed to think this day through.

10

CONVERSATION WITH THE SHERIFF

Back at the hotel, I emailed Caroline in London and told her how the case was progressing. Then I booked a flight to LA for the next day and called Chris on FaceTime. His face looked thinner, and he sounded a little distant.

"I'll be home tomorrow, Chris," I said cheerfully. "Is everything okay?"

"Yes, I'm feeling better. How was your day?"

I recounted the events of the day, the trip out to the stately house; how, because of a mix-up with a realtor, I had been invited to have lunch with Giovanni's widow Rosemary, her brother, and granddaughter, and how they slowly revealed that Aldo Bandini was Rosemary's nephew, her brother's son.

"They invited you to lunch just like that?"

"Yes, and it really didn't surprise me too much. I've never been in an Italian home without being offered food. It's really a nice tradition. The food was good too, and they seemed good people as far as I could see."

"You really are too trusting," he said reproachfully.

"Maybe, but I'm okay. Let me talk to JP."

JP told me about a new friend, and I told him I loved him and that I would see him tomorrow.

I turned on the television while I thought about what to tell Ed. The local news announcer droned on about the antics in North Korea and the Middle East interspersed with the usual inner-city shootings.

Ed was not immediately available, so I left a message for him to call me back, which he did shortly afterward.

"You're busy," I said apologetically.

"No, it's all right," he said. "I had to give an update at the advisory council meeting about a string of burglaries. We have to be so careful to collect evidence and make sure we have a case before we make any arrests. It's ludicrous. We take a guy to jail, and he's out of there and driving up the highway before the deputy can finish his report."

"I guess it's difficult to be in law enforcement these days," I said.

"There's constant scrutiny, but it's all right. My deputies are pretty sharp."

"That's good. What else is new?"

"There are some deliberately set fires on opposite sides of the county depleting our resources. One member of the advisory council who has followed ISIS's and Al Qaida's activities brought up that this type of arson is the MO of some Islamist terrorists all over the country. Well, we know they're out to put a stress on local resources, but we can't always publicize everything. We don't want people to live in constant fear, but that makes it hard to get extra funding."

"Yes, there's a fine line there, and the public is watching your every move."

"That's right." He cleared his throat. "So, are you still in London?"

"No, I'm in New York. I got in yesterday, but I was too tired to call you. And besides that, you would have interfered with my plan."

"What plan?" he exclaimed. Then he continued almost inaudibly under his breath, "I was crazy to let you get involved in this murder case."

"Did you learn anything about the name Aldo Bandini through your computer search?" I said.

"No, and you said it was probably not his real name so I didn't spend much time on it."

"Okay, but now I know it *is* his real name. I told you my friend Caroline and I went to Scotland Yard and talked to Commissioner Percy Simmons. He found that the address Franco had given me was the address of the Moravia family, so I took a taxi to the address I was given. It turned out to be the estate of Aldo Bandini's aunt, a gracious widow by the name of Rosemary Moravia who had taken her nephew in when his parents divorced. She called her brother, a New York lawyer by the name of Frank Artusio, and we all had lunch together."

"They invited you to lunch just like that?" Ed said sounding surprised.

"Yes, that's exactly what Chris said too, but this is an Italian family, and in my experience, when Italians have visitors, there's always food involved." I paused and waited for Ed to respond. However, he remained quiet so I continued, "I strongly suspect that Frank Artusio is Aldo Bandini's father, even though he had a different last name. Rosemary said her nephew Aldo, who was also a lawyer, had taken his mother's last name after his parents divorced. Being a lawyer, Artusio didn't admit it directly and said he had no interest in coming out to California to give a positive identification of the victim unless he was subpoenaed."

"You've really done a piece of detective work there, Megan."

"From the general comments I heard, I have to assume that Aldo Bandini was a lawyer for the mob. He evidently traveled to Chicago and the West Coast often, but Rosemary maintained that Aldo was a good kid and wanted to drop these 'nasty clients,' as she called them. Her brother reminded her that you don't drop the mob. They drop you—in a lake somewhere or else in a coffin. He insinuated that Rosemary's deceased husband also had ties to the Mafia."

"Okay, Megan. It's past the time to call in the FBI," Ed said authoritatively. "I've let this investigation go too far."

"Yes, I agree," I said. "But are they going to do anything, do you think?"

"I don't know, but I have to follow protocol."

"Yes, I understand," I said with resignation.

"I will grant you that I can't figure any of this out, but whatever it is, it seems likely that it has something to do with the drug smuggling that goes on around here," he said, and I could hear a loud sigh.

"What I can't understand is why a lawyer for the Mafia would choose our idyllic little resort town and our lake to get himself killed in. How do you think this ties in with our drug problems?"

"I'm not sure, Megan, but in any case, we don't have the resources out here in San Bernardino to follow up on this case. This is a federal case. It's the federal government's job to secure our borders and prevent drug smuggling."

"I know."

"You're on your way home now, I hope."

"Yes, I'll be home tomorrow."

"Do you need someone to pick you up?"

"Thank you, but no, I'll use Uber. It's really very convenient. The traffic around LAX is so horrendous, a real zoo, and I don't want to subject any of you to such an ordeal."

"The entire city of Los Angeles is a zoo. I'd never want to live in a big city."

"Yes, I hear you, Ed, and I see your point, but many people have no other choice, and we have problems in our little isolated bubble too."

He didn't answer.

"I read the other day that some rape cases have now been reclassified as misdemeanors," I continued. "That's outrageous, and it doesn't bode well for women in our community."

"Yes, it makes me mad. It was brought up in the community meeting yesterday. It's especially unsettling since we have so many reports of rape and domestic violence around here now. But all I can say is that people need to get out and vote when these propositions appear on the ballots."

"I agree." Then in an abrupt change of subject, I went on, "How's James?"

"Busy getting ready for graduation. I think he misses you. He especially misses his mother right now, of course, but he has taken to you as a substitute, and I'm grateful to you, Megan."

"Thank you. I like James, and I think I know what he's going through, although both of my parents were around when I graduated."

"Chris and I lost our mother early too, as you know."

"Yes, but I think it's even worse at James's age."

"That may be."

"I think his idea of a gap year is a good one at this time, considering the circumstances, especially since you can well afford it. We'll talk when I get back tomorrow. Tell him I said hello."

"I will." There was a long pause, and I was ready to hang up when he continued, "I probably won't be home tomorrow when you get in, but I'll tell James. He may go over to see Chris and John Patrick."

"Ed," I said sternly. "Are you sure you have your priorities right?"

"What do you mean?"

"You know perfectly well what I mean," I said irritably.

"I think we've had this conversation before."

"Yes, but it warrants repeating."

"I assure you I can take care of myself."

"I'm not worried about you, Ed. I'm worried about James. I'm a teacher, and I know how much teenagers are affected by the loss of a parent. If you could just be a little patient. James will be John Patrick's role model, so I have an extra stake in James's well-being."

"I appreciate your concern. I've been there."

"Yes, I'm sorry, but you were barely thirteen. Sixteen is the worst possible age to lose your mother."

"Nevertheless, I will be down in Los Angeles tomorrow and won't be home until late. And it's not what you think," he said stubbornly. He remained silent for a few moments before he continued in a more conciliatory tone, "Megan, I'm really impressed by your detective work. But you have taken too many risks. Something could have happened to you. You have a son and a husband. You've put them at risk too. Who knows what's going to happen with this case?"

"I guess you're right now that I think about it. Thanks for the reminder."

"You're welcome."

"I guess I should have something to eat and then get ready for my flight tomorrow."

"Have a safe trip, and thank you for some good work."

Instead of going to bed early, I went downstairs and asked the concierge to round up a ticket to see a new play I had read about called *The Play That Goes Wrong*. It turned out to be a hilarious comedy and a wonderful production, something that our small college could handle. I took a picture of the marquee and secured a couple of extra playbills to give to our theater director. This time I ordered a taxi from the hotel, and with a generous tip I asked the driver to pick me up after the performance, which he did.

Before I went to sleep, I thought about Aldo Bandini lying cold in the morgue and no one caring. I realized that I didn't like the idea of giving up on him so readily. I'd have to figure out a way to stay at least partially connected.

11

COMING HOME

Flying commercially is no fun and flying into LAX is especially harrowing. Robert had avoided it when he flew home from Africa or the Middle East with royals and other dignitaries. He preferred Long Beach or Burbank, or even Ontario or John Wayne Airport in Orange County. At $4,000 an hour—small change for many of these sheikhs—he had built a booming business, but he was a risk-taker, and that finally got him killed.

Outside the terminal I finally hailed and caught my Uber car, gave the driver directions, and called Chris as we merged onto the 105 Freeway. Chris picked up right away, but his voice sounded groggy.

"Hi, Chris," I said lightly. "I'm on my way home, and I can't wait to see you. Are you okay? You sound sleepy, or have you been drinking?"

"No, I'm doing all right. I'm just a little tired. I'm getting used to the new van. Yesterday I spent the day in Redlands and signed the contract for another big construction job for the Redlands School District again."

"That's good news. That's the third or fourth year in a row you've gotten a contract with them, isn't it?"

"Yeah, that's right."

"And so, I guess the guys took you out to celebrate? I remember the first contract you signed with this district and how drunk you were when you came over to my cabin."

"No celebration this year, but the guys are happy."

"What else is new?"

"Nothing really. I let the physical therapist go a couple of days ago. They don't really do anything that I can't do myself now."

"Yes, I remember you said something about that. I didn't think too much of him either. Actually, I think physical therapy is overrated."

"James just left. He's been over to play with JP, who follows him around like a shadow and mimics his every move. It's really funny. Of course, we watched cartoons this morning." He paused. "And how are you holding up, honey? You must be tired."

"I am, but I took a nap on the plane. Do we have anything for supper, or should I stop and get something? They don't serve anything anymore, even on long flights."

"I'll see what I can round up. When will you be here?"

"In less than an hour."

"I'll get busy then. I love you."

"I love you too."

Driving up the familiar mountain highway made the world seem farther and farther away. London, New York. It all seemed like a dream. But the rest of the world was encroaching on our resort town too. Drugs. Crime. Undocumented immigrants. And what was a lawyer for the Mafia doing up here in the mountains? How was Ed going to handle all of this? Would FBI agents come out here? And if so, how would they deal with Ed? He was not one to be pushed around.

JP came running toward me as I walked in the front door. I set down my suitcase and carry-on before I picked him up and carried him over toward Chris, who watched us with a big smile as he wheeled himself across the floor. I set JP down and bent over to hug Chris.

"I missed you, honey," he said softly.

I kneeled down by his side and laid my head on his lap. He stroked my hair as if he were petting Duchess. Then he started to undo my braid. "Your hair is a mess," he said and laughed. "Let me braid it before we eat. French or fishtail?"

"French," I said.

He was an expert at braiding my hair, a skill he had learned when his little daughter, Emily, who had Down syndrome, lived. When Chris had finished the braid, I turned to JP. "I have a gift for you," I said and took his hand. We walked over to my suitcase and pulled out the stuffed rabbit I had bought at Hamleys in London. "And give this to Daddy." I handed him the daddy cup I had picked up at the airport in New York at the last minute. "But carry it carefully."

He tiptoed over to Chris with both the rabbit and the cup.

"Daddy," he said with excitement in his voice as he handed over his loot.

"That's nice," Chris said simply and then turned to me. "I have something for you too," he said. "But it can wait until after we eat."

Chris had set the table in the kitchen. He had grilled salmon and served it skillfully with mixed vegetables and white wine, moving himself around in his wheelchair like a pro.

After we had put JP to sleep, and I had thrown myself on the couch in front of the fireplace, Chris wheeled himself into his office and brought out a small box. "I bought this for you after I signed that Redlands School District contract. It should provide a good profit," he said and watched with a wide smile on his face as I opened it. Inside was a sparkling ruby on a gold chain.

"It matches my ring," I said and reached out to give him another hug and a kiss.

"You have to have jewelry that befits the wife of a successful businessman," he said teasingly.

I just smiled at him and held the chain around my neck for him to fasten the clasp in the back.

"It will go great with my new suit that Franco is making for me," I said. "It cost me a fortune, but I felt I had to give him some business for helping me out."

"Yeah, why not? You might as well spend some of your hard-earned money," he said sarcastically and looked at me with a crooked grin. "All right. Let's see the expensive suit. Model it for me."

"It's not finished yet. Franco will send it over here when it's all done. At least he offered free shipping," I said and laughed.

We were both tired, so we decided to go to bed early. I lay comfortably on Chris's arm, but then he suddenly pulled himself toward me and kissed me profusely as he cupped one hand over my breast. Then his hand moved sensuously down past my waist and between my legs as if he wanted to arouse me, something he had certainly been good at before his accident. I laid my hand on his and let him play with me for a while.

"I love you," he said passionately. "What I wouldn't give to have some good sex with you right now."

"Don't torture yourself, Chris," I said and pulled his hand away.

"We're at a different stage of our lives right now. Sex is overrated. I love you just as much without sex. It really is not the most important part of a relationship." I paused. "I'm fine with or without sex. I love your kisses and your embraces, and I'm so happy to be home. We have a perfect little family and a beautiful house. Every day I wake up I thank God that I live in this amazing place in Southern California. I have seen a lot of poverty around the world and often think of all the people who do not know if they'll have something to eat for breakfast or lunch. We're so fortunate here. Sometimes we don't seem to realize it."

"I guess that's a good way to look at it."

"Traveling does that to you, especially coming home from a trip."

"But people in London are not poor, are they?"

"No, of course not. I was thinking about other places I've seen."

We lay still for a while. "Oh, I meant to tell you," I said. "I want to invite Susie, my friend from graduate school, to spend a few days with us next week. Is that okay with you? You remember Susie, right?"

"Yeah, of course. That's fine. Is she bringing her daughter? Ashley, wasn't it?"

"Yes, I think Ashley will come too."

"I still have the wallet she made me out of duct tape. She was cute." His tone was nostalgic and distant again, maybe remembering the time when he could walk, go fishing, and make heads turn. Chris was good with children. He and Ashley had hit it off right away.

"Great. I'll email her tomorrow." I looked at him and gently removed his arm. "Ed said he and James will be over tomorrow too. Maybe we'll go out for brunch again."

"Yes. Ed has been over almost every day since you were gone. He has a lot on his mind with all the crimes and deliberately set fires around here…"

I must have drifted off to sleep while he was still talking because when I woke up, it was already light.

12

BAD MANNERS

We rose to an unusually hot Sunday morning. The humidity was much higher than normal for this altitude, especially at this time of year, and like most people around the lake, we didn't have air conditioning.

Already at nine o'clock, perspiration was running down my back as I was trying to help JP put on a light tank-top, although he was quite adept at dressing himself. "By self," he kept saying while pushing me away.

While JP went over to watch Chris dress, something my handsome but disabled husband had become surprisingly adroit at, I walked out on the deck, where there was a slight breeze. The lake lay there shiny and dark, with a handful of sailboats gliding elegantly back and forth in the distance. A squawking blue jay flew overhead and landed brazenly on the railing, where he sat perched unperturbed, paying no attention to me. A woodpecker pecked furiously at a big pine tree below us. A bald eagle winters in that tree. What a sight to see it swoop down on the lake to pick up a plump duck near the little commercial center at the south end of the lake. The tiny village with shops, restaurants, and a hotel has become a popular resort for both day-trippers and weekenders who need to escape from the hustle and bustle of Los Angeles.

I took a deep breath of fresh mountain air. It felt good to be home and not have to be somewhere or have to wait to board another plane. And today the deck was surely the best place to be. I decided we'd have our breakfast out here.

The sound of rattling pots and pans came from the kitchen. I went back in and made two cups of coffee and poured a glass of milk in a plastic cup for JP to bring outside, while Chris was whipping up his special scrambled eggs with tomatoes and spinach that he served with toast.

We took our time eating. Afterward JP and I walked down to the dock while Chris followed in his wheelchair. No sooner had we reached the water than James coasted up the driveway in Chris's old Range Rover. He jumped out, waved, and came jogging down the slope toward us. He seemed to have grown taller while I had been away, and he was sporting a new haircut, very short on the sides with long bangs pushed to one side. Despite his awkward age of seventeen, he let me envelop him in my arms. "Welcome home, Megan," he said as he let go of me. "How was your trip?"

"Good," I said. "How's school?"

"Fine."

"Waiting for graduation?"

"Yeah."

"Actually, I've been thinking about a trip for you too, James, if you want to travel someplace safe."

"Oh, yeah? Where?"

"To Scandinavia later this summer."

"Scandinavia! Where's that?"

"Oh, come on. You know. Norway, Sweden, and the small countries in Northern Europe. I still have some second cousins over there who I think would be more than happy to have an American student come and visit. And there are some summer courses you could take at the university in Oslo. What do you think?"

"Sounds good. Are you going too?"

"No, you'd be on your own. It will be good for you to get away from here for a while, see some other places, another country."

He frowned and seemed to have some doubts. "Do they speak English over there?"

"Yes, and very well too. And you'd be quite popular there, maybe meet some Norwegian and Swedish girls, see some well-managed countries."

"I don't know about leaving Dad here by himself."

"We'll talk to him later. He said he'd be over this morning, and then we might all go out for brunch again."

"I didn't see him this morning. I spent the night at my friend Thomas's house, and when I stopped by home on my way over here, Dad wasn't there."

He turned away and walked toward Chris.

"I'm sure Thomas is welcome to come with us too," I said lightheartedly, not wanting to speculate where Ed could be, although I suspected he was with his unpleasant girlfriend, who was sure to come with us as well. "Why don't you text Thomas to see if he can make it?"

"Okay," he said and turned to Chris. "Where are we going, Uncle?"

"I think your dad mentioned something about Settlers Inn," Chris said and glanced over at me before he continued, "if that's okay with Megan."

"I love that place," I said. "They have the best lobster bisque but probably not for brunch, although I kind of remember them serving a lobster quiche there one Sunday."

Ed came over around noon with his realtor girlfriend, Vee, as I suspected. She was elegant enough but in a cheap way with her hair too red and too much make-up. Her stark black eyeliner set off her light brown eyes. She wore a white sleeveless top and a tight blue and white striped skirt that showed off a shapely figure. While she breezed right past me, Ed stopped and gave me a good squeeze. "Welcome home, 006," he said cheerfully. His embrace was hard, and my body shuddered just a little.

"I'm really glad to see you," he said more seriously, shaking his head as he continued, "I can't imagine what drove me to let you go off like this. If something had happened to you, my whole department would have been in trouble. I've called the FBI, and I imagine I'll hear something from them tomorrow. We may have stepped into a real hornet's nest here." He held me at a distance to look me over. "You look good."

"You look good yourself," I said. I looked at him and smiled. His face was more rugged than Chris's fine feature. He was a bigger man altogether, but his gentle eyes indicated a kind and caring man.

He let me loose and turned to Chris, and the two of them went out toward the garage. James and JP were in the kitchen, while Vee had flung herself down on the couch, her white handbag next to her.

"This frickin' heat is killing me," she announced. "Excuse me, but I have to take off my panties."

"The bathroom is free, Vee. You know where it is," I said frostily.

However, to my disbelief, she remained where she was and actually removed her black, silky underwear right then and there. She placed them on the armrest as I glared at her. I resolutely walked over to the couch and picked up her underwear with the tips of my thumb and middle finger. Her jaw dropped.

"What are you doing with my underpants?" she asked as I was walking toward the kitchen and laundry room.

"I'm taking them out to the laundry room and throwing them in my washing machine," I said acidly. "I don't particularly appreciate people leaving their dirty underwear in my living room."

She didn't say anything, and I hurried out as Chris and Ed returned to the living room.

"What's going on?" Chris said innocently enough, but I heard his snicker. He had had some of his own undesirable relationships before I met him and had suffered criticism from his family. Now he was apparently relishing in his brother's bad choice of girlfriends.

Ed looked at me accusingly as I came back in. "Is this girl talk that we're not supposed to hear?"

"I think your friend here has to go home and change," I said, looking coolly at Ed. "I think she lost her underwear." Ed's face reddened and he looked away.

"I know when I'm not wanted," Vee smirked. "I'll be out of here right away, Miss. But first I'll say hello to James."

I walked behind her into the kitchen.

"Do you want me to fix you a drink, big guy?" she asked James a little too seductively, I thought, as she edged toward him. James backed away.

"I can get my own drink," he said more sharply than I'd ever heard him speak before. "This is just as much my house as yours. I will ask Aunt Megan when I want something."

Ed stood in the doorway, looking on. "That's enough, James. Watch your manners when you talk to my friend."

"Manners? What kind of manners does your friend have? You didn't see what she did in front of Megan just now. It's disgusting."

I was horrified that James had witnessed the underwear scene.

"I'd better go, Ed. I'll see you later," Vee said calmly.

She walked over to the couch and picked up her purse as I walked over to the door to let her out. As she passed me, she evidently couldn't resist a last parting shot. "Ed and I have already talked about selling this house," she said triumphantly. "You should know it's too inconvenient for

Chris with all the stairs. He needs a place where everything is on one level, and I know I can get several million for a property like this, right on the lake with a dock and everything."

"I'm sure you can," I said coldly. "How are you going to get home?"

"I came in my own car. I'll see you all later."

"I'll have Maria wash your underwear. She can give it to Ed," I called after her.

I walked over to James. "I'm so sorry you had to witness all of this, James. But I'm proud of how you spoke up, even if it embarrassed your dad." I looked over at Ed who seemed a little crestfallen.

"Have you and Chris talked about selling this house, Ed?" I asked. I looked over at Chris, but he appeared just as startled as I was.

"Vee may have mentioned it," Ed admitted. "I agreed that Chris would be better off in a one-level house."

"I'm doing fine right where I am, big brother. And I plan to walk again soon."

James and I went into the kitchen to get a drink of water. "Your dad is a great guy, James, and he can do a lot better than settling down with this realtor. I agree she's good-looking, but has she really sold any real estate? I can't imagine anyone wanting to buy anything from her."

JP came and dragged James away.

"You look tired, little brother." I heard Ed say.

"I am tired," Chris answered. "And I don't know why. I exercise and eat well, and I don't drink anymore." He looked up at his brother as I returned.

"I know I've had a lot of floozies in my time as you've often pointed out." He shot me a quick glance. "Until I found Megan," he added with a big grin. "But don't you think this one is a little over the top for an old man like you?"

"I'm still healthy, little brother."

James was no longer within earshot as he and JP were out on the deck where JP had left his toys. Chris seemed to enjoy the drama, but Ed avoided looking at me.

A little later, we left for Settlers Inn. James and Thomas drove over in separate cars, as neither one was allowed to carry passengers yet, but Vee didn't show up.

"How was your trip to England, Mrs. Cronin?" Thomas asked politely, seemingly making an effort to sound worldly. His parents had done a good job raising him.

Although I was used to being addressed by Chris's family name, it was not my legal last name, and I almost always introduced myself as Megan Viets, my real name and pen name. "You can call me Megan, Thomas." I told him my trip was good but tiring. "Would you like to travel one day, Thomas?" I said.

"Naw, I don't know. I haven't thought about it much, I guess."

We gorged ourselves on smoked salmon, different kinds of meat, salads, and breads—no lobster today. After we had eaten our main meal and James and Thomas had taken JP for a short walk outside, I told both Ed and Chris in more detail about staying with my friend Caroline in London, and, for Ed's benefit, how Caroline and I had first met in Nigeria. Chris, of course, knew the story. Although I had kept Ed somewhat up to date about the case, I recounted my visit to Franco the tailor and Scotland Yard, what had happened in New York, how I had learned that the victim was a New York lawyer and that his name was indeed Aldo Bandini. What he was doing out here was still a mystery.

When the boys returned and sat down expecting desserts, I broached the subject of James going abroad.

"Ed," I said cautiously. "What do you think about James taking a trip to Europe, or rather Northern Europe, to take a late summer or fall course at Oslo University in Norway? He'll be eighteen right after graduation, right?"

Ed frowned and looked at James. "I know, and I guess it's time for James to see the world too," he said unexpectedly and shot me a quick glance before he continued, "as Chris and I had to do when we graduated high school. But I don't know that he's quite ready to go by himself."

I wasn't sure if Ed thought I would go with his son.

"He should absolutely go by himself," I said authoritatively. "So that he's forced to make new friends over there. He could also visit some of my second cousins that I've kept in touch with. He could hang out with them sometimes, at least at first."

Everyone remained silent.

"And what about you, Thomas?" I asked. "What are your plans?"

"I'll take classes at San Bernardino Community College since I don't know what I want to do yet."

"That's a fine idea," I said encouragingly. "Maybe you and I could go over and meet James in London or some place after his courses are over." I looked around at all the raised eyebrows around the table.

Chris cleared his throat. "Megan is trying to make world travelers out of you guys," he said jokingly. "What about the rest of us? How about we all go over and meet James somewhere?"

"Yeah, maybe we all need to get out more," Ed said thoughtfully. "I'm sorry about Vee's behavior earlier, whatever it was. I guess the women around here are a bit crude—and the men too," he added almost as an afterthought. "Do you want to travel to Europe by yourself then, James?"

"Do you think I should, Dad?" James answered in a conciliatory tone.

"Well, if you want to." Ed remained silent for a moment. Then he looked at me. "Maybe we should take advantage of Megan's offer to help with the travel arrangements. And I like the idea of all of us going over to meet you somewhere over there before you come home."

"Okay, I'll start to look into it," I said. "There are nonstop flights from LAX to Norway, and I'll email one of my cousins to give me some contact numbers at the university over there. Homestay would be nice. When the courses are over, we could meet up in London or Paris and fly home together." I looked at James. "How does that sound, James?"

James flushed. "Wow! That sounds awesome," he said and looked at his father who smiled benevolently.

We took our time with coffee and dessert, talking about the high school sports teams and local events. I didn't want to go into too many specifics regarding our study-travel plans until I had done a little more research.

13

SUSIE'S VISIT

Although Chris still drove around in his special van to check on his workers at the various job sites, he often complained about being tired, but I didn't have much time to think about it. I was busy preparing for Susie and Ashley's visit. I also had to go down the hill for both a doctor's visit and a dental appointment. On my way home, I stopped by the sheriff's station to inquire about any further development in the Aldo Bandini case.

Ed was in his office, and when he saw me in the doorway, he waved me in. Although the heat had subsided, his office was airconditioned. He was dressed in his light brown long-sleeved shirt and black tie. His large mahogany desk was scattered with papers, while his computer sat on a smaller desk on one side. A large American flag stood in the corner; a map of the San Bernardino mountain area with red and blue pins all over it covered an entire side wall. I sat down in a chair opposite him.

"As I told you, the FBI has been notified, but I haven't heard back from them yet," Ed said gloomily without an introductory hello. "These guys are not exactly known for cooperating with local police forces as you may know." He looked at me sternly. "You stay out of it from now on, though. This case is for the professionals."

I didn't answer and remained silent for a moment. "My friend and colleague from school is coming up to visit on Thursday to stay for the weekend. We went to graduate school together. I think you may have met her when she was up here last fall. I hope you can come over while she's here and get reacquainted with her."

He looked at me curiously.

"No, I'm not trying to set you up, but she's single, divorced, and she has a daughter, Ashley, who's about fourteen or fifteen. I thought perhaps James and Thomas could show her around a little."

"Okay, I'll stop by, and I'm sure James will come over. He seems to spend more time at your place than at home."

"He's always welcome. He's a nice kid, Ed."

"I know, and I'm not a good father or role model. Isn't that what you want to say?"

"No, not at all. I know it's hard to lose a spouse. I've been there. But you'll get over it." I rose, ready to leave. "I'll let you get back to work," I said.

He sighed. "Yeah, I'm seldom out of work."

"I smelled smoke in the air on my way up 18. There must be a lot of fires around." I walked out the door and turned around briefly. "Come over whenever you can." Then I waved good-bye.

On my way home I stopped at the post office to check my mailbox, and to my delight I saw that a package was waiting for me. My new suit had arrived from Franco the tailor. When I came home, I modeled it for Chris and we had some good laughs because we both knew that I would have few occasions to dress in such a fine garment up here.

Thursday afternoon Susie texted me from the car. She was stuck on the 210 Freeway. There had been an accident, and traffic had come to a standstill. It was after dark when she and Ashley finally arrived. They were dead tired, and after a quick bite to eat, we all went to bed.

The next morning, we rose early. I helped Chris whip up his special scrambled eggs and toast since there was no nursery school today, and Maria worked for Joe down in San Bernardino.

"This is the best homemade jelly I've ever tasted," Susie commented after we had sat down at the patio table on the deck.

"I picked it up at a fundraiser at the Presbyterian Church," Chris said proudly. Then he turned to Ashley, who was walking around with JP. "How would you like to go with me and Duchess to check on my job sites?" he asked.

"I guess," she said without much enthusiasm. She seemed a little more surly than last time we saw her.

"We call her 'old salty,'" Susie whispered to me.

"We'll take JP too. That way your mom and Megan can gossip in peace and quiet."

"We don't gossip, Chris," I said reprovingly. "We talk about important issues like literature and global warming."

Chris just grinned. Ashley looked at him and nodded in agreement as if the two were conspiring against us. She had grown taller since I had last seen her and was now about the same height as Susie, but not as tall as me yet. Her hair was long and blonde, and she tied it back in a ponytail as she was getting ready to go with Chris.

"You're sure you want to go, Ashley?" I asked.

She nodded in affirmation.

After they left, we went over to the railing and watched the lake.

"What a gorgeous view," Susie said admiringly. "I could stand and look at the water, the boats, and the birds all day. How do you get any writing done?"

"Well, I write at night as you know." I paused. "But what have you been up to lately?"

"Grading papers," she said with a laugh. "Remember those days? You will not believe how poorly the students write these days. I brought some samples to show you so that you can see what you're missing."

She went inside and returned with some typed and stapled papers. She gave me one to read:

Causes of Crime

People who create crimes has a higher risk of becoming offenders because of the circumstances into which they were born into. Crimes can be a action that offend or hurt another person and someone who acts upon illegal activities. Poverty, family backgrounds, and low self-esteem are factors which can be explain why some people causes a crime.

Poverty levels certainly play a big role for the reasons why crimes are created...

I put the essay down and looked at her. "How do you even begin to correct something like this?" I said in disbelief.

"I don't know. This is an American student who has gone through twelve years of school."

"Actually, I think this student has a severe learning disability. Is Ruth still there?"

"Yes, and I've given a copy to her, so we'll see."

"Well, if she can't do anything, no one can. She's good."

"True." She paused. "But tell me about your trip to London."

"All right," I said. We sat down, and I took a sip of cold coffee before I started. "It all started one very early morning while it was still dark. I was sitting under the gas lamp over there, and I was trying to work out the plot of my new novel. An unpopular principal of an elementary school in Los Angeles, a light-skinned big black woman, has been murdered. She had been married three times, and at least two of her husbands died under mysterious circumstances. She often boasted that when she was a classroom teacher, she was so strict that two of her students allegedly committed suicide. And so there are many suspects."

"And who dun it this time?'

"You'll find out when you read the book." I paused and smiled coyly. "Anyway, the moon was out. In fact, the moonlight was unusually bright that night, and I saw something being dumped in the lake, which later turned out to be a body. I went to London to track down the tailor who had made the victim's clothes to confirm the name of the person." I took another sip of cold coffee. "You know that my brother-in-law is the sheriff here, right? I think you met him when you were up here last fall."

"Yes, I seem to remember him. Big guy, right? Looks like Chris."

"Yes, that's right. He's coming over to see you again. I don't remember if I told you his wife died of breast cancer not too long ago."

"Oh, I'm sorry."

"He's had a rough time getting over it, but he has a son to take care of, so he's doing better." I paused for a moment before I continued, "Well, I talked him into letting me take the clothes to England to see if the tailor could remember the guy."

"That's the craziest thing I've ever heard. Was it even legal?"

"I don't see why not."

"And your brother-in-law was onboard with that?"

"Yes, albeit reluctantly." I took another sip of coffee. "Ed, my brother-in-law, told me that the FBI has now taken over the case."

The sun was already high in the sky and flooded the deck with its burning rays, so I rolled the umbrella out from its corner of the deck to shield Susie's face. Her hair was reddish and shiny with a new color job, and her face was pale. I went inside and brought some sunscreen for both of us.

"Dr. Frederic Pagel is back from Africa," she said suddenly.

"Really? Is he teaching summer school?"

"No, but he came by the other day, and he asked about you."

"What did he say?"

"Oh, nothing special really. He hoped you were happy. He had heard about Chris's accident and said if you wanted anything to let him know."

"That's nice."

"Yes. He's a good guy."

"I know."

"Actually, I asked him to come up with me to see you, although I really don't know what I would have done if he had said yes."

We both laughed heartily at the possibility.

"I guess I could have pretended that he was my date," Susie said finally, and we laughed even more hysterically.

"You remember he asked me to go to Africa with him, right?" I said.

"Yes, I remember."

"My life would surely have been different."

"Yes. 'How singular is life, how fickle, how little is needed to change a person's life,' to quote Guy de Maupassant." She remained silent for a little while seemingly in meditation. "Actually, he's getting ready to go to Mongolia," she said. "Evidently, most of the people outside the cities are farmers and goat herders who move from area to area with their flocks grazing, but because of climate change, their patterns of movement, tracked by satellites, have changed. The sheep are kept too long in one spot, ruining the grass, which normally absorbs half as much carbon as the rain forest in Africa. As part of the carbon offset trade, Fred will pay the farmers to move their sheep sooner."

"It sounds complicated, but that, of course, is just like Fred."

"Yes, it is very complicated, and I'm not sure I understand it completely, but Fred is a smart man. I think when he met you, he figured you'd be the perfect companion for him with all your crazy travels."

"Maybe. But traveling ain't what it used to be, especially traveling on commercial airlines. I liked traveling with Robert in his private jet, and I think you'll see more and more people choosing to pay more for that kind of service."

Just then, I heard Ed drive up in his patrol car, turning on his siren for just a fraction of a second to announce his arrival. A few minutes later, he came out on the deck, looking his usual imposing self in his black boots, brown summer uniform, dark sunglasses, and no hat. I noticed Susie do a double-take, her cheeks flushing, and I gave her a stern look.

"Are you ladies safe out here all by yourselves?" he said jokingly. "Chris has taken the kids out, I see."

"Ed, this is my good friend and colleague Susie," I said.

"How do you do, ma'am?" he greeted her formally.

"I'm well, thank you, and you?"

"Fine. And I do remember you from last fall."

"Yes, I remember you too, but I don't think you were in uniform then."

"How would you like to take a ride in the patrol car?" he suggested.

"That would be an exciting adventure," Susie agreed readily. "What do you think, Megan?"

"If you want to." I looked at Ed. "Do you want me to come too?"

Ed scowled at me, and Susie's eyebrows rose.

"Where did Chris and the kids go?" Ed inquired gruffly.

"They're out looking at Chris's job sites and won't be back for a while," I answered. "We'll leave him a note."

Susie slid into the front seat after Ed removed a giant flashlight that he stuck between his man-spread legs, making him look even more sexy. For some reason it irritated me. And as if that wasn't enough, Susie seemed to be smitten. But wasn't that what I wanted? Wouldn't it be great if Susie moved up here? We would really have some adventures then, and we could both teach at the local high school. Ashley would have a little brother or sister, and JP would have another cousin. No, stop it. My imagination was running away with me as it often did.

14

THE MISSING SHOE

Ed was busy with four area fires, once again deliberately set at opposite ends of the county, presumably so as to put a stress on our local resources. However, James and Thomas came over mid-morning the next day. Both boys had grown tall and were athletic. James had just had his dark hair cut in a new "cool" style, but Thomas's fair hair was longer and wavy. They both wore matching black T-shirts. After introductions, James wanted to make "Frappuccino" in my coffee maker for Thomas, Ashley, and himself, and I immediately nodded in approval. To Susie's delight, Ashley now finally looked up from her cell phone and actually put it away.

"Do you want to take Ashley and show her around a little?" I asked James and then looked at Susie.

"Do you both drive then?" Susie asked. Her voice held a certain doubt.

The two boys nodded.

"They're good kids," I said reassuringly. "James drives Chris's old Range Rover, and Thomas drives a Toyota 4Runner." I turned to Thomas. "Right, Thomas?"

"Yes," Thomas said and nodded.

"Mountain kids prefer rugged vehicles," I explained to Susie.

Ashley livened up. She stood by the counter with her Frappuccino. "Can I go with them, Mom?"

Susie looked at me, her eyebrows raised and her mouth partially open.

"Well, actually, I didn't mean for you to drive together. I'd take you down to the resort, and you could hang out there for a while."

James looked a little crestfallen but soon recovered.

"It's not that I don't think you're a good driver, James," I said apologetically. "But I believe it's illegal for you to take a minor as a passenger right now." I hesitated for a few seconds. "Yes, I know, your father is the sheriff, and no one would probably stop you, but we should hold ourselves to a higher standard, not lower." I stopped to think for a moment. "Actually, I have another idea. How about we ask Uncle Chris to take you over to the new amusement park on the highway?"

Chris and JP came into the kitchen from the bedroom. He was willing and offered to take JP as well.

"Thank you, Chris," Susie said and breathed out a sigh of relief.

"I brought hiking boots," Susie announced after they had left.

"Good," I said. "I suppose the function of that statement is that you want to hike one of the many trails around here. Am I right?"

Susie smiled. "Yes, I remember the lectures on the functions of language too. Was it in Dr. Hertz's linguistics class or was it Dr. Ross's class?"

"Both, I think."

We laughed as we reminisced about our graduate school days.

"I always wanted to walk the trail around the lake," Susie said. "Are you up to it?"

"It's about twelve or fifteen miles," I cautioned her. "It will take us all day, but that's fine with me. We'll pack a lunch and water, and I'll take my little rucksack."

"Are these shorts and a T-shirt okay?"

"Of course, that's what I wear around here when it's warm like today," I said. "But we should also take a jacket. The weather, like everything else in the mountains, can change quickly."

We slathered ourselves with sunscreen and stuffed our hair into wide-brimmed hats.

"We'll take Duchess with us too," I said.

Then we started out toward the Resort.

Susie continually commented on the mansions along the trail. "But it doesn't look like anyone is living in any of them," she said finally.

"No, they're mostly second homes. It's the caretakers who get to enjoy them the most."

We took a short break at the Resort, already bustling with visitors. To rejoin the trail afterward, we had to pass through a locked gate. I had forgotten my card that gave us permission to walk through, but fortunately, I remembered the code, punched it in, and the gate opened.

The houses were even grander on this side. I let Duchess loose, and she soon discovered gophers and squirrels to chase, but I reined her in and put her back on the leash when other hikers came toward us with their dogs.

By early afternoon, we'd reached the halfway point and found a pretty spot and a couple of rocks to sit on. I had made ham and cheese sandwiches that we ate with our bottled water.

"Life seems to move at a slower pace up here," Susie commented. "But I don't think I could live here full time."

Another couple with a dog passed us, but Duchess paid no attention to them or me when I called her back. She was busy digging under every root and rock, bringing us rags and sticks that she evidently found interesting.

"There's certainly little diversity in this place," Susie continued. "I suppose you have to have money to live around here."

"True," I said. "But farther away from the lake we have people of different ethnicities." I looked at her. "Your thighs are lobster red. You didn't put on enough sunscreen, and now you have a bad sunburn," I said and rooted around in my rucksack for my big tube. I gave it to her and she covered herself with the white cream.

"You certainly belong to the white race," I said and looked at some ultra-white spots that were not yet burned. I made sure she had covered all the bare spots. Her face was fine as it was shielded by her hat and her dark sunglasses.

"When are you going back to work?" Susie asked.

"I don't know. I was thinking of getting my PhD first. Do you think it's worth it?"

"Absolutely."

"You're not teaching summer school, I take it. Do you want to stay up here a little longer?"

"Well, maybe another time. Ashley and I are going on a river cruise from Switzerland to Amsterdam next week. We'll leave on Saturday, and I need several days to prepare. I'm not like you who can take off at a moment's notice."

Duchess was running a little too far ahead. I called her back but to no avail, so we rose and continued our trek.

When we reached the north side, I showed Susie a 16,000 square-foot home and told her about the underground parking garage with turn-tables for about twenty cars.

"That's obscene."

"That's what I thought the first time I saw it. And who on earth would want to live in such a monstrosity?"

"Not me," Susie said, albeit with a sigh.

Although the trail was partly shaded by the tall trees around the lake, it was warm. Many properties were fenced in all the way to the water, and the trail zigzagged up and down the slopes around them. The back of Susie's T-shirt was soaking wet, and drops of perspiration rolled down her cheeks. She was not used to the altitude, of course, although I felt sweaty too.

We soldiered on in silence and stopped often to catch our breaths and have sips of water. I texted Chris where we were and told him not to expect us home any time soon. Fortunately, he texted back that he and the kids were having a great time at the park and had no plans to return home any time soon either. He loved to spend time with the children.

Suddenly I discovered that I had completely lost sight of Duchess. I called her and whistled but she was nowhere to be seen.

"Susie, did you see which way Duchess ran?" I asked desperately.

"No, I guess I have just enough energy to put one foot in front of the other. I know you said the hike was twelve or fifteen miles, but I didn't realize the hike was going to be this hard since it's all flat, except for a few minor slopes around these spectacular properties."

"It's the altitude, Susie. But you take a break here while I search for the dog."

A young couple passed us, and I asked them if they'd seen a German shepherd, but they shook their heads with a quick "sorry," so I walked on, calling, whistling, and clapping my hands as I'd seen Chris do at times, not noticing a man walking toward me in the opposite direction. He looked at me curiously as if thinking I belonged in an asylum.

"I'm looking for my dog," I said sheepishly. "A German shepherd. Have you seen her?"

"There's a German shepherd up ahead less than a quarter mile, but it's behind a fence that goes all the way down to the water. You have to go around the property to get through."

"Well, no, that's not mine. My dog just broke away from her leash." I held up the leash to show him that I wasn't a complete lunatic.

A little farther on, I finally saw Duchess inside a large fenced estate. The pale yellow, mansion-like house sat perched about 300 yards above the lakeshore. I walked all the way down to the water to see if I could wade in, climb up on the dock, and walk up the wide path to the house. No boat was parked in the slip, but, to my surprise, I saw a canal of sorts that went in under the grounds. A padlocked gate stood between the dock and the path. However, Duchess had to get through somehow. She was furiously digging in the dirt near the house. I knew she wouldn't be able to jump the fence, so I walked up the slope to see where the entrance was. Not until I reached the other side of the enormous house did I see a gate with a big chain.

Susie was ambling along at the bottom of the slope. "Duchess is behind the fence," I called out to her. "I have to figure out a way to get in. The only gate I've seen is right here, but it's locked."

The house was shuttered up, and no one seemed to be home, but I walked up to the front entrance anyway and knocked. No cars were parked in the driveway. I fiddled around with the latch at the top of the gate beside the house and unfastened it. The chain was long enough to provide a narrow opening, and I managed to squeeze through. How and why Duchess had decided to squeeze through I don't know, but as I entered, I saw gopher-holes and a gopher scurrying along the outside of the fence. A large green trashcan near the house had been tipped over, and the trash was strewn all around. Duchess was sniffing and digging, although at first I didn't see what could be so fascinating.

To show that I only wanted to repossess my dog, in case someone had noticed me, I called Duchess and whistled. Duchess, however, paid no attention. She growled and would not let me come near. I could not put the leash on her collar. She bit into something black and leathery. It was a muddy shoe. She shook it wildly from side to side until a petrified gopher fell out. As soon as the gopher started to scurry away, Duchess let go of the shoe and chased after the frightened animal. My heart stopped for a moment, for the shoe bore a striking resemblance to the shoe found in the lake near Aldo Bandini's body.

When I finally caught up with Duchess, I was able to grab her by the collar, and, with some effort, I forced the leash on her. Then I went back to look at the shoe more closely. Yes, it looked like it could be the same shoe as the one found in the lake by Aldo Bandini's body. I took the empty sandwich bag out of my rucksack, turned it inside out and made sure it was clean. Then, sticking my hand in the bag, I gingerly picked up the shoe, shook off most of the dirt, and carefully folded it into the bag so as not to leave any fingerprints on it. I was not sure how important the shoe would be as evidence since we already knew the victim's identity. However, I knew from researching my books that one does not tamper with any kind of evidence. I wrapped the plastic bag in my jacket and stuffed it into my bag.

Meanwhile, the weather had suddenly turned colder. The sun had disappeared, and ominous clouds were building up over the ridge.

Susie had missed the gate and sat forlorn on a fallen tree trunk on the other side of the property.

"How did you get in?" she called out.

"Through a gate that was only partially secured. Wait for me there. Duchess has dug up something quite amazing, but I need to tidy up the ground to make the place look less disturbed."

I didn't worry about the trashcan because a coyote could have come through the gate to look for food, but with my fingers I straightened out a few sticks and dispersed some leaves that Duchess had dug up.

Then came the trick of squeezing back out through the gate again. Duchess crawled through in no time, while I took a little longer.

"We're only a mile or so away from home," I told Susie when Duchess and I caught up with her. "Look at those clouds over the ridge," I said and pointed to the northeast. "And here comes the wind. You're shivering. Put on your jacket, and let's hurry. Rain and thunder will be here shortly."

"So, what did the dog find?" Susie inquired.

"A black men's shoe, but not just any shoe. It looks like the mate to the shoe someone found near the body in the lake, and we think they may have belonged to the victim, whose name I'm pretty sure is Aldo Bandini. I put it in my rucksack"

"But isn't that evidence then? Should you have removed it?"

"Well, I'll call Ed. Duchess dug it up, so I took it from her."

The first lightning struck the lake followed by a loud clap of thunder. No more than a minute later, the cold rain came at us in sideway gusts, and we were soon drenched. Duchess was howling. She was afraid of thunder and fireworks, and we ran with Duchess on the leash all the way home.

15

TRAGEDY STRIKES

The sudden wind had whipped up the dead leaves, and the rain soon made the dirt trail muddy. As we reached our house, Duchess started shaking herself, spraying even more water onto me. I put her in her pen and followed Susie into the mudroom, where we kicked off our boots and Susie tore off her wet jacket. "Where's your jacket, Megan?" she wondered suddenly.

I pulled my jacket out of my rucksack. "I used it to wrap up the plastic sack with the dirty shoe," I explained.

"What?"

"Well, as I told you, Duchess had evidently made her way through the narrow opening in the chained gate and was rooting around in some trash from a knocked-over trashcan. I think she was chasing a gopher that had hidden in the shoe. The gopher fell out when Duchess was shaking the shoe and as soon as it scurried away, Duchess lost interest. I picked up the shoe and placed it in our empty lunch bag. Then I wrapped it all in my jacket that I stuffed in my backpack."

Susie shook her head and looked straight at me. "What a bizarre story!"

We walked into the living room where Chris and the big kids were playing cards. They barely looked up. JP was helping Maria in the kitchen, so I returned to the mudroom with the dirty jacket and the shoe in the plastic bag.

"I cannot believe how quickly the weather changed," Susie continued as I came back in. "One minute I was feeling hot, and the next thing I knew I was miserably cold." She started up the stairs. "I'll be in the shower if anyone wants me," she called down to no one in particular.

I walked into the kitchen where Maria and JP were preparing pulled-pork tamales. It smelled delicious, and I realized that I was hungry, although I, too, needed to clean up first.

As soon as I had showered and dressed and Susie had come downstairs again, all fresh with glowing cheeks, her auburn hair pinned up in a bun, we sat down to dinner at the big dining room table overlooking the deck and the lake. The thunder and lightning continued, casting ghostly shadows around the darkened room. Chris asked James to switch on the big chandelier, which lit up the dark walls, but Chris also brought out candles in case the electricity went out.

Everyone commented on the tamales, and I told Chris about the shoe. Like Susie, he was skeptical.

"You should have left the shoe there," he said reprovingly.

"But if the owner returned and saw it among the trash, he would have tossed it back in the can," I countered. "The trash truck would have picked it up, and the evidence would have been lost forever." I paused. "I'll call Ed and tell him what happened."

But Ed didn't pick up the phone. I left him a short message, "Call me back when you can. It's not an emergency."

———

James and Thomas were already there when Ed came over the next day. He was in civilian clothes with the ever-present sports coat concealing his gun. We all had a quick lunch, and then we said good-bye to Susie and Ashley. James and Thomas also left.

After they had left, Ed and I sat down on the couch while Chris sat in his wheelchair, his eyes closed. I asked Ed how he liked my friend.

"She's very nice, I'm sure," he said neutrally without looking at me.

"No spark?" I said with a smile.

He just glowered at me. "What do you mean?"

"You know what I mean."

"She's too much of a delicate snowflake for the mountains, don't you think? And too conventional for me." He looked at me with a grin on his face.

I remained silent, although I wanted to comment on his fancy snowflake metaphor. It did really describe Susie in a way.

"What did you call me about last night?" he asked. "It was too late to call back when I finally got home from the fires."

"Well, here's what happened...if I made a mistake, I apologize." I took a deep breath before I continued. "Susie and I took Duchess on a walk around the lake yesterday. When we reached the north shore, Duchess found a shoe in some trash by one of the big estates, a pale yellow house. The shoe looked like the pair to the shoe your deputies found in the lake near Aldo Bandini's body. I put it in a plastic bag and brought it home. I hope you saved the pair. It was a black Italian dress shoe."

Ed looked at me with raised eyebrows.

I went into the mudroom to fetch the shoe in the plastic bag and gave it to Ed. "Do you remember what the other shoe looked like? Isn't this the pair?"

Ed took the bag and looked at the shoe carefully.

"I know it may be evidence," I said apologetically, "but if I hadn't brought it with me, it would have gone out with the next trash pick-up."

"That's okay. I'll take it down to headquarters and see what the FBI agents make of it."

"Do you know that under that property is a kind of man-made inlet or canal with concrete walls and I think an iron gate that was open. What on earth can that be for?"

"I don't know what house you're talking about," Ed said. "But many properties have these subterranean boat slips. That's just the way it is."

"They do? I guess I've never seen any before."

"You can only see it from the water when you drive by in a boat." He smiled indulgently. "But I am really concerned that you're meddling in this. This case is now out of our hands."

"I'm not trying to meddle. It was really a freak accident that I found this shoe. Actually, it was Duchess who found it anyway."

Ed turned to Chris, who was still in his wheelchair with his eyes closed. "You look tired, little bro. Are you all right?"

"I'm good," Chris said and opened his eyes slowly.

I walked over to Chris and looked at him closely. His face was pallid and drawn. "Did you overdo it yesterday, Chris?" I asked.

"No, I'm all right." He smiled faintly, and he sounded tired.

Ed left, and I didn't see anyone or do anything all afternoon. Maria had taken JP out to a playgroup at the library, so we made our way upstairs to the media room. We sat down on the couch and watched a documentary on the Nicaraguan countryside, with peaceful, green meadows and hidden rivers. A lone riverboat was puttering upstream toward remote villages, untouched by the rest of the world.

"We should travel there sometime," I suggested. "With your fluent Spanish skills, we could venture into these faraway places."

However, as soon as I finished speaking, I noticed that Chris had dozed off.

The next day, he complained about feeling cold, but when I put my hand on his forehead, he felt hot and sweaty. I gave him two aspirin and helped him lie down on the couch. He said he felt better, although he didn't move around much all day. The next couple of days, he stayed in bed and was too sick to get up. He had a fever of 104 degrees, but I assumed it was just the flu. Out of habit, I wanted to call Ed but I came to my senses and called the doctor's office instead. I talked to one of the nurses who knew Chris. Because he didn't have a sore throat or a cough, she said to come in right away in case it was an infection.

Unfortunately, Chris had told the therapists and caregivers to take a break, so no one had checked his legs and when the doctor removed Chris's pants, he found an ugly, infected sore on the back of his right thigh. I was horrified when I saw it. It ought to have hurt, but Chris didn't have any feeling in his legs, so it had gone unnoticed.

"We have to do surgery right away to remove the infection," the doctor said gravely and called the hospital to prepare them for Chris's arrival.

I was speechless and took Chris's hand. "Oh, Chris, how could we not have seen this? I'm so sorry. And you can't feel anything, of course."

"No, I haven't noticed anything. I showered on Monday, but I guess I didn't wash back there."

"Do you need an ambulance?" the doctor asked.

"No, I'll take him."

I wheeled Chris out and drove over to the hospital right off the highway, overlooking the lake. An orderly came out to help me wheel Chris into the small clinic to start the paperwork before anyone would touch him. When that was done, two nurses put him on a gurney and helped him undress. They put a hospital gown on him and warm socks before they covered him with a warm electric blanket. After looking at a chart, they turned him on his side and motioned for me to come over.

They pointed to a red line that had started from the infection and was moving up his torso toward the heart. They shook their heads and didn't say a word. My jaw dropped, and tears welled up in my eyes. "Where's the doctor?" I finally asked.

After what seemed like an eternity, the doctor finally came rushing in. I stood by Chris's bedside, gave him a kiss, and told him I loved him before he was wheeled into the operating room.

I don't know how long I sat in the waiting room. Two or three other people sat along the wall. They looked sullen and tired. No one was reading the magazines placed on the little tables between the seats. At one point I called Joe, my father-in-law, and then Ed, but Cheryl, Ed's sister-in-law by marriage—a nurse who worked at the hospital—had already called them, and they were on their way.

Cheryl came in first.

"He's in the operating room," I told her as my voice broke into a sob.

"I know," Cheryl said and put her arm around me. It wasn't long ago that her sister, Ed's wife, had died in this hospital.

"I can't believe we didn't see this earlier." I cleared my throat and swallowed to regain my composure. "He has complained about feeling tired for some time, but he always made light of it."

Ed came in his uniform followed by Joe. Cheryl updated them. Joe put his arm around me without saying a word.

Ed kept his distance. "He'll be all right," he said consolingly, but Cheryl and Joe looked at me full of sorrow and remained silent.

The doctor finally came out with his "shower" cap and scrubs still on. He shook hands with Ed and Joe. "We think we got to all the infected area, but the poison has already spread to the bloodstream. It's too late to amputate his leg, but we've shot him full of antibiotics. We'll just have to wait and see."

"What's the prognosis, Doc?" Ed asked.

"Fair."

"I guess that means neither good nor bad but not hopeless," I said pessimistically.

"That's right. I'm sorry I can't be of more help. He's in the recovery room now. You'll soon be able to see him."

He left the room.

Ed's face had turned ashen. He shot me a quick glance. Did I see accusation in that look? I honestly don't know.

"I'm sorry I haven't looked after your little brother as well as I should these last few days. I was so busy with my friend and what not."

"It's not your fault, Megan," Joe said softly.

Ed moved toward me. "I have been busy too, hunting down crazy people who run around setting fires all over," he said with bitterness in his voice.

"Has anyone been hurt?" I asked.

"In the fires, you mean?"

"Yes."

"No, and no structures have been damaged."

Cheryl's face looked sad, but she finally spoke up. "I'll give you something to sleep tonight," she said. "We'll set up a cot for you in Chris's room as soon as he's assigned one." She paused. "I'll go and check."

When she returned, she told us to follow her as she led the way to Chris's assigned room. As soon as we had seen Chris resting peacefully in his bed, Cheryl told Joe and Ed that it would be too much stress for Chris to have so many people around. Grim-faced, they gave Cheryl and me perfunctory hugs and quietly left.

When I mentioned that I had to go home and take care of JP, Cheryl assured me that she'd check with Maria and ask her if she could take JP home with her.

"I'll explain everything to her. She'll understand, and she'll want to know Chris's prognosis."

I thanked her. Then I pulled a chair next to Chris's bed and sat down. His eyes were closed, and he was breathing quietly. I closed my eyes. An image of another hospital room appeared in my mind. It was after the accident. I was sitting by his bed then too, looking at his handsome face. We weren't married then, but I was pregnant and wondering what would happen, not only to Chris, but to me and the baby. He was just as handsome now, even if his hair was matted and his skin pallid. How would it have been if he hadn't run into the flaming house and gotten himself hit by that burning beam? Who knows? I remembered the literal version of Susie's paraphrased quote about the singularity of life: "How singular is life and how full of changes! How small a thing will ruin or save one!"

Yes, physically Chris had been ruined in a sense, but he had also shown what a fighter he was. Could he fight through this incident as well?

I must have fallen asleep because the next thing I knew it was daylight. Chris was awake, but he looked exhausted. An assistant nurse came in with breakfast for both Chris and me, but Chris could eat only a little. A team of nurses came to wash him and spruce him up for the doctor's visit. After he had looked at the chart, he took Chris's hand and asked him how he felt, but Chris barely answered.

"What do you think, doctor?" I asked apprehensively.

"We'll have to wait and see." He felt Chris's feet and left.

I sat by Chris's bedside and waited one more day. I didn't feel like reading. A television was mounted on the wall so that Chris could watch from his bed. I turned it on but there was not a single program on worth watching. The nurses came and went. Some kept feeling his feet. I did too, and his feet were ice cold.

Throughout the day, people entered and left. The cleaning crew came in with rags and mops ready to clean, nurses' helpers came with lunch and supper, and Cheryl popped in before she started her shift. Joe came and sat with me for a while, his face pale and drawn. He didn't say much, and Chris barely responded to his touch. Ed came in, looking stern and official, but that was just his mask to the world.

"How's he doing?" he asked gruffly.

"The same," I said. "Are you out making your runs?"

"Yes, but I have a little leeway to visit my brother."

"Thank you," I said quietly. I was tired. "How are the fires?"

"Oh, they're pretty much contained, and my deputies have located the whereabouts of the arsonists. There are several of them."

"I'm not surprised. I'm glad they've been caught. Who are they?"

"Foreign names. I can't remember them off hand."

He went out in the hallway and brought in another chair and sat down next to me. I looked at him seriously, and he reached over to hold my hand.

"You're a strong woman, Megan," he said. "You'll get through this too." If there had been bitterness or gruffness before, it had vanished. Ed was a good man at the bottom of his heart.

The next night, I woke up sometime after midnight hearing Chris calling my name. He was awake and was trying to say something and pointed to his plastic urinal. I finally understood that he wanted to relieve himself. While I held the urinal between his legs, he was able to go, but as I was about to get up and empty the bottle, he started shaking. His eyes appeared glassy and were moving around in their sockets. I set the urinal down on the floor and held him up awkwardly before I pushed the emergency button. Nurses and staff immediately came rushing in, then the doctor. They were frantically trying to insert tubes and attach nodes while I was still holding him. In a flash I remembered a scene from the Long Beach hospital where one of my Japanese students was kept on a life-support system after a car crash. There was no hope, and when the parents arrived from Japan—the father was actually a doctor—they gave the order to pull the plug. I was horrified, but the parents just stood there so stoically.

I heard a rattle in Chris's chest and remember screaming. He convulsed but the doctor did not ask me to move, and I cannot remember anyone trying to make me. To my horror, there was another rattle, the death rattle, before he took his last breath and died in my arms. I cried and I lowered my head. I felt numb. He was all of a sudden so heavy that I couldn't breathe. I kissed him before the doctor and a nurse slowly and carefully helped me over to the chair. I don't remember seeing them wheeling Chris out. I was shivering but lacked the willpower to stand up. It all seemed so impossible. How strange death is! One moment he was alive, going to the bathroom, and the next moment he was dead. Dead and lifeless. I could not believe that I would never see him alive again, and my thoughts immediately went to JP, who would not see his father again or even remember him.

16

ARRANGEMENTS

Death hung in the air like a pall. Outside it was still dark, and the stark neon lights gave the hospital room a cold and sickly ambiance. As if chained to the chair, I just sat there, unable to move. At some point a stout, middle-aged nurse came in and rummaged around.

"Do you want to call someone?" she asked and put a blanket around my shoulders.

I looked at her and realized that Ed and Joe should know.

"What time is it?" I asked.

"Three o'clock."

Joe would be asleep, as would Ed, but Ed would have his phone on in case of an emergency. I pushed Ed's number in my contact list, and he picked up right away.

"Ed," I said in a shaky voice. That was the only word that would come across my lips, but he knew immediately what it was all about.

"I'll come right over," he said and hung up.

The nurse came over and stood by my side. "I'm sorry," she said kindly as she put her hand on my shoulder. "There was nothing we could do. He's at rest now."

"Do you know him?" I asked and realized immediately that I'd used the wrong tense. "I mean, did you know him?"

"Yes, I knew both him and his brother, the sheriff. Good-looking guys both of them, but Chris was exceptionally handsome. He could have made it in Hollywood. Instead, he chose you," she added cheerfully.

"Did you know his first wife too?"

"Sure, and she was crazy. Her whole family is crazy. I guess a deputy shot her before she could get to Chris. If she could have, she would have killed him on the spot."

"I know. I was there. That's how Chris got hurt. She had run away from the asylum and somehow had entered the house and set it on fire. A burning beam fell on Chris and injured his spine."

"Yes, that's what I heard. He may have tried to save her. Who knows?"

As Chris had often commented, everyone knew everything about everyone else in this small town. It wasn't that different from Wisconsin. When I went out to California to go to college, it was a big news item in the local paper. Then, when I moved to Africa with an adventurous bush pilot, I became the talk of the town. Actually, it was the same in our small ex-patriate community in Lagos. I guess it's part of human nature all over the world.

It was only a few minutes later that Ed stood in the doorway in a T-shirt and jeans.

"How are you, Judy," he greeted the nurse with a steady voice.

"I'm sorry, Ed. There was nothing we could do."

"I know." He turned to me. "How are you holding up, Megan?"

I rose, and he came closer and put his arms around me. I buried my face in his shoulder, but I couldn't get a word out to greet him. Tears ran down my cheeks and made his shirt wet. He didn't say anything more, and after a few minutes, I looked up at him. His eyes were filled with tears too. I'd never seen him or Chris cry, but losing his only brother like this was probably too much even for Ed.

"I'll take you home," he said finally.

"But I have the van parked outside," I objected.

"We'll pick it up tomorrow. You need some rest."

"I've done nothing but rest all day here," I said. "And I actually did sleep some last night."

Judy, the nurse, still stood by the door and walked us out to Ed's white sedan. Ed was used to taking charge, and if he said we'd go in his car, we would go in his car.

At the house, Ed parked in the driveway and came in with me. I walked over to the big fireplace and sat on the couch, but Ed started for the kitchen.

"I'll look in Chris's wine cabinet. He surely kept a bottle of brandy handy."

For some reason, seeing Ed head for Chris's wine collection made me break down into a sob. Chris liked to have a drink or two or three in the evening. However, after the scene I made one time at my old cabin before we were married, he never drank enough to get drunk. I sighed and slowly regained my composure. Ed brought two glasses of brandy and sat next to me. We both took a couple of small sips, and the strong brandy burned my throat.

"Chris was more than a brother to me," he said contemplatively as I stared at the enormous fireplace that still showed some black spots from the fire.

"I always felt responsible for him after Mother died. When he had trouble in school, I came with him to try to straighten everything out for him. My father was busy with his various girlfriends of the month and was often away, so it was just Maria, Chris, and me. We spent many summers at a beach house in Malibu, learning to surf and sail." He paused for a moment and took a deep breath. "In the winter, we'd go skiing at the many ski resorts around the mountain." He took another sip of brandy and cleared his throat. "Maria took care of the house. She's very loyal, and my father has paid her well over the years too. You probably know that she's a beneficiary on our trust too."

"Yes, Chris told me about your trips to Malibu. He often talked about how he relied on you for everything, and how important it was for him to have your approval."

"I guess. But he was also really good at whatever he tried." His lips drew back into a faint smile as if he were recalling something. "When he married his first wife, we were not happy with him," he said.

"I know. He told me, but he got his little girl from the marriage, and he loved his child, even if she suffered from Down syndrome. He said she used to call it the 'Up syndrome.'"

"Yes. That was cute. She was really loving."

We drank up, and Ed went back to refill our glasses once more.

"Death is strange," I said bitterly as he returned with full glasses and sat down. We drank in silence for a few minutes.

"It happens so quickly," I continued. "A moment before he took his last breath, he wanted to relieve himself. As I put the warm urinal away, he convulsed and died. Gone. And here we are alive, drinking brandy. Cheers!" I said and took a big sip. "Yes, we're here, alive," I continued, "while Chris is dead, dead, dead. I say it over and over, you know, but it has no meaning. It's just a funny word. It rhymes with bed, fed and red. It really should be pronounced 'deed.' We used to say that 'when two vowels go a-walking, the first one does the talking.'" I took another sip. "I know I should now be gently crying. Then you could hold my hand and comfort me. But nothing seems real. It's like a nightmare." I looked up at him. A frown had crept between his brows. "I don't even feel grief. I'd like to grieve for Chris, but I don't know what it means. Did you grieve when Elizabeth died?" I asked.

"I did," he said thoughtfully. "But she'd been suffering for so long that it was in many ways a relief. James took her death harder." He stopped for a moment to finish his drink. "We'll tell him about Chris tomorrow."

After I had finished the second glass, I started yawning.

"Why don't you go to bed," Ed suggested. "I'll sleep here on the couch. I don't think you should be alone tonight."

I got up, feeling a bit unsteady.

"Tomorrow, I'll call our undertaker, our local funeral bureau," Ed said. "They'll handle everything. They took care of Elizabeth's funeral, and they made it so easy. James and I will pick up your van."

"Thank you, Ed," I said and walked slowly, first to the bathroom and then to bed.

Maria brought JP over the next morning, and JP came over to my side of the bed and woke me up. "Daddy?" he said simply and looked at the side where Chris should have been.

"Daddy is gone, JP," I said and reached out for him.

"Daddy gone," he repeated and crawled up next to me.

We joined Maria in the kitchen. She looked at me inquiringly. She hadn't heard, of course, and when I told her, she broke down. "Chris was like a son to me," she sobbed.

Ed came in. He put his arm around the weeping woman and held her for what seemed a very long time. He spoke to her in Spanish as was often his and Chris's custom. She was, as Chris had often told me, the closest they'd had to a mother, and Joe had decided that she should speak to them in Spanish rather than broken English.

We each had a bowl of cereal, and Ed called Joe.

"He's in disbelief," Ed said after he'd hung up. "He'll be here in an hour."

We walked around the house and were reminded of Chris's presence everywhere.

While Maria, Joe, and Ed handled all the funeral arrangements the next few days, I took care of JP. He didn't understand completely what was going on naturally, and he kept me from breaking down and feeling sorry for myself. James was a great help as well. One day, James, JP, and I went down to the big shopping center on the 210 Freeway and bought new clothes for the funeral, a simple but fine black dress for me, a dark blue suit for James, and a little coat and a pair of slacks for JP. I realized it would be a big event; I would be watched and criticized as an outsider, so I wanted us at the very least to be appropriately dressed.

I called my mother in Wisconsin and had a good cry with her, but we agreed that it would be better for her to come out after the funeral. Then I emailed Caroline in London and, of course, Susie. Cindy and Chad came by, as did Cheryl and Jonathan. Flowers and cards poured in from everywhere. Some people even brought food.

The day of the funeral came and went in one big blur. The chapel was packed with close to 200 people. Chris and his family were well known around the area, and this was a tragedy of epic proportion, in which everyone, it seemed, wanted to participate. I'm sure there was a certain amount of *schadenfreude* too. Money was involved as was scandal. People still remembered Amanda's violent death, and there was even a dash of sex in the mix.

Vee, Ed's realtor girlfriend came up to me, looking elegant as usual in a pastel blue suit and black heels.

"I'm so sorry, dear," she said with a somber expression on her face.

"Thank you," I answered mechanically.

Joe, James, Ed and I sat together in front, and when Ed went up to the podium to speak for the family, she tried to take his seat.

"My dad is going to sit there," James told her firmly. Did she really want to use this occasion to show how close she and Ed were? She quietly found a seat behind us instead.

Ed gave a good eulogy, looking very composed and official in his dark suit, but I don't remember anything he said. What can one say, other than clichés, in a speech like that anyway?

I felt empty inside despite a strange pit in my stomach. My thoughts went back to Robert's small and informal memorial service. I had traveled to Africa to claim his body, and I had brought his coffin back on a flight to Los Angeles, where he was cremated. His parents were deceased, and I handled everything myself, rented a plane and a pilot, and scattered his ashes over the Pacific Ocean. That, I was sure, was what Robert would have wanted as he didn't have a will. Chris's family was more conservative, and as part of the family trust and will, a regular burial with a cemetery plot was what both the two brothers and their father had already decided for themselves.

At the reception that followed in our home, Vee tried once more to attach herself to Ed. Again, she seemed intent on showing everyone how close she and Ed were, but James was right there claiming him. I looked at Ed solemnly, and for a moment his piercing eyes met mine, but he turned around to talk to one of his deputies. The pesky girlfriend finally left.

One frumpy-looking, middle-aged woman I didn't know came up to me. "You'll be all right, dear. You're still young and good-looking. You'll soon find someone else," she said. What a thing to say to a grieving widow at the funeral of her husband!

JP received much attention and had a great time. Children are wonderful to have around in times of sorrow.

Then it was all over, and everything was back to normal—sort of. Maria and some people from her church came by and sorted Chris's clothes and other items to give to needy families. Many undocumented workers had been left stranded in the area after a big employer who had hired them filed for bankruptcy and failed to pay them.

Joe came with his CPA, a grim-looking, stocky female with short black hair and turtle-shell glasses. They sifted through Chris's computer files for tax purposes. JP was thrilled to have his grandpa around. Now and then I tried to escape into my unfinished mystery novel about the brutal murder of Mrs. Luella Jones. My sleuth, the ex-nun Jule McCormick, had a cadre of suspects connected to the school, disgruntled teachers and staff, but she had now started to look closer to Luella Jones's home town in Texas. It turned out that Mrs. Jones owned 200 acres of pecan trees there, worth over a couple of million dollars, and a few disreputable relatives had been hovering around like vultures waiting for their inheritance.

My family came out from Wisconsin. Although it was hard to get my father away from home, he came too, as did my brother George and his wife, Joyce. They doted on JP. After a short discussion, we skipped Disneyland. "Too crowded," my father said, and that made it final. Instead, we all drove down to Hollywood one day, but like many tourists, they were surprised at how sleazy and run down it looked, so far from the glitz and glamor they had expected.

The weather was perfect, so we took the boat out, and I gave them the grand tour of the lake. Everyone said they preferred our little resort town in the mountains to the big city.

17

WHAT THE SHERIFF SAID

Maria took JP to various playgroups since the nursery school was on hiatus until the end of August. He loved to play with children his own age and not just adults. However, James came over every day whether JP was home or not, and we talked about travel plans for him. Joe was in and out, looking for one more paper, and Ed stopped by on his many rounds around the county.

"Your grandpa will pay for your plane tickets, won't you, Joe?" I said cheerfully one day when everyone was there. "The rest of us will chip in to pay for tuition, room, and board. How's that, James?"

"But who will look after my dad?" he wondered and looked smilingly at his dad.

"I guess you mean so that none of his girlfriends tricks him into marrying him," I said teasingly.

Ed scowled at me.

"Yeah, that too," James said.

"Well, what else are you worried about?"

"Lots of things. He's not very good at taking care of himself, are you Dad?"

"Oh, we won't let him out of sight," I said reassuringly. "Maybe your dad and I will start our PhD programs at USC. We've talked about carpooling one day a week and then take classes online or hybrid classes, half in-class and half online."

"That would be so awesome," James said. His face lit up in a big smile, but Ed's face didn't reveal any particular emotion.

"But why USC?" James asked after a while. "Wouldn't it make more sense to be at UC Riverside?"

"True, but they don't have the programs we want," I explained.

"What does that mean?" James wanted to know.

"USC has a renowned PhD program in Criminal Justice that your father is interested in. USC also has more choices in literature."

"I see." He rose and moved toward the door. "I promised to pick up Thomas," he said. "His car is in the garage."

Ed left with him. Shortly afterward Joe also said good-bye.

When no one else was home, I took Duchess for long walks. Summer weather was here; the oak trees sported fresh green leaves, and the daffodils and tulips were gone. The weather was still mostly temperate but warming up, and tourists were arriving in droves every weekend.

One warm Friday afternoon Ed came over. He was in his full uniform and dress shoes and flung himself down on the living room couch with a groan and an expletive. When he removed his sunglasses, I could see dark shadows under his eyes. That in addition to his droopy eyelids made him look tired and sad.

"You look exhausted, Ed," I said worriedly. "Is everything all right?"

"I'm okay. A little tired. That's all."

"How about we take a little walk and get some fresh air," I suggested. "Chris's hiking boots are still here because I thought maybe James or you could wear them. He bought them right before the accident. I have a couple of new T-shirts too. It's a warm day."

"Sounds like a good idea." He reached for his phone. "I'll call the office and tell them I won't be back until later."

He stood and faced me as he started to unbutton his uniform jacket. To my surprise, he had nothing underneath. His bare chest, accented by small tufts of black hair reminded me of Chris's body—the tanned look actually not caused by the sun but by their Italian mother's background. My jaw dropped, and I couldn't take my eyes away from him. He pushed the sides of his uniform jacket back, slowly, first the right side and then the left, to loosen and remove his heavy gun belt, revealing a strip of his white underwear. I looked up at his face and, as if in slow motion, I took a step toward him. He slowly put his belt on the couch and smilingly floated toward me, holding out his arms. Spellbound, I touched him, but as he tried to touch me, I stood there as if glued to the floor.

"Oh, Ed. You look so much like Chris," I said as he was about to embrace me, and the spell was gone in a poof.

"Yes, that's always been my luck," he said flatly. "He was always the handsome one who got everyone's attention. I was just the big clumsy oaf of a brother, always cleaning up after him when he made a mess out of things."

"Oh, Ed. I don't believe that," I said resolutely, realizing that I had hurt his feelings. "I didn't mean it that way. You're just as good-looking and just as nice, even though you put on a gruff and intimidating façade in public. In fact, that combination is probably why you were appointed sheriff."

"Nice guy. Yeah, that's me. And nice guys finish last. Isn't that what they say?"

"That's ridiculous. It was really meant as a compliment."

"Was it?"

"I think it was, and that's why I don't want you to waste it all on someone who's not worthy of you."

"What do you mean?"

"Ed, you have everything going for you—good looks, money, status in the community. What more do you want me to say? You can have any woman you want. Anyone."

"Anyone?"

"Yes, anyone."

He looked at me curiously as I turned and walked into the mudroom to get his boots. Then I went into the bedroom to find a T-shirt and an old baseball cap. I put on my own boots and put the leash on Duchess, who was ecstatic to go out again. Impulsively, I took Ed's hand as we walked down the rough, stony path to the trail, where I let it go again. I led the way toward the north side of the lake. I had in mind to walk up to the pale yellow house where we had found the missing shoe.

"How's the investigation going?" I asked after I had let Duchess loose to chase after squirrels and gophers, and everything else that moved. "I thought we'd walk up to the house where Duchess found the shoe."

"Okay." He watched Duchess. "We should keep the dog on the leash," he said and added smilingly, "Otherwise, I'll have to give you a ticket."

"Oh, come on, Ed. She won't hurt anyone."

"You're starting to sound like my brother," he said accusingly.

"Sorry. I'll put her back on the leash in a minute."

We walked on in silence for a few minutes.

"So, was the shoe the missing mate to Aldo Bandini's shoe?"

"Yes, I believe so. The agent on the case sent it to the FBI lab."

"Really? What does he expect to find?"

"He sent the other shoe too."

"To look for what?"

"Mainly DNA I presume. DNA testing is almost always done today." He paused and reflected for a moment before he continued. "The agent sent all the clothes to their lab too, the underwear, the jacket and slacks that you took to London. Even the socks. Although we know that the clothes belonged to Aldo Bandini, who most certainly is the victim, they may find DNA from someone else, perhaps the killer."

"I suppose you're right. But if Aldo Bandini was shot execution style, only his blood will be found on his clothes. Of course, my DNA may show on the coat and slacks. Wouldn't that be interesting?"

"I don't think you have to worry, but today we have to be so careful and collect all possible evidence—cross every 't' and dot every 'i' to make sure an arrest will stick before we actually make one. And if a prosecutor discovered that we hadn't bothered to test for DNA, he or she would have a field day."

We were close to the lakeshore now, and Ed picked up a flat rock and threw it sideways toward the lake so that it skimmed the water and created ripples along the way.

"Good throw," I said admiringly and picked up my own rock and threw it, but my throw was not very elegant.

"I used to be the pitcher on our high school baseball team," Ed said consolingly.

"Are we going to start our PhD programs in the fall then?" I asked.

"We?" He turned and looked at me but continued walking.

"Well, you then."

"Maybe. I've been accepted."

"I haven't officially, but I can take one course in the program I want to enroll in without a formal acceptance. We could carpool, as I mentioned to James." I stopped and looked at him. "What do you think?"

"It's an idea," he said slowly and kept walking.

I didn't pursue it any further.

"There's the house," I said and pointed as we came closer to the goal of our walk. "Any idea who owns it?"

"No idea."

We walked through dead leaves and other debris down to the water's edge.

"I wonder what's hidden in that fortified underground canal that seems to run far in under the property." I pointed in that direction.

Ed now became interested in exploring it. "I'd need a warrant in order to go on the property, but we could take the boat out and go in as far as we can."

"Let's walk around first," I suggested and led the way along the outside of the fence.

The house was still shuttered and looked deserted. We reached the chained gate and scanned the property from there. The trash had been picked up, and the trashcan was placed neatly against the wall.

"Someone has been here, I see," I said. "That trashcan was tipped over and trash strewn all around."

"There's probably a caretaker somewhere," Ed said.

"Well, you have realtor friends. Can't you find out who owns the place?"

"That's in the public records."

"I know, but it may be leased or rented."

"It may be an out-of-state agency, but I could find out. Of course, you could call my realtor friend, as you call her too."

We walked all around and down to the shoreline on the other side. Ed again took an interest in the underground waterway.

"It looks like the big gate at the entrance is closed." He paused. "You had the boat out when your folks were here, didn't you?"

"Yes, but I don't really like to go out by myself."

"I'll take it out, and we could drive around sort of surreptitiously and see what this canal business looks like from the water."

I called Duchess, who was sniffing and digging everywhere, and put her back on the leash.

When we returned to our property, Ed walked straight down to our dock while I put Duchess in her pen and found the keys to the boat. It was a perfect day for a leisurely swing around the lake, and Ed was already onboard when I joined him. As soon as I gave him the keys, he opened the side bench and took out two life jackets that he shook and brushed off. Cobwebs are everywhere up here, but spiders had, fortunately, not been able to find their way into the bench.

"In that orange life vest, Chris's baseball cap, and sunglasses, I doubt anyone will recognize you, Ed," I said and laughed.

"That's sort of the idea, isn't it? I don't want anyone to get a hint that a law enforcement officer is snooping around. That would spread like wildfire and make it difficult to proceed with this whole investigation, wouldn't it?"

He started the engine and carefully backed the boat out.

"That's where I come in to cover for you, don't you think?"

He nodded. "That's true."

"How's the gas tank?"

"Not great, but I don't think I want to fill it up right now. Someone would for sure recognize us."

"Being a celebrity is a real challenge, isn't it?" I teased.

"And I could do without your sarcasm, thank you," he said in a feigned hurtful tone. "That's life in small town."

We cruised around the south shore of the lake, close to land, before we cut across to the north end. It was hard to find the house, even though it was the only house in that pale yellow color. However, it sat on a bluff a distance from the water, partially blocked by oaks and tall cedars.

Ed pulled the boat up close, as if we were planning to dock at the pier that partially hid the entrance to the canal and drove all the way up to the iron gate that was now closed. It was too dark to see what was on the other side.

"Yes, this is definitely interesting," Ed admitted thoughtfully. "But this is not my case anymore." He started to back the boat out again. "I'll report what we've seen to the FBI."

"Because that's procedure," I said flatly. "Maybe *you* don't want to interfere, but I'll try to find out. I'm not concerned with procedures. I just use common sense."

"No, I don't want you to step into this case more than you already have," he said sharply. "You're really too naïve. You don't seem to realize the danger here." He paused. "I don't want to take care of two motherless boys."

"How else am I going to get fodder for my next book?" I said pleadingly.

"This is not a book. This is real life. You seem to have trouble distinguishing between the two."

"Okay. I'll be careful," I said. "I'll first search the public records to find out who owns this place. Then I'll ask your precious realtor friend to find out if the house has been leased. She seems desperate to want to make friends with me anyway."

He drove the boat carefully into its dock, and I threw the big rope around the post to secure it.

"You're really too independent for your own good," Ed said conclusively and looked at me searchingly. "I'd better get back to the office," he added as we walked together up to his car. "I'll be in touch." He got into his car and left.

18

GRADUATION

I was sitting outside on the deck one warm morning when James drove up in the familiar brown Range Rover. I had been reading to JP from a picture book about anteaters and other peculiar animals, but JP now turned his attention to James.

"Here are some tickets to my graduation," James said breathlessly as he came rushing up the outside stairs like a sudden fresh breeze and handed me four tickets. "Are you coming?"

"Of course I'm coming," I said and slowly counted four tickets. "Maria, JP, and me," I said. "Who's the fourth one?"

"Oh, I guess I forgot that Uncle Chris won't be coming."

"He'll be there in spirit." I smiled at him. "And I have the perfect present for you."

"What is it?"

"You'll see."

JP came over and gave James his heavy bright green dump truck, an invitation to play.

"Hi, buddy," James said cheerfully. "I can't stay right now, but I'll be back."

He turned to me. "I'm helping decorate the auditorium for the big day."

"That's nice. Good luck," I said.

He bounded down the stairs and ran around to the driveway.

After he left, I took out my cell phone and started searching the public records for the owner of the pale yellow house, but I wasn't entirely sure of the address and lot number.

"How about we take Duchess for a walk, JP?" I suggested.

JP was immediately excited, as was Duchess.

Once again, we made our way up to the pale yellow house. By now, the trail was tinder dry, so the fire hazard was extremely high. The lake glittered in the sunlight, and sailboats bobbed along, looking more like little paper boats than real ones. JP was running after Duchess, sometimes falling but bravely getting up by himself. We hiked up from the trail to the road long before we reached the fenced property, and I finally found the number 24 nailed to a gigantic pine tree in front of the house. A little farther down was a wooden sign announcing that this was Deerskin Lane, but the lot number was nowhere to be seen. A new silver Porsche was parked in the driveway, and the shutters had been taken down. Clearly someone was living there now. I walked a little farther down the lane before I turned around so as not to arouse any suspicions. It was an advantage to have a child—and a dog.

When we returned home, JP had his lunch and was ready for his nap while I went out on the deck with my laptop. I quickly found the address and learned that the lot number was 201. The owner was listed as Leo Smith; he had purchased the property seven years ago. The name sounded so made up that I immediately suspected it was a pseudonym, although I knew that many immigrants from Eastern Europe were given names like "Smith" when coming to this country because their real names with their unfamiliar consonant clusters were difficult for Americans to pronounce.

I called Vee.

"How delightful to hear from you, honey," she greeted me with forced cheerfulness.

I most definitely disliked being called "honey" by this woman, but I calmly stated my case.

"Sure, I'll look it up," she said amicably. "Just give me a few minutes. Are you thinking of buying it?"

"Is it for sale?"

"Yes, I think I saw one for sale on Deerskin, but let me check. I'll call you back in five minutes."

It was over half an hour before the phone rang, but Vee confirmed that one Leo Smith was listed as the owner.

"Do you know if it's leased?"

"No, it's not leased at present and not on any short-term rental list." She paused. "If you're interested in buying, I could inquire whether or not Mr. Smith would be interested in selling. Actually, there's another property for sale on Deerskin that I could show you."

"Thank you, but no, not right now. I'm just looking around to see what's available."

"I'll be glad to take you on a tour. I'm free this afternoon or tomorrow."

"Thank you, Vee, but not yet." I was starting to worry that I might be jeopardizing the case. Who knew what this crazy woman would do? If Leo Smith, whoever he was, got wind of someone being interested in this house, he might decide to bail out and destroy evidence if any remained.

I told her not to do anything quite yet. "I'm really more interested in something closer to the Resort, but don't tell Ed."

"Oh, I won't. It will be our little secret."

What an insufferable woman! I felt sure she'd tell Ed. Actually, maybe if I had asked her to be sure to tell Ed, she might have forgotten. But it was over and done with now. I had always been a master of "should've and could've," and wondered how Leo Smith could be connected to Aldo Bandini.

———

Graduation was at 11:00 a.m. a week later. Maria was coming, of course, and we dressed JP up in a white shirt and red bow tie. Maria put on make-up, which she ordinarily didn't use, and it made her look different. Actually, it didn't suit her since she already had good coloring and truly looked better without anything artificial.

The auditorium looked festive, decorated in blue and white banners and balloons—the school's colors. It was quickly filling up with parents, grandparents, and friends.

Joe and his lady friend Sandy, who had just recovered from cosmetic surgery, had come early and had saved seats for the rest of us. Ed, Cheryl, and her husband, Jonathan, came shortly after us They left an empty seat next to Ed; I assumed that Vee would sit there. No sooner had I finished the thought than there she came strutting down the middle aisle in high heels and her signature tight flowered skirt and jacket. Ed greeted her by kissing her on the cheek. I wondered if James had given her a ticket, but it was probably Ed. I tried to ignore them and focused my thoughts on

James. I had ordered a top-of-the-line suitcase and carry-on set for his graduation present, and I was excited about helping him purchase his plane tickets, arranging for a homestay in Oslo, and filling out paperwork for summer courses at the university over there. I had been thinking of accompanying him. I had second cousins over there that I could visit, but I changed my mind. It was time for him to try something on his own. We'd put him on a nonstop flight from Los Angeles and have someone meet him at the airport in Oslo.

The students soon came walking down the middle aisle to the strains of Elgar's familiar graduation march, the girls in white dresses and the boys in dark suits, filling the rows of chairs set up on the stage. JP stood on his seat and waved. Since Cronin was toward the beginning of the alphabetized list, James walked relatively early, so as soon as we'd seen him shaking hands with the principal, I took JP for a stroll while all the others were called.

At the reception for the graduates at the small country club in the next town, Ed and Vee greeted and bantered with everyone. They were certainly a good-looking couple, and, of course, they knew everybody. The rest of the family had found a table to the side, and Joe brought drinks for everyone while a waiter came with snacks. Although I was surrounded by many people, I felt lonely without a companion.

James soon left with his friends to continue the party elsewhere, and we all went back to our house. Ed came too after a while, *sans* Vee.

"Where's Vee?" I asked frostily before he had time to sit down. "She was swarming around you like a pesky wasp."

"Oh, she likes to network at the country club with me at her side, but she's not much of a family person."

"I see," I said thoughtfully, but I wondered if that was the whole story. "Did she mention anything about my interest in real estate?"

"No. Are you? Interested I mean?"

"Not really, but I called her about the pale yellow house. I walked by the house a couple of days ago because I didn't remember the exact address, and I wanted to look it up and find out who lived there."

"And what did you find out from Vee?"

"Well, I first looked up the address in the public records and learned that the owner for the past seven years is listed as one Leo Smith."

"Leo Smith? Is that his real name?"

"That's what I thought. It sounds so made up, but Vee confirmed it and told me that it's not leased." I paused. "Of course now she thinks I'm interested in buying the house, but I told her that I was actually more interested in something closer to the Resort. I pressed upon her not to contact the owner because I'm not really interested in that location. I was just curious because I'd never seen anyone there."

"She'll soon forget."

"Do you think so?"

"I know so," he said gruffly.

"Well, actually, my point is that when I walked by with JP and Duchess, I saw a relatively new silver Porsche in front. The shutters were down, and the house looked lived in."

"What do you want me to do?"

"Somehow, I believe that there's a connection between Leo Smith and Aldo Bandini, but what?"

"Okay, I'll notify the FBI agent who's on the case."

"There's got to be more evidence on that property than the missing shoe, don't you think? Can we get a search warrant?"

"We?"

"Well, you, then."

"This case is no longer mine. And besides, *we* have to have probable cause."

"I know, but isn't the fact that we found the shoe on the property, a shoe that most probably belonged to a murder victim, enough cause?"

"I'll share the information with the FBI agent and see what he says. In the meantime, be careful." He looked at me seriously. "Do you know how to handle a gun?"

"I went hunting with my father and brother back on the farm in Wisconsin. Do you mean I should carry a gun to protect myself?"

"It wouldn't hurt. They're offering courses especially for women at the shooting range on the 173 this summer. After you pass the course, you could apply for a permit."

"Okay, although I wonder if that's such a good idea." I paused. "You know I'm nosy, and I hate to leave loose ends, but if I carried a gun, I might accidentally shoot someone." I smiled and left it at that. "Can I get you a drink or something?" I asked in an effort to change the subject. "Maria is making sandwiches in the kitchen."

"I'd take a cup of coffee first, if you don't mind."

"Have a seat, dear brother-in-law, and coffee will be coming right up. Black, right?"

"Yes, please."

I went into the kitchen and made two cups. Then I returned to the living room, where Ed had found a seat on the chair next to the fireplace. The others were squeezed together on the couch.

"Anyone else for coffee?" I asked cheerfully.

"I'll help you," Cheryl said, and we made coffee for everyone, and Maria soon brought in chicken sandwiches.

I shared the progress with James's travel plans. Everyone was excited about this opportunity for James, even Joe, his grandfather, but Ed was uncharacteristically silent.

19

AT THE SHOOTING RANGE

The Fourth of July came and went. JP had a slight cold, so I watched the fireworks from the deck while the rest of the family took the boat out, as was their custom.

Then came the day of James's departure. His passport had come in the mail several weeks ago. The nonstop flight to Oslo didn't leave LAX until early evening, so we took our time getting ready before we started out for the airport.

I was happy that James wanted me to come for the grand send-off. Ed drove, and on the way, we picked up Joe, who lived down in the flatland. James rode shotgun so that he and Ed could have some final words together—mostly instructions and admonitions from Ed.

"Relax, Ed," I said cheerfully. "The Scandinavian countries are safer than California, and James will be well taken care of."

"Yes, Dad," James said with a demonstrative sigh for the umpteenth time. He looked at his father for a brief moment.

I told James about the good hiking trails north of the city and how accessible they were. "You can ride up to the trailhead on a streetcar. It's a really pretty ride. And all the girls are sporty and smart."

Joe glowered at me. "Do you have to make us more worried than we already are?" he said with feigned anxiety.

James turned around and looked at me. "Will many of them look like you?"

"Well, maybe, but they're not all tall and blonde. You'll see Africans from Africa and Middle Easterners as well. I read that many Pakistanis now serve in the armed forces over there, and some of them even guard the king's palace. It's as multicultural in Oslo as it is elsewhere in Europe, and everywhere in the world for that matter, except in our little mountain resort town."

The traffic was horrendous and worsened the closer we came to the airport. In addition to the usual snarls, the police had set up check-points at the entrances to the terminals so that all the cars had to stop and submit to inspection. It was stop-and-go all the way in.

We left James off at the International Terminal with some last-minute instructions from all of us on what to expect.

"Be sure to look after Dad." Were his last words to me.

"I will, and don't worry," I said and smiled encouragingly. "We'll see you in a few weeks."

We watched him disappear into the cavernous building; then we drove off.

"He'll have a great time," I said cheerfully, but Ed and Joe remained silent.

We stopped for a bite to eat in Fontana, another town along the 210 freeway where Chris and Joe had done a lot of work during the winter months, before we dropped Joe off at his house and drove on up the mountain.

The setting sun was playing peek-a-boo with us as we drove up the winding mountain road. It dipped behind the many mountain tops, creating ominous shadows, only to come out in blinding force in the valleys between.

"The sun is relentless, isn't it? You'd think after all these billions of years it would dim a little," I said in an effort to wipe the gloom off Ed's face. I waited for a reaction but none came. "I understand that it's hard for you to see your only son leave home, Ed," I continued consolingly. "Especially since you just lost your wife, but I'm positive that this is what Elizabeth would have wanted for James."

"I know," he said and stared straight ahead as if trying to concentrate on the road. His radio kept making crackling noises, so he turned it off.

"It's really a good move on his part," I continued. "You cannot expect him to spend the rest of his life in the mountains just because you've spent most of your life there."

"I know, and you're right. But James is so naïve about the world, especially with all the stuff that's going on around airports these days. I don't feel he's ready for it all." He paused. "It's not easy to be a single parent of a teenager."

"He'll be fine," I assured him. "Remember, you see only the underbelly of humanity, Ed, but most people are actually good and honest."

Ed just grunted and shot me a quick glance.

"It will be good for you to go back to USC this fall," I said. "I'm going to take a course there as well, a hybrid course, so I don't have to come to class or even go down to the campus more than once a week. It would be great if we could carpool if our class schedules coincide."

"That sounds like a good idea. I'll be taking two classes, and I believe they're both on Tuesdays and Thursdays."

I made a mental note of the days.

"Have you had any time to check on the Aldo Bandini case?" I asked after a while.

"We're working on it."

"But no plans to actually get a search warrant and enter the pale yellow house?"

"Not that I know of," he said without much enthusiasm.

"I feel strongly that clues are waiting for you in that house."

"You mean more shoes?" His tone was slightly sarcastic, and he turned toward me with a grin on his face.

"No. Other things. Maybe cash from the gambling casinos. We're pretty close to Las Vegas."

"You be careful about snooping around on your own. We don't know yet what kind of people we're dealing with here." He kept his focus on the narrow, winding road.

"I think I'll take your suggestion and enroll in that weaponry course at the shooting range," I said after a while. "I see it's advertised all over, and it will be offered over and over again all summer. It's not because of this case, but living alone among drug dealers and other shady characters, stabbings and shootings around here, I need to know how to defend myself."

"Is this a criticism of me and my guys?"

I ignored him.

"We cannot be everywhere, you know," he continued. "And that's why people need to learn how to take care of themselves too."

"Yes, and that's the reason why I just said that." Why did he always feel I was critical of him? "Is Vee signing up?"

"Not that I know of, but I don't think so. She's not into this kind of stuff and probably has no need for it."

"I see. Does she live alone too?"

"No, she lives with her daughter, who's a junior in high school, I think."

I left it at that, and we drove on in silence.

"Do you want to stop in at my house?" I suggested as we came closer to our resort town. "Actually, I guess it is your home too, since you grew up there."

"I wouldn't mind a cup of coffee after the long drive, but then I'd better stop by the station and then go home and get used to living alone." His tone was wistful.

I didn't answer.

Maria and JP met us as we walked in the door. JP was ready for bed, and I tucked him in while Maria made coffee. She and Ed talked in Spanish about James, from what I could understand. All three of us sat on the couch for a few minutes before Ed left.

A few days later, I perused the local newspaper and saw a big, colorful picture of Ed and Vee on the society page. They had attended a charity event together a couple of weeks earlier, and I had to admit they looked good together, a handsome couple that a photographer would want to take a picture of.

On the last page was an ad for the gun safety and self-defense course for women on the mountain. I decided then and there to enroll and called the number. It was time for me to learn to live independently.

There was plenty of space in the next course the following week, a woman with a gruff, no-nonsense voice informed me, and I gave her my name and number and told her I'd be there. She said she remembered me. No surprise there. Then I put the paper away. I didn't want to save it for James. Ed had probably not seen it. He was not much into reading the local newspaper, "the Bartlett family update," as he and Chris had called it since the publisher's family members, the Bartletts, were featured in every issue.

The drive out to the shooting range is a pretty one, with the glittering lake on one side and majestic pines on the other. The vegetation thinned out eventually, however, as the high desert came into view. Clouds were rolling in.

Growing up in Wisconsin, I had been against any gun control. But after I moved to California, I changed my mind. There were too many crazy people running around with guns out here, and gun control made more sense. Now I was slowly reverting back to the Second Amendment and the right to bear arms. The Wild West is still with us, and as Ed had said, the police cannot be everywhere.

The range is close to the highway and hard to miss. I parked my Subaru outside the high fence alongside several all-terrain vehicles and walked through an open gate to a low, drab building where the range master directed me to a small group of women gathered over to the side. A prominently displayed sign announced, "Stupid people should not have guns." Most of the women seemed a rough bunch, in their thirties probably, husky without being fat, in sweatshirts and jeans, but three of them were younger and more feminine looking in tights and long shirts.

A deputy joined us and demonstrated self-defense methods, which we practiced. Then he issued us earplugs. Some of the women had their own guns, and I was issued a small pistol and was shown how to clean it and load it before we went downrange facing the targets.

My thoughts went back to my father's gun collection that he kept in a locked gun cabinet. One snowy winter day when I was about seven years old, Dusty, my white horse, had evidently stepped on a rusty nail and contracted tetanus and a high fever. The veterinarian came in his big, white Jeep, and he and my father led my poor Dusty out in the snow to cool him off. He was foaming not only at the mouth but all over his body. It looked like someone had put patches of shampoo all over him. I sat at the kitchen window overlooking the snow-covered yard and watched it all. Soon the vet shook his head, and my father came walking toward the house. Grim-faced, he went straight to his gun cabinet, unlocked it, and removed a shotgun that he loaded before returning to the horse. I saw the vet nod his head. Then my father took aim and shot my horse dead with a single bullet.

Now I stood aiming at a target with a handgun, ready to shoot. It was not the first time I had shot a gun, but the first time with a handgun. I held it with both hands as instructed, aimed, pulled the trigger, and unexpectedly jerked back as the gun went off. I missed the bull's eye, but I was close, and the others cheered as we all cheered for each other whether we were near to the target or far.

Unbeknownst to me, Ed had stopped in while I was getting ready for my turn. "Well done, Megan," he said. "You're a natural."

He gave me some extra pointers and talked to the other women, who all seemed to know him. Ed left, but we all shot a few more rounds.

Inside the building several gun catalogs were on display in case we wanted to purchase a gun online. I ordered a small handgun with a rose-colored mother-of-pearl handle that looked like it would fit in my purse. After we filled out applications to carry a concealed weapon, we went on our way.

20

SOLICITING FOR A HUNDRED-DOLLAR BILL

My new "toy" arrived a few days later. It was cute, definitely a woman's firearm with a faint rose-colored glow from the mother-of-pearl handle and soft pink rivets and other pink decorations. It was not anything like the guns I had seen in Wisconsin. I weighed it in my hands. It was extremely light, no more than a pound, and, according to the advertisement, it had a reputation for accuracy. Frightening to think about the power such a small thing had. After admiring it for a while, I took it down to the sheriff's station to register it as instructed.

Vee came walking through the wood-paneled lobby on her way out just as I was entering. As usual, she looked very professional in her light blue suit and matching heels while I was in my gray work-out clothes. She stopped and greeted me.

"Is Ed here?" I asked casually.

"No, he left. We just came back from lunch." She watched me and smiled condescendingly. "I'll be happy to give him a message. I'll see him again later."

"No, thanks. That's okay. I'll speak with the deputy on duty." I walked away and into the office, where a deputy sat at his desk. He gave me more forms to fill out in triplicate, and, as instructed, I scrawled my John Hancock in several places. Then I left.

Ed stopped by the house later, and I showed him my new acquisition.

He looked at it and picked it up, smiling indulgently. "Let's go out to the range and try it out then," he suggested.

"But I thought you were meeting Vee?"

He looked at me sharply as if taken by surprise. "Where did you hear that?"

"Well, one hears a lot of things in this small town," I said a bit sarcastically, watching him. "But, actually, I saw Vee at the sheriff's station earlier this afternoon."

"Yeah, I heard you'd been there." He paused. "We were going to some real estate dinner, but it was canceled."

"Okay. Let's go then," I said and grabbed my purse, tucked my small "Chic Lady" inside, and we hurried outside. Ed's marked car was parked next to my Subaru.

"Do you mind if we take your car?" he asked politely.

"No problem," I said and took the keys from my purse. He got in on the passenger side, an unusual spot for him.

The traffic was light, and it didn't take us long to get to the range. I parked next to the gate and we walked onto the grounds. Ed stopped to talk to a couple of young men who were standing outside the low, nondescript building before we went inside to get our earplugs and safety glasses. We lined up downrange, and Ed took out his gun, aimed, and hit the target smack in the middle.

"Wow, Ed! What a good shot!" I exclaimed. "But, boy, if law enforcement officers are such good shooters, why do we have so many police killings? Why don't you guys just aim at the shoulders or knees, or something? That way the prey would at least survive."

"It's not that easy when you're in a situation," he replied sternly. "They're moving targets. That's why there are so many shots. If we were bad shooters, they'd get away. As a matter of fact, we're trained to aim at the middle of the body to allow for error. That way, we'll usually hit somewhere." He put his gun back in the holster. "Now, let's see you try." He obviously didn't want to continue the conversation any further in this direction.

As I took aim, he corrected my stance and positioned both my arms before I could pull the trigger, again recoiling, but at least less than before. It wasn't too bad a shot but far from a bull's eye. Ed made me try a few more times, and I actually improved.

"I don't know if I feel any safer," I said laughingly on the way back and glanced at him briefly.

"Well, if you carry it consistently, it may save your life that one time when you're confronted by someone who hasn't just come to borrow a cup of sugar."

Maria had picked up JP from the summer program that the nursery school ran, and after Ed left, we went through our usual bedtime routine of reading and singing. I put my "Chic Lady" on the top shelf of my wardrobe. A gun in a house with children is not really a great idea, and I visualized with horror various possible scenarios. I made a mental note to look for a small cabinet with a lock.

———

While Maria was running errands and JP was in his summer playgroup, I often hiked the trails around the lake area, trying to think up an excuse to enter the pale yellow house. I had also returned to playing the piano daily, practicing scales to limber up my fingers and taking out old music that I had partly forgotten. I played some Chopin waltzes, some etudes by Beethoven, and pieces by Schumann and Brahms. I did my best thinking when playing, and one day a plausible idea finally came to me.

A big charity event was planned at the Neighborhood Church. I volunteered to help with marketing. I designed flyers to be sent digitally to the newspapers in the area but also to be printed and passed out. In addition, I made colorful posters that I put up around the resort.

Leaving Duchess at home, I took a few flyers with me and knocked on doors along Deerskin Lane. Most of the houses were second homes and empty, but I left flyers anyway. At number 24, the same silver Porsche was parked outside, but this time, next to it stood a new white Range Rover.

My heart beat faster as I walked along the cement driveway and up three or four steps to the solid oak and beveled glass front door. I didn't see a doorbell, so I rapped on the glass and finally heard footsteps and other noises inside. I knocked again. A young woman in her late teens opened the door slowly. She was petite with long dark hair and a cute face with small, regular features and large brown eyes. Behind her, wagging his tail excitedly, stood the same white poodle mix that I had seen with the older, taciturn couple on the trail a few times.

I cleared my throat. "Hi." I smiled, trying to look as friendly as I could.

"How can I help you?" the girl asked.

"Is the owner of the house home?"

"Who are you?" she asked, ignoring my question.

I introduced myself and told her I was a volunteer for the upcoming charity event for recovering alcoholics and drug addicts. "Are your parents home? I have seen them with the dog out on the trail a couple of times." I held out my hand for the dog to sniff me, but the girl pushed the dog away and told him to go inside. I stepped back but held up my flyers and gave her one. Then I took another step back but missed the top step. I fell sideways without really hurting myself. I had played enough softball in high school and college to know how to fall without getting injured. The young girl rushed over and bent down to help me up. The dog followed her. Human nature is strange in this way, for, no matter what, we instinctively stop to help when someone falls right in front of us. Even chimpanzees, who cannot swim, will jump into the water to try to rescue another chimp from drowning. The girl put her arm around me and steadied me as I limped into the cluttered living room where she positioned me on the couch.

The large room was filled with large and small boxes as if the people had just moved in or were getting ready to move out. The high vaulted ceiling was stained a natural wood color, while the solid wooden beams were painted brown. Big picture windows provided good lighting and a view of the lake through the trees. The humongous rock fireplace that covered most of one wall resembled the one in Chris's house...now my house. The furniture was hardly visible because of all the boxes.

The young woman and the dog left but soon reappeared with what I assumed to be her mother, a middle-aged woman of average height in black slacks and a loose patterned top. Her elegantly coiffed brown hair had blonde streaks, but I didn't immediately recognize her as the woman with the little white poodle mix that I had seen on the trail earlier in the spring. Her hair looked darker, but it could have been her.

"I'm so sorry to inconvenience you," I said apologetically. "I'm afraid I took a fall on your front steps. I'm so sorry."

"Are you all right? Do you need me to call 9-1-1?" she asked in a polished East Coast accent.

"Oh, no, thank you. I'll be fine. I don't think I've broken anything. I'll be on my way shortly. I'm sorry to have caused trouble."

I looked around at all the boxes. "Are you moving?" I asked as I raised myself up.

"Here. Let me help you," the woman said, ignoring my inquisitiveness. "Can I get you something to drink?"

"Oh, no, thank you. I'm good. I'm volunteering for the big charity event at the Neighborhood Church to benefit recovering alcoholics and drug addicts," I continued, "and I'm wondering if you'd care to donate something, anything, for the flea market…or just money."

I gave her a flyer, and she looked at it while I got on my feet.

"All right. Wait just a minute. I'll give you something." She disappeared but returned after only a moment and gave me a hundred-dollar bill.

"This is really generous of you," I said. "I really appreciate it." I started toward the front door, remembering to limp just a little.

"Is drug addiction a problem around here as well?" she asked as she walked me to the front door.

"Probably no worse than any place else," I said.

"It seems so tranquil around here, and people look so wholesome." She smiled benignly enough but remained cool and aloof.

"Yes, I agree, but there's an underbelly here as there is everywhere, especially among the young. Your daughter probably knows more about it than we do."

"That's my niece," she said and glanced at the pretty teenager. "She's staying with us for the moment. She just graduated from high school." She held the door for me. "I'll help you down the steps this time," she said with a smile. "Good luck with your charity event."

I limped down the road until the house was out of sight, and then I resumed my normal gait but walked a bit more slowly. At home, I put the hundred-dollar bill in an envelope before taking the envelope into Chris's office. I would present the charity with another bill, give this one to Ed, and ask if he could trace it. It would require some work to convince him. In addition, I somehow had to figure out a way to explain what I was doing in the house by myself, although it was hardly against the law as I was just there to solicit for a charity.

I wandered restlessly around the house for a while. Then I sat down and tried to work on my novel. My sleuth, Jule McCormick, had discovered that the victim, Mrs. Jones, had a nephew who was in big financial trouble. He was Mrs. Jones's oldest living relative, and he had a mentally challenged younger brother who worshiped his older brother and would do anything for him. They now became the main suspects.

After a while, I sat down at the piano again and improvised on Mozart's piece "Twinkle, Twinkle, Little Star." At the same time, I thought of ways to persuade Ed to have the hundred-dollar bill traced. Las Vegas was my guess.

21

THE FBI

The lights that dotted the hillsides around the lake like little pinpricks grew steadily fainter as dawn crept over the mountain ridge in a russet glow. I was sitting outside on the deck the next day with my laptop, writing out more plot details of my novel. By nine o'clock, the sun had cleared away any stray clouds, and it was clear that it was going to be a perfect day, not too hot with a light breeze. I put down my laptop and tried to figure out how to tell Ed about my visit to the pale yellow house and the hundred-dollar bill. I decided to call him on my cell phone. "Hi, Ed," I said chirpily. "It's Megan."

"Hello, Megan. What's going on?"

"Can you come over sometime today? I think I have a new clue in the Aldo Bandini case that I want to show you."

"Really? Is it urgent?"

"No, any time today is fine."

"I'll tell you what. The FBI agent will be here for a meeting this afternoon. Why don't you come over and meet him?"

"What time?"

"Between one and one-thirty."

"Okay, I'll be there."

Maria had gone home after taking JP to his playgroup, so I put on a short white skirt and a blue top, took some flyers with me, and went out grocery shopping. Afterward, I decided to have lunch at the Lakeside Café before I headed over to the sheriff's station.

A middle-aged man who looked like an officer of the law was sitting in Ed's office but stood as I entered, as did Ed. The agent was of average height with short cropped dark brown hair, a square jaw, and piercing dark eyes. He was dressed in a blue and white short-sleeved shirt and black Dockers. Next to him was a woman in her thirties, about my height, athletically built with thick auburn hair that framed a pleasant face with large blue-gray eyes. She also sported a short-sleeved shirt and black slacks. Ed introduced them as Agents Carrie Jensen and Andrew Wells.

"And this is Megan Viets, our local mystery writer, who also gets herself involved in real-life mysteries."

"That's very interesting," Ms. Jensen said and held out her hand. "Are you a published author then?"

"Yes, I'm actually working on my sixth novel at the moment. And I understand you're working on our mystery victim Aldo Bandini."

"That's right. Ed here says you may have some information for us," Ms. Jensen continued. She spoke with a familiar Midwestern accent.

"I don't know, but maybe," I said slowly and looked at her. "I can hear you're from the Midwest. Would it be Wisconsin by any chance?"

"No, Minnesota, close to Minneapolis." She smiled. It seemed to give her pleasure to mention her home state.

"I understand that you discovered the body," Agent Wells said.

"Well, not exactly," I replied. "I saw a boat drive out to the middle of the lake and dump a big bag overboard. The bag turned out to contain a body, and we found out from his clothes that the victim's name was Aldo Bandini."

"*You* did," Ed corrected me.

"Okay, I did, and I reported it to the sheriff." I looked around. Their faces were all turned toward me. "The victim is evidently from New York, or at least he has family there."

Both Wells and Ms. Jensen were watching me intently, eyebrows raised. Ed was just sitting there, looking self-satisfied, like a cat who had just gotten to the milk jug. The only thing lacking was white whiskers around his mouth.

"And how did you find all this out?" Wells asked skeptically.

I didn't know how much Ed had told them, so I tried to watch my words.

"I saw the label in his jacket and traced it to a tailor in London. This tailor, Franco is his name, recognized his customer from a picture—he even looked up the address he had sent the finished clothes to." I looked from one to the other, but their faces showed little emotion.

"Why don't we all sit down," Ed suggested and placed chairs in front of us.

"So, you went to London to do all this?" Agent Wells said. He appeared to be the senior of the two.

"Well, actually, I was going over to visit a friend who, as it happened, had used this tailor, and we both went to Franco's, where I had a new suit made." I looked at Ed, who knew I was stretching the truth a little, but he just smiled.

Before they had time to reprimand me for meddling, I turned to Wells and Ms. Jensen. "And now I understand that you have sent the clothes to your lab for DNA testing. Have you found DNA belonging to anyone other than the victim??"

"No, not yet," Agent Wells replied stiffly.

"The deputies also found a shoe in the water near the body—the body was shoeless. Then one day, my dog found the match in some scattered trash outside a house near my own home. It could have been the house where the boat with the body came from, and I understand you've also sent both shoes to your lab for analysis as well."

"That's right," Agent Wells said. "And what exactly is your interest in all of this?" Agent Wells asked in a sharp tone.

I shrugged my shoulders. "Nothing more than a concerned citizen," I said firmly as I looked straight at him.

"I encourage everyone around here to report anything suspicious," Ed said kindly. "See something, say something. This is a huge area with a vast National Forest. My deputies cannot be everywhere."

"Right," Agent Wells said with a sigh.

We sat in silence for a few moments.

Ed turned to me. "So, what else have you found out?" he asked. "What did you call me about this morning?"

"Well, it's a strange story."

"How come I'm not surprised?" Ed said.

"I'm volunteering for the charity event at the Neighborhood Church," I continued. "It's a benefit for alcoholics and drug addicts. I've made posters to put around the resort and flyers to send to the newspapers around here and also to pass out to people. I brought some with me, in fact." I pulled three from my purse and gave one to each of them. They looked at them politely.

"I went around my neighborhood and stopped by the house where I'd found the missing shoe. It's an expansive property with a big house and an underground dock." I watched them. They looked at me rather doubtfully.

"An underground dock?" Ms. Jensen asked.

"Yes, many properties have dug out a dock under part of the property to protect the boats from storms, especially in the winter," Ed explained.

I continued, "An elegant woman who spoke with an East Coast accent and her niece invited me into a cluttered living room filled with all kinds of boxes. The woman agreed to contribute to the cause. She went into another room and soon reappeared with a hundred-dollar bill." I took out the envelope with the bill from my purse and handed it to Ed, who passed it on to Wells.

"You're very observant, aren't you?" Wells said. He took out the bill and scrutinized it. "So, this hundred-dollar bill came from the house where the boat with the body came from," Wells said.

"No, I don't know for sure that the boat came from that house, but my dog found the missing shoe there, the shoe that matched the one found near the shoeless body."

"The bill looks authentic enough," Wells said slowly.

"I have no doubt about that," I said. "I'm wondering if it's worth tracing."

"Where do you expect it will lead us?"

"I would guess Las Vegas, to some gambling casino or drug dealers or some money-laundering scheme."

Ms. Jensen and Wells looked at each other and then at me.

"It's not that far out," I said irritably. "Las Vegas is only a couple of hours away. And no, I do not confuse real crime with plots in my books, if that's what you're thinking. Of course, most of my plots are actually based on real cases anyway."

They looked at me sorrowfully, probably thinking, "Cuckoo."

I continued unabashed, "The victim had an Italian name, and, as far as I know, was a New York lawyer. The people I met in the house where my dog found the shoe were olive-skinned and looked Italian. I know you have to have probable cause to get a search warrant to enter the property, but isn't the shoe enough? With all these boxes everywhere, it looked to me like they were about to move out. That's why there may be a certain amount of urgency here and not enough time to wait for a positive DNA match." I looked over at Ed, who still seemed amused by the whole scenario.

"Well, we could try," Ms. Jensen said. "What do you say, Wells? I could present the case to Judge Schaller tomorrow. What do we have to lose? We haven't had any other breakthroughs in this case."

I smiled at her encouragingly. She seemed to have a little more imagination.

"I could show you the house," I said eagerly, watching them. "For a start, we could just drive by surreptitiously."

"Yes, okay, I'm all for it," Ms. Jensen said. "Let's take a drive, Wells."

Ed's phone rang, and he answered.

"You don't want me to go along, anyway. I have another fire to deal with. I'll see you when you get back."

We walked over to a white, unmarked sedan.

"You ladies drive," Wells suggested as he walked around the car to the front passenger side and opened the door for me, taking a good look at my legs as I maneuvered my way into the seat in my short skirt. Men! Do they ever let up?

Ms. Jensen took the driver's seat, and Wells sat in the back. We drove back toward my house, and I directed Ms. Jensen to turn into Deerskin Lane.

"Slow down," I said worriedly. "The roads around here are narrow and winding."

As we neared the house, I pointed. "There it is. It's an odd pale yellow color, isn't it?"

Neither the Porsche nor the Range Rover was anywhere to be seen, and the place looked deserted.

"They may have gone already," I said, feeling a bit crestfallen. Of course, this was not my case, so why should I care? But I really hate loose ends.

"Where exactly did you see the boat?" Wells asked.

"From my deck." I turned and looked over my shoulder at him. "We can stop by my house if you wish. It's only a couple of minutes away."

"Okay," Wells said without much enthusiasm.

I directed Ms. Jensen to my driveway, and she parked next to my van. Maria and JP would be back by now.

JP met us at the door. "Mommy!" he greeted me and followed us around.

"I see you have a son," Wells commented.

"Yes, I'm a single mother. My husband died a couple of months ago."

"I'm sorry about that," Ms. Jensen said and looked at me.

"Thank you," I said. "He was disabled after a serious accident."

Ms. Jensen remained silent and looked around. "You have a beautiful house," she commented. "Is that a Steinway?" She pointed to my piano.

"Yes, do you play?"

"Just a little."

"Oh, you have to come back and try it some time. It's really quite good. It was my husband's."

"Oh, thank you. I might just take you up on that."

We walked out on the deck.

"What time did you see the boat with the body?" Wells asked.

"Between three and four in the morning. There was a full moon and good visibility."

"What were you doing out here in the middle of the night?" He looked at me suspiciously.

"Thinking and writing."

"In the middle of the night?"

"Yes, I often do." I looked at him curiously. He surely didn't think I had staged all of this, although I realized that he had to keep an open mind.

We walked back inside where I picked up JP and told him I'd be right back.

Then I went back out with the agents. "I guess I have to return to the station with you guys to pick up my own car," I said. Ms. Jensen took the driver's seat again, and I got back in beside her. We drove in silence, and I thought about what we had just seen. Could Leo Smith, or whoever he was, and his family already have moved? Although the Porsche and Range Rover were gone, I hadn't noticed whether or not the shutters were up. Back at the station, I didn't see Ed's car, so I said good-bye to the two agents and drove home in my Subaru.

22

A SHOOTING ACCIDENT

One day I met one of the women from the self-defense and gun safety class in the parking lot of our little commercial center—a stout woman in her late thirties, with short brown hair, brown eyes, and a rugged complexion. Her name was Donna, and she was wearing maroon sweats that gave her a masculine look. She updated me on all the recent crimes in our area and told me she lived alone, which I remembered, and how happy she was to now have her gun with her at all times.

I said that I, too, was in the habit of carrying my gun with me at all times.

"It's crawling with drug dealers," she said authoritatively. "And the poor addicts are desperate. You have to be extra careful."

I nodded in agreement.

"A break-in happened just two days ago in a house down the road from me," she continued. "A computer and two TVs were stolen, and you know they weren't interested in just watching the news." She paused and looked at me righteously. "If they try anything at my house, they'll soon find out they've chosen the wrong address."

I agreed and told her I was sorry about the crime rate up here and that I kept my doors locked on advice from the sheriff.

"Good for you, darlin'," she responded.

We said our good-byes and went on our way.

James, my dear nephew, emailed me as soon as he had settled in with his host family, Ingrid and Thomas Andersen.

They are really nice. They met me at the airport with a sign that had my name on it. Ingrid is a nurse, and Thomas is a retired doctor. The university is full of students from all over the world. They all speak English. The classes are easy. Are you taking good care of Dad?

It really warmed my heart to hear from James. It appeared all had gone as planned, and that he had adjusted well. The question about his dad reminded me that I hadn't seen Ed since he introduced me to the FBI agents, Andrew Wells and Carrie Jensen. Fires were constantly raging in various parts of the county again, often intentionally set, and he probably had his hands full trying to catch these pesky arsonists, whoever they were.

I spent some time with JP, who, however, much preferred to play with friends in his playgroup. Even when I came to pick him, he was not ready to leave and ran away from me, so that I would have to chase him.

I was working steadily on my mystery novel, but one day when I was sitting on the deck with my laptop, the lake was beckoning to me. Small and medium sailboats glided back and forth, and speed boats pulled water skiers of all skill levels around in circles. The weather was particularly gorgeous, so I decided to take a break. I went back inside and into the mudroom to pick up my hiking boots and the fanny-pack I used as a holster for my gun when I didn't want to lug my purse around. As soon as Duchess heard me getting ready, she started whining. Of course, she had to come along too.

We went down to the dock first, but I didn't feel secure enough to take the boat out by myself. I had all good intentions of following the trail to the resort, but the pale yellow house, located in the other direction, pulled on me like a magnet, and I changed my mind. I kept Duchess on the leash, and when I came nearer to the house, we cut across to Deerskin Lane once again. At number 24, a new black SUV was parked next to the silver Porsche, and I passed quickly, looking at the forest rather than at the house, while Duchess pulled on the leash, urging me on.

Instead of returning the same way, I left the road in order to cut across the mountainside up to the next lane. It was an arduous task. Bushes with sharp thorns and thistle-like weeds covered the ground, and trees grew everywhere on this steep hill. I was not as familiar with the terrain as I had thought; I had trouble holding on to Duchess, so I let her loose. She'd find her way home by herself anyway.

The area is part of the National Forest, and although people had cabins and houses around here, they were few and far between. Most appeared to be empty. Trudging uphill through the brushy undergrowth was tiring. I didn't see anyone else around, for this was bear and coyote country. It was probably not a good idea to trample around this territory alone.

All of a sudden, I heard a thud and a whooshing sound. Another thud followed, and I felt a jolt in my left shoulder. It reminded me of swimming in the Indian Ocean once and having sea lions fly by like rockets or cannon balls. I hid behind a large tree, but I was too stunned to take out my own gun until several minutes had passed. Then I came to my senses. I took the gun from my fanny-pack, undid the safety lock, and aimed at something I thought was moving in the direction from where the shots had been fired.

I didn't see or hear anything more for the next several minutes, so I put my gun back in my fanny-pack, waited some more, and then started for home. Duchess caught up with me, and we both ran back side by side.

Well inside, I put the dog in her pen and made sure she had water. Although I felt a little faint, I had not felt any pain in my shoulder until now, but all of a sudden it was hurting so badly that tears came to my eyes. I pulled my T-shirt off, and blood ran down my arm and shorts, all the way to the floor. No one was home, and I realized I needed help with the bandaging. After rolling the blood-stained T-shirt around my shoulder and arm and throwing a button-down shirt over my other shoulder, I grabbed my purse with my keys and walked out to my Subaru. My fanny-pack with my gun was still around my waist as I drove myself to the emergency room at the hospital, only a short distance along the highway.

Only three other cars were in the spacious, newly asphalted parking lot, and as soon as I entered the lobby, I was shown to the emergency room. A young nurse, tall with long straight blonde hair led me to a spare room with a chair and an examination bed. I sat down, and the nurse went straight to work, rolling back my T-shirt.

"What happened here?" she asked. According to her name tag, she was an RN by the name Hannah.

"I guess I was accidentally shot in the shoulder," I said as she put a large piece of gauze in some solution and dabbed my bloody shoulder. The cold fluid stung, which caused me to wince for just a moment.

"You shot yourself in the shoulder?"

"No, someone else shot me."

"Who?"

"I don't know. I was out hiking in the National Forest with my dog, and someone may have mistaken me for a bear or a coyote." I looked at her. "Do you know Cheryl Day, and do you know if she's on duty?"

"Yes, I know her. Let me find out." She finished the bandaging. "At least it seems to be just a flesh wound. Nothing appears to be broken."

She took her phone from her pocket to call and asked if Cheryl was there. "A friend is here in Emergency, and she's been shot," she said.

"Thank you," I said gratefully after she hung up. "Cheryl is actually my sister-in-law."

"Really?" She put away her phone and didn't sound too interested in our family relationship. "Just sit here," she continued. "I'll tell the doctor. He'll give you something for the pain and maybe an antibiotic."

"It doesn't seem to hurt as much now," I said. "Thank you."

Cheryl came in after a few minutes. "What's happened?" she asked immediately, showing genuine concern.

I explained that I'd been out hiking with Duchess in the National Forest when someone probably mistook me for a bear or coyote or something and shot me in the shoulder.

"Oh, my God, that's a strange story. This is not the hunting season." She looked at me seriously. "Where were you?"

"Over on the north side. I thought there would be some trails around there, but I was mistaken."

"That's not a place I'd go wandering off, Megan," she said admonishingly. "That part of the forest is swarming with drug dealers and other outlaws. Did you call Ed?"

"No, not yet. Should I?"

"Yes, I'll call him for you." She took her phone from her pocket and called, but no one picked up.

"I'll try his cell phone."

Ed picked up immediately. Cheryl told him what had happened and put Ed on the speakerphone.

"Where is she?" he asked irritably.

"Hi, Ed," I said cheerfully. "I'm right here with Cheryl at the hospital, but it's really nothing, just a flesh wound. I'm waiting for the doctor to give me some pain pills and release me."

"What's this about being mistaken for a bear or coyote? No hunting is allowed anywhere around here now."

"I don't know. Maybe whoever he was feared I'd attack him," I said sarcastically.

"Do you need a ride home?"

"No, thank you. I'm fine. I have my car outside. It's nothing serious, really."

"Okay, I'll stop by later to hear the story in more detail and find out what you were really up to."

"Thank you, Ed. I'll have a cup of coffee ready for you." I handed the phone back to Cheryl.

"I'll be back after you see the doctor and walk you out to the car," Cheryl offered kindly. She was a wonderful woman and surely must be a great nurse.

The doctor finally came. He was a small, spare man with wavy blond hair streaked with gray, small eyes and a mild and kindly aspect. I told him my story, and he smiled politely. My tale was probably pretty tame compared to the injuries he witnessed every day, especially now with everybody running around with guns. He sent me to X-ray, where a young male nurse with short black hair and a dark complexion took several X-rays of my shoulder. When it was over, he told me it would take only a few minutes for the doctor to examine the pictures. Then he walked me back to the same examination room and pulled the pictures up on the computer screen. When the doctor returned, he looked at them for a minute but said there was nothing to indicate any damage to the bone, so he just gave me a prescription for some antibiotics as a precaution and a sling for my arm. "You don't really need it," he said. "But it sends a message to other people to be careful and not bump into you, as that might hurt."

I thanked him and returned to the lobby as Cheryl came through another door and walked me to my car.

The van was parked in the driveway, so I knew that Maria and JP were home. They both wanted to know what had happened. JP was especially intrigued by the sling. I told them I had taken a nasty fall and that I'd gone to the hospital, but nothing was broken and I'd be fine in a couple of days.

The three of us made macaroni and cheese for supper. Then Maria left, while JP and I went to bed early. Ed didn't come by; something must have held him up. I wondered who had shot at me. I didn't really believe anyone could have mistaken me for an animal. Neither did I believe that any drug dealer could see me as any kind of threat. Could it have anything to do with my snooping? Was I now a target? That was a scary thought.

23

SOJOURN AT THE BEACH

"What really happened yesterday?" Ed demanded impatiently after bursting his way in without knocking or announcing his arrival with the usual chirp of his siren. Or, at least I hadn't heard it. I was just coming out of the bathroom and was about to put my sling back on but put it on a chair instead. Maria had taken JP to his playgroup.

I stopped and looked at him. "It was just an accident, Ed," I said calmly.

"You haven't told me the whole truth, have you? I know a fishy story when I hear one. You were snooping again, weren't you?"

"No, I wasn't. I walked by the house, yes, but I cut through the brush and was climbing uphill into the forest when I heard two shots. One grazed my shoulder. And you'll be proud of me that I shot right back but didn't hear anyone scream or anything else, so I came home." I waited for a reaction, but none came. "I wouldn't have bothered with the hospital if someone had been home to help me with the bandaging, but after I put Duchess in her pen and removed my shirt, I noticed that my shoulder was bleeding profusely, so I decided to seek help."

"This was meant as a warning to you," Ed said seriously. "These guys don't miss if they are who I think they are. They may take out JP next if you don't get out of their way."

My heart stopped for just a moment. "Oh, I can't believe that, Ed. It was probably one of the nutty hermits that live in those isolated cabins in

the forest. I heard at the hospital that there are a bunch of them up there."
I cocked my head to one side just a little. "Actually, I wonder why some
of them aren't arrested," I added with a grin.

"You can't just go up there and arrest people. Where's the probable
cause?"

"How about shooting at stray hikers?"

"Yes, we'll investigate. In the meantime, why don't you take Maria
and JP down the hill and rent a beach house or something for a few days."

"Will you come and visit us?" I asked innocently.

"Oh, you are impossible," he said with feigned exasperation, but it did
put a smile on his face. Then he glanced at the door. "And I need to be on
my way."

"Are you catching any arsonists? Quite a few of them around now,
aren't there?"

"Yeah, that's right. Copycats crop up all over the place." He opened
the door ready to leave. "And I'd better be going. Are you going to take
my advice?"

"Okay. That's probably not a bad idea. Will you report the incident to
agents Wells and Jensen?"

"Of course. That would be the procedure, and they may want to talk to
you."

"Okay. I'll be in touch, and thanks for coming over." I went up to him
and gave him a hug.

"I don't want you and JP to get hurt, Megan," he said as he put his
arms around me and kissed me on the cheek.

"Careful with my shoulder, will you."

He pulled back and looked at me grimly.

"I'm sorry to cause you more work, Ed. Curiosity killed the cat, as
they say, and that's probably me."

"Megan, this is not a game," he said in his avuncular tone. "You're a
smart woman, but you have to be careful. You have a son, remember."

"I will."

Once he left, I just stood there for several minutes, looking at the
closed door. After I pulled myself together, I started researching places to
stay near the beach.

When Maria and JP returned from the playgroup, I suggested we go
on a short vacation. "Ed told me that some bad people are out to get us,
and he advised us to go away for a few days," I explained. "You too,
Maria," I said and looked at her. "Can your husband manage on his own

for a few days? I've rented an apartment near the beach for the rest of the week through the weekend. It will be a nice break for all of us, and JP will miss only a couple of days of playgroup."

Maria's eyebrows went up. She looked at me with her big brown eyes but didn't say anything.

"Do you need to go home and pack a few things?"

"I guess," she said finally and left shortly afterward.

The next day saw us all driving down the hill in the van to Newport Beach. I had brought the stroller, a box of toys, and clothes for JP. I didn't want to drive with the sling on my arm but brought it in case I needed it in a crowd.

The apartment was on the first floor. The kitchen and living room combination was furnished with sleek, IKEA-style furniture and a lone rug on light-colored wooden floors. Maria chose her bedroom and JP and I took the other. The complex had both a wading pool and a regular pool. I texted my friend Susie to see if she was ready for visitors. After a few minutes she called.

"I get so tired of texting," she said a little breathlessly. "So I decided to call you instead. Are you free to come over this afternoon?"

"Okay, what time?"

"Oh, between two and three. How's that?"

"Great."

"And, guess what? Dr. Frederic Pagel's in town. Back from Mongolia. Can you believe it? I'm still at school and just saw him. I'll see if he's free to come over as well."

"That would be awesome. I'll bring some snacks and three Starbucks coffees."

"Super. Got to run. See you this afternoon."

Maria and I put some clothes and things away, and then I took JP out to the wading pool while Maria took out her knitting. After lunch, JP went down for a nap, and I drove the short distance over to Susie's apartment, stopping on the way to pick up some wrapped muffins, some meal bars, and coffee.

Susie and Fred arrived just as I was parking the van. Susie fluttered toward me like a butterfly in a colorful silky dress, her auburn hair pulled back in a ponytail. Fred appeared a little thinner than the last time I'd seen him. His face was tanned but a bit more wrinkled, and his blond hair had not been trimmed for some time. Nevertheless, in his black-rimmed glasses, white, short-sleeved shirt, and dark Dockers, he still looked distinguished and professional. In fact, the two of them looked like the perfect couple.

"Megan, how nice to see you," Fred greeted me. "And you look just as sporty as ever. I'm sorry for your loss, but I hear you have a little boy now." He came over and gave me a hug and a friendly kiss.

"Watch out for my shoulder," I said quickly. "I usually wear a sling, but I can't really drive with it."

"What happened?" Susie asked as she, too, greeted me with a hug.

"It's a long story. I'll tell you later. Let me get the snacks from the car."

I handed them each a cup of coffee and gave Susie the plastic bag with the muffins and meal bars. I let my eyes rest on her face for a few moments. "You look like you could do with some rest, Susie. Are you sure you're not overdoing it, taking on all these extra summer classes?" I paused. "And where's Ashley?"

"Oh, she's with her father, and then it's on to camp. How's little John?"

"He's with Maria. As I told you, we've rented an apartment near the beach for a few days."

They both looked at me curiously.

"I'll tell you all about it, but let's first go inside and enjoy our coffee while it's still hot."

Fred and I followed Susie through the entrance hall into the sparsely but elegantly furnished living room. The walls were hung with angular, modern paintings in strong, primary colors. On the glass coffee table stood a large bronze statue of a life-like deer.

"So, how's Mongolia?" I asked Fred as we sat down while Susie went into the adjacent kitchen to get a plate for the snacks.

"Well, it's actually finished. The Mongolians are not as easy to work with as the Africans. We want to pay the goat herders and try to prevent them from letting their goats overgraze the grass because that special grass absorbs more carbon than trees, but the herders are reluctant to listen to us. This grass has been the main source of food for their goats for centuries. Not so simple to change their old habits."

"Where are you going next then?"

"Back to the Congo."

"Did you ever find an assistant to help you with your reports and grant writing?"

KARI H. SAYERS

"Just locals." He took a sip of coffee and looked at me smilingly. "Are you still interested?"

"It's not so easy for me to pick up and leave now, is it?" I said quietly as Susie returned from the kitchen and put the plate of snacks on the coffee table. I took an energy bar and started munching on it.

"You're right, but there are excellent international nursery schools there as well," he said encouragingly.

"I know. It sure would be a great adventure." I looked over at Susie. "How about Susie?"

"No, count me out," Susie said laughingly. "I'm just fine right here where I am." We all laughed, for we all knew that Susie would hardly survive a day in Africa.

We talked about old colleagues, those who were still at the college and those who had left since last year.

"So, what's the story behind your injured shoulder?" Susie asked suddenly.

"Well, someone took a shot at me the other day as I was hiking in the National Forest."

"Who?"

"I don't know. I told Ed it was probably a hunter who accidentally mistook me for a rabbit or a deer." I looked at Fred. "Ed is my brother-in-law and the town sheriff," I explained. "He told me that there may be something more sinister going on. And, Susie, you remember I told you about Aldo Bandini, who was found drowned in the lake?"

"Yes, I remember."

Fred raised his eyebrows, and his eyes widened.

I told him what I had witnessed, how I had recognized the labels on Aldo Bandini's clothes, the trip to London and New York, and how I had gotten myself invited into the pale yellow house. "Ed thinks that the shot was a warning because I've been snooping a little around the house where the boat with the body could have come from. I even found a clue. You remember, Susie? I found a shoe that belonged to the victim. Now the FBI is involved, and it's turning out to be a bigger deal than I bargained for, and that's why I'm down here until they can figure out what's going on."

"They who?" Susie wondered.

"Ed and the FBI."

"Holy cow!" Fred said disbelievingly. "You'd be safer in Africa."

"I know. In Lagos, we had two armed soldiers guard our house, and we never had any trouble, even though the slums were less than half a

132

mile down the road." I took another sip of coffee and stared down at the brown liquid in the cup.

After a few moments, Fred cleared his throat. "Are you free tomorrow?" he asked.

"Yes. Why?"

"I thought we could go to the museum I had planned for us to visit last time we saw each other when you stayed over at my apartment."

"Ooooh," Susie exclaimed. "I didn't know about that."

We all had a good laugh.

"We could take your little boy. Very educational for him."

"Can you go too, Susie, or are you teaching tomorrow.?"

"Yes, I'm teaching. Some of us actually have to make a living." She glanced over at Fred. "Megan is a well-to-do widow now, Fred. She could probably fund some of your enterprises for you."

"That's what I hear, but I have government grants, not only from the United States but also from European countries. But that's not why I'm asking you to spend the day with me, although a donation would not be rejected."

"Actually. Dr. Fred, I'll take you up on your invitation tomorrow. Where do you want me to pick you up?"

"I'm still at my old apartment. I sublet it while I'm gone, but now it's empty. I don't bother with a car here and use public transportation, such as it is, and Lyft."

"That fine. It's better for me to drive my van anyway since I have to have a car seat for John Patrick, and I also have to bring a stroller for him."

"You chose a really Irish name for your son, didn't you?"

"Well, my husband was half Irish and half Italian."

"Interesting."

"What time tomorrow?"

"How about 10:30 a.m. or so?"

"Sounds good to me." I looked at my phone. "It's getting late. I should probably go back and see what Maria and her little charge are up to." I took my leave, but Fred stayed behind with Susie.

Back at our apartment, I told Maria about my date the next day. "You're welcome to come too, Maria," I said, but she declined.

"I do a little shopping at the mall down the street."

We left it at that.

24

DATE WITH DR. PAGEL

$\mathbf{M}$aria dressed JP and prepared snacks for our big outing. Then JP waved to Maria and said "*hasta luego*" and "bye-bye."

"Do you have enough money for your shopping, Maria?" I asked, knowing full well that she did.

"Oh, yes. Joe gave me a check last week, and I have my card."

My father-in-law kept paying her out of the trust fund, as he had always done. The family had included her as a beneficiary of the trust long before I married Chris. She was well taken care of and showed her appreciation with her loyalty.

I called Fred when we were close to his apartment complex, and he met us at the entrance in a blue and white checkered shirt and jeans that did not appear to come from Target. Both his shirt and pants were professionally pressed.

"Hello, big man," he greeted JP as he opened the back door and shook JP's hand. Despite being strapped in his car seat, JP made a bow as Maria had taught him.

I reached over and opened the front door for Fred to get in next to me.

"You look nice," I said approvingly.

"Thank you," he said. "So do you."

I smiled. "Thank you. You probably have servants to take care of all your needs wherever you go, don't you," I said knowingly.

"Certainly. As you're well aware of, that's an advantage of being an expat in Third World countries. And to tell you the truth, I really don't know how to do household chores anymore." He strapped on his seat belt, and we took off.

"How about you?" he continued.

"Actually, I have help. We have a nanny who is really like part of the family, a good thing as I'm not as good at taking care of children as I thought I would be."

"Are you planning to have more?"

I looked at him. "What do you mean? It takes two to produce a baby."

He laughed but then caught himself. "I'm sorry. I meant, do you want to have more children?"

"Maybe one more if I find the right man."

He was silent for a few moments.

"What are your plans?" I asked finally.

"I don't know. There are too many children here already who need care. I might adopt one or two."

Yes, that sounded like Dr. Fred. Always the idealist.

"So, what do you do when you're not writing grant proposals and reports?" I asked in an effort to change the subject.

"Well, I read and do my share of research. I'm able to use the computers and the library at school. No one seems to mind, and I love José the librarian. He's just so knowledgeable, so helpful and interested in what's going on."

"Yes, he's a doll. Who do you write to all the time?"

"Foundations, grantors, laying out plans, and basically asking for more funds. There's a lot of interest in the field, fortunately, especially in Europe, and in September I'm going to Paris for an international symposium. I've already started to prepare a paper to present there."

"Paris, France?"

"Yes. What other Paris is there?"

"There's a Paris out here in San Bernardino too. Actually, a horrendous family tragedy took place there recently. A seemingly well-educated couple held their thirteen children captive. They tortured and starved them. I guess you didn't hear about it."

"No, but that's what's wrong with the world today. People have too many children that they cannot care for. That's the tragedy all over the Third World. People can barely take care of themselves, and then they have one baby after another. Organizations from all over the Western world send food and medicines but no contraceptives. It makes the whole aid thing so pointless."

"I agree. If we could somehow educate the women, we'd see a change. The more education the women receive, the fewer children they want."

"Yes, that's right." He paused. "I have an idea. You could start a school for girls in Central Africa, just like Oprah Winfrey."

I laughed. "Actually, on my flight to London not too long ago, as I told you, I sat next to a woman who worked for the United Nations. She was going to Africa to help set up English language schools over there. She asked me to contact her if I was ever in the area." I shot him a quick glance.

"So, you already have the right contacts," he said eagerly.

"I suppose so," I said. Going back to Africa was certainly tempting, but was I ready to make such a drastic change at this time? What about JP? Was it really safe to take a small child to such a dangerous area?

Fred remained silent, and I kept my eyes on the road. The traffic on the freeway was light between morning rush hour and the lunch crowd. We soon reached the museum, and we concentrated on finding the correct entrance and on securing a parking spot..

"Can you take John Patrick out of the car seat for me, Fred, while I get his stroller ready?" I asked.

"You trust me with such an important task?"

"Yes, Dr. Fred. You can handle it. You're a smart guy."

He held JP gingerly and deftly placed him in the stroller. I gave JP a cracker and a sippy-cup with a little juice mixed with water.

"Juice contains sugar," Fred said knowingly. "It's not as good for children as people think."

My eyebrows seemed to go up automatically. "Where did you hear that, and, by the way, it's mostly water anyway. Just a tiny bit of apple juice."

"Just water is the best." He looked at me seriously.

"Well, I'll remember that next time, Mr. Know-it-all"

He smiled indulgently. "I actually try to teach young mothers correct nutrition. I often see African mothers give their babies Coke or Pepsi in baby bottles."

"That may be because they don't have access to clean water," I said.

JP appeared to be finished with his cup, so I took it away and put it under the stroller.

"So, did you stay long at Susie's after I left yesterday?" I asked as we were walking toward the huge brick building.

"No, we went out to dinner, and then I went home."

"I see," I said thoughtfully.

After we had purchased our tickets, I realized that we had to go through security, and I had forgotten to remove my Chic Lady from my purse. Fortunately, we were shown to a cloakroom first, where we left our jackets, my purse, and loose items in the stroller. Someone also inspected the stroller.

As we entered, we were met by the familiar giant rebuilt Dinosaur Rex, and Fred proceeded to read the plaque to JP, who seemed surprisingly attentive.

"See, he's already a smart little man," Fred said, looking quite self-satisfied.

"Fred, you're really amazing with children."

"I know," he replied proudly and puffed out his chest mockingly.

"And you never had brothers and sisters to take care of, right?"

"That's true, but I like children."

"You'll be a wonderful father someday."

"Thank you," he said quietly and looked at me searchingly.

It was not long before JP fell asleep, and we wended our way to the coffee shop.

"So, when are you going back?" I asked casually after we had sat down with our coffee and a sandwich each.

"To Africa, you mean?" Thinking about Africa seemed to make his eyes light up.

"Didn't you say you were going back there?"

"Yes. But not until after the Paris symposium. I'll have to have some more shots and will probably stop by Baltimore on my way to see my parents, who can actually give me at least some of the required shots. They're researchers at Johns Hopkins Hospital, as you may remember." He looked at me. "Then I'll go to France and from there directly to Kinshasa."

"It certainly takes some preparations to go to Africa," I said. "I remember it well. All those shots!" I took a sip of my coffee. "My nephew is actually in Norway at the moment, participating in an international program there, and when he's finished, I'm planning to go with the rest of the family to Europe to pick him up. Not much in the way of medical preparations to go to Northern Europe."

"Is that the sheriff's son, then?"

"Yes. And I'm looking into hiring a private jet because it's not that much more expensive if you take enough people. My first husband had a private plane service, as I may have mentioned."

"Yes, I remember you told me." He looked at me. "It's hard to believe that you've had two husbands. And I haven't even tried marriage once. How fair is that?" he said in a melancholy tone.

"Yes, and both my marriages ended in death."

"I'm sorry."

"It's okay."

"Why is your nephew going to Norway of all places?"

"Well, I'm half Scandinavian. I guess I know a little about the culture, and I helped him arrange the trip. It's clean and safe, and that's important to his father, as you can imagine."

"What about his mother?"

"She died of breast cancer a year or so ago, so my brother-in-law is a single parent too. It's not so easy, and James, my nephew, is his only child."

He looked at me curiously. "I see," he said quietly.

"No, there's nothing between us. We're just a couple of single parents thrown together. When Susie came up to visit some time ago, I tried to hook them up, but no spark evidently." I cleared my throat. "He's seeing an aggressive but fashionable realtor, who seems to be all over him." I looked at him for a few moments. "How come you aren't seeing anyone, Fred?"

"I don't know. I've had a couple of girlfriends since I saw you last, but it didn't work out."

"Did they come out to see you in Africa?"

"No, they were already in Africa."

"You mean African women?"

"Well, yes, one of them. I'm not prejudiced."

"Oh, I know, but multiracial relationships are not easy. What did your parents think?"

"Not much. They don't think much of Africa in general. Too many dangerous diseases, too much corruption and mismanagement of resources, but, as you know, Africa is a beautiful continent with the most charming people."

"No argument from me there, Fred."

"So, why not come out there with me? I care for you, Megan, always have since I met you when we were both teaching at Pacifica College. And you seemed to like me too."

I smiled. "I know, and I do. You're a great companion, Fred, but I guess I haven't thought of you in a physical sense." I looked at him and took his hand.

"I probably should have been more aggressive when you spent the night at my place that time, but I didn't want to come on too strong and scare you away."

"Fred, I really appreciated that. You're a gentleman."

At that moment JP woke up whimpering, so I gave him a few goldfish and a bit more to drink. Then we finished our coffee and got up to see more of the exhibits, which prompted Fred to give both JP and me some fascinating lectures.

I dropped Fred off at his apartment, and we agreed to get together on the weekend, maybe with Susie as well. Then I went back to our rented place. Maria was sitting on the shady patio knitting, and JP ran over to her right away.

"Ed called while you were gone," she said in what I imagined to be an accusing tone, although it may just have been my guilt playing tricks on me.

"What did he say?"

"Oh, nothing. He want to know how we like our house. He said he call back later."

"Maybe I'll call him back. He may have some news about the murder case." I took out my phone and saw that I had received a call from him, so I just clicked on the call-back button.

He picked up on the second ring. "Where have you been?" he said.

"We're okay. A friend and I took JP to a museum, and I had my phone turned to silent."

"How's your friend?"

"You mean Susie? She's fine. I saw her yesterday, and today another friend. Dr. Fred Pagel and I went to the big Science Museum by USC. Susie had to work today."

"You don't waste much time, do you?" he said accusingly.

"What's that supposed to mean?"

"Nothing, really."

"You started going out soon after Elizabeth died too, didn't you?"

"You're right," he said, and even over the phone I could detect a deep sigh.

"Any news about who shot at me?" I asked after a moment or two.

"No, but just because you're out of the area doesn't mean you're out of their sight."

"I'm sorry, Ed. I guess I have a hard time believing someone is out to harm me. Thank you for looking out for me."

"It's my job," he said dryly.

"I'll check in with you tomorrow," I said, "and see if anything has developed."

"Okay, you do that. And be careful."

"I will."

We said good-bye and hung up.

25

DEVELOPMENTS

Monday saw us driving up the mountain again. It was early enough in the afternoon to beat the rush-hour traffic out of Los Angeles. I had called Ed for updates as promised, and he deemed it safe for us to return. Besides, it was time for JP to go back to his playgroup. He talked constantly about his little friends, imaginary or real, and needed someone other than Maria and me to play with.

Maria was sitting in front, leaning back with closed eyes, and JP soon fell asleep in the back seat. The highway up among the shrub-covered mountains, now mostly brown for lack of rain, is a great piece of engineering but monotonous, and my thoughts started to drift. Dr. Fred and I had agreed to go out again, and I managed to secure four tickets online, probably from a scalper, to see the immensely popular Broadway musical *Hamilton* at the Pantages Theater in Hollywood on Saturday night. I called Susie and asked her—actually told her—to come along.

"Don't you have a date you can bring along too?" I asked hopefully.

"Actually, I do. Surprise, surprise!" she replied laughingly. "How's your Japanese?"

"Not good. Doesn't he speak English?"

"He does, and beautifully! He's my student. A little younger than me perhaps but really cute, and I know he carries a torch for me."

"Great! That's settled then. Bring him along." I thought about it for a moment. "Oh, what's his name?"

"Senji."

"Okay, I can handle that. Sayonara."

Leaving JP with Maria, I met all of them at Susie's, and after introductions, I offered to drive, but Senji insisted on taking us in his high-powered BMW. He was quick and agile at the wheel. When we complimented him, he shared that he had been a racecar driver for eight years, but he had now decided to go back to school to finish his education.

After parking on a side street, we ambled down to Hollywood Boulevard, taking in the sights. A clown on stilts took big, awkward strides beside us. A man dressed as Captain Jack Sparrow from *The Pirates of the Caribbean* begged for tips, and the perennial Marilyn Monroe lookalike stood above some kind of a vent so that her skimpy skirt could blow upward, showing beautiful legs and thighs. Crossdressers and tourists with small children mingled on the crowded sidewalks.

The simple Mexican restaurant we chose was nearly empty. Although it was early and still daylight, an empty restaurant on a Saturday evening did not bode well, but it was convenient and looked clean. It was well lit with red and white checkered tablecloths. A young girl with long, black hair and skimpy clothing led us to a table and gave us menus, and here I saw the reason for the lack of clientele. The prices were exorbitant, even for such simple food as soft tacos with beans and rice. But an energetic mariachi band with a great sense of humor played at breakneck speed and well.

The players soon paused to collect tips, and Senji continued to regale us with stories from his racing days until I nudged Fred in an effort to change the conversation to Fred's adventures in Africa. I really didn't want to hear about racecars and Senji's many close calls all evening. Fred was only too delighted to oblige as he didn't seem interested in cars either, but he passed the baton on to me, so to speak, and asked about the Aldo Bandini investigation. I told them as much as I felt was appropriate but did not say any more about the accident or my new Chic Lady and my permit to carry a concealed weapon. Anyway, Susie soon turned the conversation to school.

"And how much do we owe you for tickets?" she asked after a while. "And where the heck did you get them?"

"That's my little secret," I said. "And it's my treat." I smiled benevolently, feeling slightly noble.

"Megan is a wealthy widow," Susie confided to Senji.

Although Lin-Manuel Miranda no longer played Alexander Hamilton, the show was awesome. Senji seemed especially amazed at the speed and precision of the actors and singers, the original music, and the staging. We talked about the show and marveled at it all the way back to Susie's. I took Dr. Fred home, and he talked more about his research and how happy he was to still be able to use the library at our old college. We sat in the car outside his complex for a while, but this time, I didn't stay the night and went straight back to the apartment. I walked in the door a little after midnight.

———

JP woke up whimpering, which awakened me from my daydreaming. Maria turned around and gave him a cracker and his special cup with water. On Fred's advice, we had cut out the juice altogether, and JP seemed fine with it.

Our house stood there as peaceful as ever. I was happy to be home. JP went straight to his box of toys, and Maria asked if it was okay to go home to her husband and sons now.

"Of course, Maria. I wonder what's awaiting you at your house with all your men managing by themselves for all this time."

She just laughed, said her farewells, and left.

I sat down at the piano and played a few scales and Hanon exercises before launching into some waltzes by Chopin and *lieder* by Brahms, Schubert, and Schumann in addition to some classic rock pieces from the Beatles era.

JP wanted to watch the *Baby Einstein* DVDs, and we both sat down together. No wonder he was such an early talker. These programs are truly educational and so perfect for little tots.

It was near sunset when I heard the short chirp of Ed's familiar police siren outside, announcing his arrival. To my dismay, my heart skipped a beat and blood rose to my cheeks. I had to admit to myself that, despite denials, I had hoped he would come by. Without knocking he entered through the front door, fresh and handsome. He looked like Chris with the same kind eyes, but his chin showed more determination. He was hatless; his dark brown hair newly trimmed, and his brown uniform was pressed and suited him well.

"Where's Maria?" he said brusquely as he came toward me.

"She went home to see what her husband had been up to while she was gone," I said and looked straight at him, waiting for a "hello."

He smiled and finally opened his arms to embrace me. He was warm, and I leaned my head on his shoulder as he kissed me on the top of my head.

"I missed you, Ed," I said a little too meekly, but that's how it came out.

"I don't believe you. You had too much fun with your doctor something-or-other."

He let me go and looked me in the face while grabbing me by the shoulders.

I winced. "Ed, my shoulder still hurts."

"Oh, sorry." He loosened his grip.

"And, incidentally," I continued, "Fred is not really a doctor. He's a researcher, working in the carbon offset trade industry, mostly in Central Africa, and he's going back there in a few weeks."

"And that makes you sad, I imagine."

"No, not really. He's a friend and a former colleague, and we sometimes go out together when he's in town." I removed his hands from my shoulders.

"Come and sit down. Do you want a drink? Or coffee?"

"Coffee will be fine. It's a quiet afternoon for a change. I've hardly had time to rest since you left...fires all over, domestic violence, drug busts, you name it. We have it all up here. I might as well be working in Los Angeles."

"I didn't witness any crimes in Los Angeles while I was there," I said as I left for the kitchen to make coffee. He followed me.

"You didn't stay in Los Angeles, Megan. Newport Beach is not exactly Los Angeles."

"We went through downtown to go to Hollywood." I rummaged around to make the coffee. "I should take you to see a show there sometime. You probably wouldn't enjoy *Hamilton* but maybe something else."

He looked at me curiously. "I was never much into theater. I played both baseball and football, and there wasn't time for sports *and* theater in high school."

The coffee was soon ready, and I looked in the freezer. Maria had left half of a Mexican casserole.

"Do you want to eat with us?" I said invitingly. "This will defrost in no time."

"Might as well. No one waiting for me at home."

"Where's Vee?"

"I don't know. Out selling real estate as far as I know. I haven't seen her for a while. She's not much for staying at home."

"Any news from James?"

"Yeah, I get an email from him once in a while. You probably hear from him more than me."

"Not really." I looked at him. "He's too busy having fun."

I placed the two cups of coffee on the kitchen table.

"Have a seat and relax. I'll set the table for the three of us."

I took out clean dishes and put the casserole in the microwave.

"Any news of the inhabitants of the pale yellow house?"

"Well, the FBI agents that you met are keeping an eye on it. They think there may be some big fish associated with that house and also with the murder. It seems too many big plumbing vans and trucks with contractors' logos have business there. One truck had a pest-control name on the door. They may, of course, be remodeling the house, but I don't think so."

"Are the workers from this area?"

"They're looking into that."

"Are the 'contractors' there during normal working hours?"

"Yeah, but also after dark."

"Could they be transporting drugs? Maybe the house is some sort of central warehouse. It would be hard to discover out here in the middle of nowhere."

"Who knows?"

"I saw a lot of boxes and stuff everywhere when I was inside the house being attended to, remember?"

"That was a foolish move, Megan."

"I know. But I didn't suspect anything that sinister. I was just dying of curiosity, that's all. You know human curiosity is part of our civilization."

He looked at me and sighed audibly.

JP came in and quickly climbed on to Ed's lap and started fingering his badge. Ed took it off and let him play with it until I lifted him up and put him in his highchair.

"I don't have any dessert," I said apologetically after we finished the casserole.

"That's fine," Ed said and paused for a moment. "How about we all take a ride in my car to the new ice cream shop in the resort." He turned to JP. "How would you like some ice cream, big guy?"

JP squealed and started chanting, "Ice-keem, ice-keem."

I figured Maria had acquainted him with that treat long ago. I did a quick clean-up and got JP ready while Ed took JP's car seat from the van and strapped it into the back of his sheriff's car.

When we returned home. I put JP to bed while Ed went into Chris's office. I heard him rummaging around in there, file drawers opening and closing.

"What are you looking for?" I asked inquisitively.

"Oh, nothing really. I see that Joe has done some cleaning up here," he said as he came back out. "Play something on the piano for me." He sat down on the couch by the fireplace, his legs crossed, one arm along the back of the oversized sofa.

I sat down and played the same random pieces as I had played for Chris many times, ending my performance with a wild rendition of Scott Joplin's "Maple Leaf Rag." I went over to the couch and sat next to him, right in the crook of his arm, leaning my head on his shoulder. Neither of us said anything. I knew very well where this could be leading, but I didn't care. I felt lonely, and Ed was an attractive man. Why not? Susie had often said that when she missed the intimacy of a relationship, she wasn't shy about it and didn't hesitate to find someone, even if she may not have been interested in anything permanent.

I turned to Ed and smiled. He looked at me with his mouth slightly open. I scooted closer to him. He took the hint and put his arm on my good shoulder. Then he bent over me and kissed my ear and neck passionately.

"Are you sure you want this?" he whispered softly.

"I guess a cop can't be too careful these days," I said.

"That's right. Pretty soon no one will dare have sex anymore, and then there won't be any more children, and our race will die out."

I put my arms around his neck and pulled him toward me, but just then, his radio crackled, and his cell phone rang. I startled. An armed robbery was in progress in the resort, involving, as far as I could hear, several people.

Ed swore but dutifully got up, straightened his tie, and smoothed down his uniform pants. "Can we continue this tomorrow?" he said as he was shaking his head.

I didn't answer. I just looked at him as he hurried out the door. After a few moments, I heard his siren as he rushed toward the resort.

26

ANOTHER TRY

Maria came early the next morning to take JP to his playgroup, and mid-morning Joe showed up. After a perfunctory greeting, he went straight into Chris's office, and I heard a file drawer open and the rustling of papers.

"Shall I make lunch for all of us?" Maria hollered from the kitchen.

Joe came out. "Unless you've made other plans, Megan."

"No, no plans, Joe. What are you looking for?"

"Just some old invoices. We have a repeat customer, and I wanted to see specifically what we had done earlier and how much we had charged." He held up a folder. "They're right here. Chris kept pretty neat files."

Ed called later. "I'm sorry, but I can't make it over to see you today, Megan," he said apologetically. "I have to finish a lot of paperwork and a proposal for a new encrypted digital radio system. We need better coverage here, but people are up in arms because the new system prevents them from listening in on our conversations. We'll have a community meeting tomorrow at the fire station. Maybe you'd like to come?"

"What time?"

"At two o'clock. Hobbyists will be there to protest, claiming they have a right to know what's happening around them. The switch from analog to digital is also expensive, but many departments around the country already have the new system in place."

"I'll try."

He said good-bye and hung up.

Maria had made tuna on rye, and Joe left right after we had eaten. That gave me time to work on my novel. My sleuth, Jule McCormick, had taken another look at the pictures of the gruesome crime scene, where Mrs. Luella Jones had been found in a pool of her own blood, brutally stabbed to death. The pictures revealed a small oblong piece of what looked like foam rubber on the floor. It was so out of place that it attracted her attention, and she went back to the crime lab to take another look at this particular piece of evidence. After JP came home and Maria left, I read to JP and went to bed early.

The next day, as soon as Maria took JP to his playgroup, I put my hair in a French braid, donned my beige walking shorts and a long-sleeved beige T-shirt. Then I grabbed my comfortable hiking boots, slathered myself in sunscreen, and took Duchess for an early walk down to the lake and then up to Deerskin Lane. Not a leaf moved in the glittering morning light, and I was in no hurry. In front of the pale yellow house stood a large white van. Even with the logo, it looked like a moving van that opened in the back. It had been backed up against the front entrance, and uniformed men carried boxes and crates in and out of the house. I passed as quickly as I could since I was afraid to linger and be spotted, and as soon as I turned around the bend, I climbed up the hillside, from where I could see more men carrying more containers from the house to the car. I didn't dare hang around and hurried on. Not wanting to go back the same way, I realized I'd have to hike the full twelve miles around the lake, which meant that I would only barely make it to Ed's meeting. However, I didn't feel I had a choice, so I trudged on. Duchess was carrying on with her usual antics, chasing anything that moved but mostly gophers and squirrels. She also would constantly run down to the lake for water. I drank my water sparingly, as I had an arduous hike in front of me, but I did finally make it to the firehouse just in time.

Not exactly the epitome of elegance, I stood outside for a while wondering what to do with Duchess, but I spotted a convenient pole and tied her to it. "You be a good girl and wait for me, Duchess," I said not thinking anyone was around. "Sit Duchess, and I'll be back."

She whimpered but sat obediently. Right behind me, someone coughed softly. I turned around. One of the firefighters was looking at me, and blood rose to my face. "Sorry," I said. "I didn't know anyone was listening. My dog is pretty perceptive, and she seems to understand me."

"I'll keep an eye on her," he said in a friendly voice.

The bathroom was right inside in the hallway, so I went in and tried to spruce myself up by re-braiding my hair and wiping dust and sweat off my face.

The bright meeting room had big windows, and a large square table with chairs on all four sides occupied the middle of the room. Along the walls were more chairs, and an additional three rows had been set up right inside the door. The first person I saw inside was Vee, elegant in a loose flowered chiffon top, white slacks, and white high-heeled sandals.

"Hello, honey," she greeted me. "Where have you been? You look a mess."

"Thank you, Vee. Duchess and I just hiked around the lake," I said coldly.

She looked the other way, and I don't think she heard me or cared.

Ed was busy laying out his notes and various papers as mostly senior citizens trickled in, but he did look up briefly to acknowledge me as I found a seat. Vee sat down next to me.

"I just brought Ed some lunch since he didn't have time to take me out today," Vee announced self-righteously.

"Oh, that was nice," I replied dryly without looking at her, but I suddenly realized that I was hungry. There was a tub filled with ice and water bottles by the door, and I walked over and grabbed one.

"Oh, did you want one too, Vee?" I asked as I returned to my seat.

"That's okay, honey. I'll get one later."

An older gentleman in a light summer suit cleared his throat and waited until the room was quiet. Then he introduced Ed, who told everyone about the importance of switching from analog radios to a new digital system, emphasizing the enhanced safety it would afford our mountain residents.

Both Vee and I spoke up in favor of switching after a few lame protests and complaints. "With all that is going on in our community, we need law enforcement to have the best equipment available. Our safety is priceless," I said. Vee emphasized that she couldn't sell real estate if law enforcement could not provide safety for our citizens.

The rest of the meeting bored me, with people asking questions whose only function was to say, "I'm here, and I'm important." It was just like a faculty meeting.

After the moderator concluded the meeting, several people flocked around Ed, but I needed to get back to Duchess. However, I went up as close to Ed as I could, and, as if I was encouraging one of my students, I called out, "Good job, sheriff."

Ed acknowledged me with a nod and a smile. Vee remained seated but waved good-bye. Duchess was ecstatic to see me, and we jogged and walked the rest of the way home.

I had barely stepped out of the shower when Maria and JP returned from their outings. I quickly dressed in a short denim skirt and a white tank top, and with my hair still wet, I met them in the kitchen. Maria and I had supper ready in no time.

Ed did not come by until after Maria had left and JP was ready for bed. After the meeting he had gone home to change into jeans, slip-on black canvas shoes, and a tight black Golf shirt that bore witness to his daily work-outs. He had even shaved off his usual five-o'clock stubble.

"You look like you're ready for a work-out in the gym," I said and smiled.

"You look pretty sporty yourself," he countered. "Shall we give it a try?"

He came closer, put his arms around me, and squeezed me as if he were tightening a vice. I looked at him, and he bent over me, kissing me lightly on the forehead and cheeks.

"How did you like the meeting today?" he inquired.

"It was all right, except I got stuck with Vee. She said she had brought you lunch because you didn't have time to take her out."

He shook his head but didn't answer. Instead, he held me and buried his face in my almost-dry hair.

"Ed," I said cautiously and pushed him away. "Do you mind if we wait a little with our secret tryst?"

He lifted his head and looked at me inquiringly. "Uh-oh. You've had second thoughts."

"No, not really, although if we're going to have a relationship, we should probably keep a lid on it. Some people may think it's a little too soon."

"Joe won't mind. Cheryl and Maria won't either."

"That's good to hear."

"And who cares about the rest?"

"Yes, that's true." I paused and wondered why he hadn't mentioned James. Would James mind? Maybe he felt safe with me. After all, his father couldn't really get involved with a relative, so to speak.

"Have you had any supper?" I asked in an effort to change the subject. "You must be hungry. Maria and I made chicken Alfredo Maria style, and there's plenty left."

I took his hand and led him into the kitchen. "Did you know, I hiked all the way around the lake before joining you at your meeting? It took me five hours because I was afraid to go back the same way I'd come early this morning."

"Why?"

"Duchess and I went for our usual hike along the lake and then up along Deerskin Lane this morning. I saw a white van in front of the pale yellow house. As I passed the van, I read Mission Care Medical Service in big letters on the door, and uniformed men were hauling equipment back and forth."

"What time was that?"

"It must have been around nine o'clock."

"Did you see anybody else?"

"No, not a soul. I hurried on. I didn't dare go back again for fear someone would recognize me or Duchess."

Ed frowned. I heated up the chicken dish and set the table.

"But you didn't see anyone else?" he continued.

"No, should I have?"

"No, but an agent was there. He was evidently well camouflaged since even the dog didn't notice anything."

We sat down and ate in silence for a while. Ed had two helpings.

"The two FBI agents that you met are coming up tomorrow. I believe they'll have something to show you. Are you free tomorrow morning? I could send them over."

"Will you come with them?"

"Probably not. I have another meeting in San Bernardino tomorrow, and I'll most likely stay down there till the evening."

We got up, and I left everything on the table and followed him into the living room.

"I guess I should be going and let you go to bed," he said with a wink.

"Alone?"

His eyebrows rose, but he smiled. Then he came over and embraced me as he kissed me lightly on the forehead. I put my arms around his neck and tried to hold him close. Although I wanted our relationship to cool and develop more slowly, I did not really want to go to bed alone another night, but life does not always turn out the way you want to. He removed my arms carefully and held them for a while. Then he said goodnight and left.

27

VISIT FROM THE FBI

The next morning the telephone rang while I was working out in the gym. I didn't recognize the number, so I ignored it and continued my routine on the elliptical. Since it was raining, I had decided to skip my usual outing with Duchess and had instead opted for the weights, the ropes, and the bicycle that had not been used much since Chris died.

Suddenly I remembered that the phone call may have been the FBI agents. There was no message, but I hit *69 to return the call. Agent Carrie Jensen picked up.

"I think you may have just called me," I said. "And I'm returning the call."

"Oh, yes. Thank you for calling back. Agent Wells and I would like to meet with you sometime today to show you some photos. Are you available this morning?"

"Yes, that'll be fine. The sheriff alerted me that you might call. Where would you like to meet?"

"Can you suggest a private spot?"

"Well, you could come over to my house. You drive an unmarked car, don't you?"

"Yes, that's right. We certainly don't want to compromise you in any way."

"That's all right. There's plenty of space here, if you can find it again." I hesitated for a moment, remembering that the GPS didn't always give accurate readings in this area.

"Oh, don't worry. We'll find it."

"Can you give me half an hour?" I continued. "I just finished my workout and need to take a shower."

"That's fine. How about we come over in an hour or so?"

"Good enough."

I gave her the address again and explained how to find my house.

An hour later, I heard a car door close. I met the two agents at the door. They both carried black attaché cases, and, as before, they were dressed in similar light-colored button-down shirts tucked into darker, nondescript pants. They could have passed for two Mormons on a mission, except for the female presence, although Ms. Jensen didn't exactly look like a typical American woman. If they carried guns, which I assumed they must, they did a good job of concealing them.

"Hello, and come on in," I said, trying to sound welcoming, even though I was far from impressed by the way—particularly the speed—at which the FBI in general seemed to operate. We shook hands.

"Thank you, Mrs. Cronin, I guess the sheriff is busy with meetings down in San Bernardino and couldn't come with us today," Agent Wells said apologetically.

"That's all right, and please call me Megan. Can I offer you a cup of coffee?" I asked.

"That would be lovely," Ms. Jensen said.

I led them both into the kitchen. They put their attaché cases on the table and looked around while I made the coffee.

"Cream and sugar?"

"No, thank you. Just black, please."

I placed the cups on the table, and we all sat down opposite each other.

"What a nice and spacious kitchen," Ms. Jensen commented.

"Thank you."

"It's a really beautiful house," she continued.

"My father-in-law built it pretty much himself as I understand it. He started a contracting business up here. My husband ran it until he died."

"Yes, we heard about the accident and all. Pretty awful. I'm so sorry," Agent Wells said.

"Thank you. Actually, my father-in-law stepped back into the business again, although he had already retired. Maybe my nephew, the sheriff's son, can take over when he gets old enough. He just graduated from high school though and is taking a gap year before going on to college. He's participating in a summer program in Scandinavia right now."

"In Scandinavia? That's pretty far away, isn't it?" Agent Wells said, taking a sip of coffee.

"Yes, but that's one of the few countries the sheriff approved of since it's relatively safe. I still have some second cousins there and helped him arrange for a homestay." I took a sip of coffee and turned to Ms. Jensen. "You're Scandinavian, aren't you, Ms. Jensen, or can I call you Carrie?"

"Yes, by all means. And this is Andrew." She smiled. "And yes, I am Norwegian on my father's side and Irish on my mother's."

While sipping coffee, Agent Wells had laid out a series of black and white photos on the table, and he passed them over to me. "Take a good look to see if you can recognize any of these people."

I stopped at a photo of a man in his fifties with graying hair and piercing dark eyes. I scrutinized it more closely.

"This could possibly be the guy I've seen walking with his wife and dog, but I'm not sure," I said cautiously.

He showed me more photos of the same man but with different hair color, different styles of beards, wearing dark glasses, yet there was something familiar about all the pictures—the high cheekbones, the same nose and shape of the mouth.

"This is the notorious New York gangster John Frazzano Junior, the son of the big Mafia boss John Frazzano," Agent Wells said. "He's been on the FBI's most wanted list for some time, and he's reported to be holed up out west somewhere. He's a notorious drug smuggler, heroin especially."

"Yes, there's definitely something familiar about him," I said slowly.

"Do you think you'd recognize him if you saw him again?"

"Possibly, but out on the trail he was always wearing sunglasses and a baseball cap, and he was not particularly friendly, so I never got a good look at him. Do you have any pictures of his wife?"

"He's not married but has a live-in girlfriend. He was born in 1960 or so, and his girlfriend is a little younger."

"Yes, it might be them," I said. "But I cannot swear to it." I shook my head and looked from one to the other. "It may be too late now anyway. Yesterday, when I was out walking my dog, I saw a big white moving van outside the house I showed you last time you were here. Several workmen were carrying crates and boxes from the house and loading them into the back of the van."

"Yes, we know," Wells continued. "We had an agent stationed above the house."

"Did someone follow the van when it left the house?" I asked hopefully, but I had no illusion that they had someone ready to move. It would have been too logical for any government agency.

"As a matter of fact, we did," Agent Wells countered a bit sarcastically, as if he were reading my thoughts.

"What happened?"

"Well," Ms. Jensen said earnestly and hesitated a moment before continuing, "the agent followed carefully out on the 10 freeway. He exited onto Santa Monica Boulevard, but road workers had blocked all lanes except one. The designated road worker held up a stop sign right in front of our guys to let the opposing traffic through, and by the time our agent was allowed to pass, the moving van was long gone."

I was not surprised. These people seemed to have a knack for bungling things.

"But the van was obviously going to some place in Santa Monica then," I said.

"Possibly, but not necessarily. The van was nowhere in sight and could have continued on to Malibu."

"Not really," I thought to myself. They would have taken another exit if they were going to Malibu. I wondered how well they knew the area, but I remained silent for a few moments.

"How long have you guys been working out here in the Los Angeles area?" I asked finally.

"We've been working out of Long Beach for a couple of years," Ms. Jensen said.

"It seems to me that they might have been going to an apartment in Santa Monica," I said stubbornly.

"Maybe," Ms. Jensen agreed.

"Well, how many apartments or houses are for rent or lease around there right now?"

"We're looking into it," Agent Wells said quickly.

"Anyway, Mr. Frazzano, or whoever lived in the house, would most likely not have gone along in the moving van in any case," I said. "Unless, of course, he was dressed as a workman, which I highly doubt."

"I agree," Ms. Jensen said. "He was somewhat of a dandy."

"And so, in that case, he and his girlfriend might still be in the house."

"Possibly. We know there are still people in the house, and we have an agent stationed there," Ms. Jensen said.

"Has the agent seen anyone leave?"

"No, not yet."

"So, what happens now?"

"We'll have to wait and see. A young girl is still walking the dog."

"I see."

"And please do not go near the place with your dog," Agent Wells admonished me. "It could compromise our agent."

I promised to be good. Of course the agents didn't know I had a secret path from where I could spy on the house without being seen.

"I heard you got shot at the other day," Agent Wells said.

"Well, it was nothing," I said, making light of the incident. "A bullet grazed my shoulder, that's all. It was probably a crazy hunter who took me for a deer, or it could have been one of the crazy hermits who live in isolated shacks around the National Forest. He may have thought I had come a little too close to his man cave."

"Or, maybe not," Agent Wells said. "We urge you to stay away. I'm sure the sheriff has told you what you could face if you end up interfering with an ongoing investigation."

I remained silent but thought to myself that someone might need to light a fire under them as they were awfully slow to act. They might end up trying to keep an eye on the entire city of Santa Monica instead of our small resort.

We finished our visit with some small talk about the changing weather up here in the mountains, and Ms. Jensen and I reminisced about Wisconsin and Minnesota, where she was originally from.

The two agents left a little after noon, and I spent the rest of the day working on my novel. My sleuth, Jule McCormick, was now in Texas, trying to talk the police there into searching the homes of the murder victim's brothers. So far, the evidence was purely circumstantial, but the piece of foam rubber so oddly left on the floor could turn out to be the tangible evidence that was missing.

I thought Ed might call later in the evening, but he didn't. Nor did he call the following day. He might be having second thoughts about developing a relationship with me. Because of the weather, he might also have decided to stay with his father down in the flatland for a couple of days. I was tempted to call him, but the cooler side of my head told me to restrain myself. He needed time to figure himself out as well as me.

I tried to bury myself in my novel, but I missed Ed more than I was willing to admit, although I kept telling myself that I was at a vulnerable point in my life, having just lost Chris. I missed the happy two and a half years Chris and I had spent together. What a fluke accident! Running into a burning building to save his crazy ex-wife, so to speak, although they hadn't officially been divorced, and then getting hit by a burning beam which paralyzed him from the waist down. Maybe death was the best way out for him. He might never have recovered.

28

DATE WITH THE SHERIFF

I had just put down my laptop and was watching the driving rain streak the windows when Ed finally called later in the afternoon. I recognized his number and took a deep breath before picking up.

"Hello, Ed," I said cheerfully enough.

"Hi," he said and continued without pause, "how would you like to have dinner with me tonight?"

"Well, yes. Of course. Here? I guess I could scrounge up a few things."

"No, at Settlers Inn."

"Is anyone else coming?"

"No, just me."

"Really? You mean just the two of us. Like a date?"

"Yes, I guess that's what it's called."

"That would be nice, Ed, but what about JP?"

"I'll ask Maria to stay."

"What if she has other plans?"

"Actually, I've already asked her."

"You were that certain that I'd say yes?"

"Yes, but if you have other plans, I'll just tell her to cancel it."

"No, I have no plans." I hesitated for a moment. "You told her you were going out with me?"

"Yes, and she's all for it."

"You really surprise me, Ed."

"So, you do want to go out with the then?"

"Of course. What time?"

"How about seven?"

"Okay. Do you want me to meet you there?"

"No, I'll pick you up at quarter to seven. How's that?"

"Okay, I'll be ready, and Maria will stay later then?"

"Yes. I told her we'd probably be back by nine."

"You're a good planner, Ed."

"Thank you. I'll see you at quarter to seven then. I've got to go."

Maria and JP came marching in from the deck singing something in Spanish.

"So, you know Ed is taking me out to dinner tonight, Maria," I said when she eyed me.

"Yes, nice. He's alone. He's a nice man."

"I know, and I agree. He is a nice man."

I decided to put on a flowery summer dress paired with a cropped white furry jacket that I had ordered online. I put my hair up in a bun and found an old pair of silver flats.

The rain had subsided when Ed arrived. He knocked but entered without waiting for me to let him in. He looked good in a light beige sports coat over a button-down dress shirt and brown slacks. He smiled and gave me a perfunctory kiss on the cheek and headed straight for the kitchen, where Maria and JP had just finished supper. He gave JP a high-five and Maria a bear hug, like a son would hug his mother, as he said something in Spanish. He finished with something like *mamacita*. Then he returned to the living room.

"You look nice," he said.

"Nice?" I cocked my head a little. "What do you mean nice?"

"Different." He hesitated. "Isn't the correct response a simple 'thank you?' Or are you playing games with me?" He gave me a quick hug. "How about strong and sporty but nice."

"Thank you, Ed."

We walked out to his car.

"Don't you like to go out?" he asked after we had buckled our seat belts.

"It depends," I said teasingly.

"On what?"

"On the company I'm with."

"Oh? And is the present company acceptable?"

"I hope so. We'll see, won't we?"

"I'll be on my best behavior, I promise."

"I guess I'm going to have to try my best too. And I do look forward to some good lobster bisque."

As usual, Settlers Inn was crowded. The restaurant had new management but didn't look noticeably different. It was still light outside but cloudy, and the paneled walls and small windows made the room look dark. Al was still the host and greeted us by name like old friends. He was in his forties, not too tall but slim and professional in his black suit and white shirt and tie. Chris and I had often come here for lunch or dinner, and Al always had a table for us no matter how crowded.

"Would you like a glass of wine at the bar, Mrs. Cronin? I'll have your table ready in a few minutes."

I looked at Ed. "That would be wonderful. What about you, Ed?"

"I'll have a beer."

I ordered a glass of Chardonnay and had just taken my first sip when Al came and steered us to the same table by the window overlooking the lake that Chris and I had shared not very long ago. Al took my glass and set it on the table before holding out the chair for me.

"Hey there, sheriff?" someone hollered from a large table in the middle of the room where about six men and two women were seated. Ed hadn't had time to sit down yet and left me to go over to greet them, shaking hands and bantering with everyone. It was a rowdy bunch.

"Sorry," he said as he returned. "Those are people I need to get along with. Some of them are members of the San Bernardino City Council on a weekend retreat up here. They wanted us to join them, but I said we'd have our meal first and then join them for coffee. Would that be all right?"

"Of course."

The waitress came and took our order. We both had the famous house lobster bisque, and Ed had filet mignon, while I asked for a second helping of the lobster bisque.

"Are they all staying here at the inn?" I said, looking over at the local government members. "Or are they staying at the hotel in the commercial center?"

"Oh, at the hotel."

"Are you going to give them a ticket if they drink and drive?"

"No, not personally. But I may call one of my deputies to look out for them…for their own safety as well as for others."

"That's a good idea."

We ate in silence for a while. The lobster bisque was delicious as usual.

"So, what gave you the idea that we should go out on a date?" I said as I started on my second helping of the soup.

He put his hand on mine. "I thought we ought to get to know each other a little better before we jumped into an intimate relationship. It could be awkward if it didn't work out."

"That's a good point, but you've already known me for a couple of years. There's not much more to me than what you've already seen."

"Oh, I know there's much more to explore." He looked at me and smiled mischievously as he squeezed my hand.

"Do you mean what I think you mean?"

"Maybe," he said slowly and looked down. "As you know, I don't exactly sit peacefully at my desk all day like an accountant. My job carries with it a certain amount of risk although I don't go out in the field as much as I used to anymore. But you've lost two husbands. Maybe you'd prefer an accountant or your doctor friend."

"He's not a doctor, Ed, and he's going to Central Africa, not exactly a peaceful place. In addition to wars and killings, there's Ebola, malaria, yellow fever, typhus, typhoid, and cholera all around."

Ed laughed but then caught himself. "Sorry, it's no laughing matter, but you're right. Life is a hazard."

"And I could have an accident on the freeway or develop a rare form of cancer, and who knows what?"

"Yeah, I guess you're right. And on that happy note, let's have our coffee with the city officials." He motioned to the waitress and asked her to bring our coffee to the city council's table.

Ed introduced me to everyone as his younger brother's widow and told them I was a mystery writer with five published books to my name. They made room for us to sit next to each other, offered condolences on my loss, and made the usual comments on my writing, not appearing to suspect there was anything between us other than an older brother taking care of his deceased younger brother's family. The coffee came, and I took a sip.

"I heard you'd lived in Africa," the woman sitting opposite from me said in a rather loud voice. She was in her late forties or early fifties with short brown hair and a plain face with very little make-up.

"Yes," I said. "Mostly in Nigeria but also in the Middle East, Dubai and Saudi Arabia."

"Dangerous places both," the woman sitting next to me commented. Her name was Susie, like my friend, but this one was a full-figured, middle-aged woman with short gray hair and glasses, and now all of the members were looking my way.

"True," I said. "We had two armed guards outside our gate, and a block or so down the road were the slums, but everyone I met was friendly and helpful. Africans in general are gracious and honest. My husband was a bush pilot stationed in Lagos and flew all over the continent until his plane crashed in a sandstorm."

I saw faces with raised eyebrows all around me.

"How awful," Susie said and shuddered.

"We probably have more crime here," Ed said and put his arm around me. "And some really stupid ones at that. The other day, someone tried to steal money from one of those gumball machines at one of the cafes in the resort. The thief had pried the machine open, taken the pennies, and tossed the broken machine out on the street. On the counter a few feet away stood a basket full of paper money, tips from customers, untouched."

Smiles and laughter followed. Ed seemed to have these people in the hollow of his hand.

The room was noisy, and I continued my conversation with Susie, who was telling me about council affairs—dealing with permits for gateposts and other building proposals, in addition to the rise in crime, and I answered her questions about living in Africa. By the time we had finished our coffee, she and I were good friends.

Soon Ed turned to me. "We should probably be leaving so Maria can go home."

"Yes, I'm ready."

I got up, and we both said good-bye and left. Ed shook hands with some people at the other tables, while I followed quietly behind, waving to Al as we walked out the door. Ed took my hand and led me to the passenger side of the car, but out of habit I grabbed the door handle and slid in before he had a chance to open the door for me.

"Sorry about forcing you into the unwelcome party," he said apologetically as he started the car. "But you carried yourself well."

"Thank you. People are pretty much the same all over. They like to talk about themselves and what they do and politely ask questions about what you do." I looked at him. "They all seemed to like you and approve of what you're doing."

"Yes, I think you're right. At least I hope so, but maybe I won't be in this business for many more years. If I could get my degree, I'd like to teach criminal justice at a small school."

After he stopped in the driveway and turned off the engine, we remained seated. I stared straight ahead, wondering what to say. Should I invite him in? It was, after all, his old home. It surely would be strange to just leave me at the door. I glanced over at him. He sat bent over with his hands on the steering wheel.

"Do you want to come in for a drink?" I said finally.

"Do you want me to?"

"Are we all of a sudden becoming so formal now? This is your home, and you'll want to say goodnight to Maria."

"You're right."

He removed the car keys and stepped out, as did I, and we both walked inside. Maria was ready to leave. We both wished her goodnight, and then there were only the two of us left. I went into the bedroom to check on JP, who was fast asleep.

"I've poured us both a drink," he said when I returned.

"Okay, but what about driving?"

"I think I'll just crash on the couch tonight," he said and laughed.

"Well, you still have your old bedroom upstairs."

"Right," he said. "I might as well move right back home."

29

INTIMACY

Once again, I was sitting on the big couch facing the stone fireplace, taking small sips of my drink. Ed was lying next to me with his head touching my thigh, and his eyes closed. He had kicked off his shoes, and his empty glass stood on the coffee table. I looked down on his handsome face. What made him look different from Chris, apart from his short, military-style haircut, were his bushy eyebrows, his broader nose, and his more defined chin.

He opened his eyes and pushed himself toward me, so that he could put his head on my lap. I stroked his forehead.

"Did you know that in some Arab countries it is an ancient tradition that an older brother marries a younger brother's widow and takes care of her children?" I said. "It's an obligation."

"Really? Poor guy. Two wives at one time and more kids."

"Poor guy? I guess I haven't really thought about it that way. I've been thinking more about the poor woman. What about her? If her brother-in-law so chooses, she has to move right into his bedroom." I looked at him to see if there was any reaction. There was none. "But it's true that the children are taken care of right away," I continued. "And they get to share rooms with their cousins, probably quite exciting, at least at first." I reflected for a moment. "It happened to a friend of mine. Well, she wasn't exactly a friend but someone I had met at an American Embassy event. She was quite a bit older than me, probably around forty and from New York. She had Scandinavian roots, and that may have been why someone thought we should get to know each other. She had married an Arab businessman that she had met in Geneva, where she was working as a secretary. He was a short, fat guy with a round face and glasses, not exactly the epitome of good looks, but neither was she. However, he had a lot of money—I mean a lot. She moved with him from Switzerland to Saudi Arabia, one of the more conservative countries in the Middle East, where they lived in a big mansion full of servants. She had her own private plane, a big one too, with an American pilot on standby, and she would fly up to London to go to the dentist or to Paris to go shopping."

"They didn't have shops and dentists where she lived?" Ed interjected.

"Yes, but I guess not always the latest Dior or Cartier designer fashions, and she'd had her teeth beautifully capped too."

"And did that improve her looks?"

"I'm sure it did."

"Maybe I should have that done."

"You have beautiful teeth, Ed." I assured him. "Just like Chris."

"We both had braces when we were in our teens."

"Good. Everyone has braces, Ed. Anyway, one day her husband was killed in a car accident in the French Alps, and my 'friend' told me that her husband's older brother, a big oaf of a man and uneducated, came over the next day and started telling her what to do so that he could come and get her and marry her. He would then take her and her two children with him to his house to live with his other wife and kids. She fought it, claiming that her son would soon be of age and would be able to take care of her." I looked at Ed to see if he was listening.

"Yes, I'm listening," he assured me and smiled.

"Actually, she was quite capable of taking care of herself *and* her children by herself because she had stashed money away in a Swiss bank account and could live independently in Europe, which she did."

"You're quite a storyteller, aren't you?" Ed interjected. "What was the name of that princess again who told the sultan, or whoever he was, stories every night, always stopping at a suspenseful place so that he would let her live to continue the story the next night? My mother used to read to us about her and Ali Baba and Aladdin in *Arabian Nights* or *1001 Nights* or something like that."

"Yes, Scheherazade."

"Oh, yeah. That's right." He paused and smiled indulgently. "And so, your friend lived happily ever after?"

"Maybe, although I found out later that there was a French woman in the husband's car when it crashed and she was also killed. So, what was a French woman doing driving around in the French Alps in his luxury car?"

"I can think of a few reasons," Ed said sarcastically.

"Right."

"And now I'm supposed to feel obliged to take care of my younger brother's widow?" he said, feigning a hurt tone.

"It's funny in a way. Maybe the custom isn't so far out after all because here we both are, the older brother and the younger brother's widow. It was certainly practical for them in the olden days, when single women really couldn't survive in the Arab world without a male protector."

"So you think you need a male protector?" he asked and looked at me innocently. "I could make myself available if you need one."

"No, I don't think so."

"I didn't think so either."

"But I will admit that it is lonely to be a single mom, especially at night," I said after a while, making my tone sound melancholy. "Going to bed every night alone is not exactly wonderful."

It wasn't exactly meant as a hint, but he sat up and looked at me. "Well, we won't go to bed alone tonight, will we," he said emphatically. He stood and took my hand, pulling me up as well. "We'll have to get rid of that gloomy expression on your face somehow," he continued and embraced me, kissing me all over my face and on my mouth.

I put my arms around his neck and kissed him back.

"I wonder if there's going to be another emergency call about an armed robbery tonight," I said, pulling myself away a little.

"No, I don't think so. I've actually turned off both my radio and cell phone," he said smugly. "I have a good guy in charge. He can handle anything."

"You're a smart guy, aren't you?" I said and loosened my arms.

Ed began to take out some pins and clips from my hair that he placed neatly on the coffee table.

"How do you untangle these unruly curls?" he said as he ran his fingers through my messy hair, trying to straighten it out some.

"With Tangle-Free® and a good brush," I said. I must have looked like a Scandinavian *huldra* or wild siren.

He took my hand and led me into the darkened bedroom.

"It sure is a spacious room," he commented to no one in particular. "I had forgotten how big it really is." He looked over at JP's crib, which had a tall screen beside it so that JP had a little cubby hole to himself. I went over to my own bed, pulled the covers back and sat down, but Ed pulled me back up and started to undress me, folding my clothes slowly and putting them on a chair. I watched as he took off his own shirt, pants, and underwear, which he put on the same chair. He truly kept himself in good shape. Watching him standing there naked, perched in all his virile glory, gave me goosebumps. I held out my arms toward him, and he came closer and embraced me. Then he pushed me down onto the bed slowly, gently, and spreading my legs, he lay down on top of me. I pulled the cover over us, and it all felt so natural and wonderful.

When I woke up the next morning, Ed was gone. I was disappointed but I knew he'd be back, if not today, then another day, although another day now seemed so far away. I dressed in a tank top and shorts and walked over to JP's crib, but JP was gone as well. I knew JP could climb out, but I thought he would have come over to crawl into bed with me. I quickly went into the living room and kitchen, then out on the deck and out the front door. Ed's car was gone, but where was JP? Had he already learned how to play hide and seek in his playgroup or from Maria? I went out to see Duchess, but JP was not there either. I called his name but no answer. Had Ed taken him? I wondered.

Then I heard Ed's car, and pretty soon he and JP came in with Starbucks coffee and breakfast muffins. Proudly carrying his own muffin, JP came running toward me.

"I thought you'd gone home, but when I couldn't find JP, I was worried," I said seriously.

"Sorry, Megan. I thought we'd be back before you woke up. You were so sound asleep that I thought you'd sleep at least another hour."

"What if you'd had an accident?"

"Oh, don't be so dramatic. I used to do this all the time when James was little. I thought you'd be happy. Elizabeth loved it."

I realized I would constantly be compared to Ed's former wife, but I also realized that I, too, compared Ed to Chris.

"I'm very happy, Ed," I said. "Especially now that you're back safely. I just had a small shock when I didn't see JP, that's all." I looked at him and smiled. "Next time I'll know."

"Sorry," he said again while holding the two coffees and the muffins in both of his hands. He gave me a quick kiss on the cheek as he made his way to the kitchen. "Let's have some breakfast," he said amiably.

He set the coffee and muffins down on the kitchen table. "How did you sleep?" he asked.

"Great. And you?"

"Very good." He paused for a moment. "It's gonna be a nice day. I thought we could take the boat out and perhaps go swimming, if it's not too cold. What do you think?"

"I'd like that very much," I said and gave him a hug on my way to the fridge to get some milk for JP.

"Do you have a safety vest for JP? If not, I could go and get one at home. I think we have one that James used."

"No, we have one here," I said and looked at him. "Were you thinking of stopping by the station too? I don't want you to go near that place. They'll for sure grab you for something."

"No, I don't think so. I did check in earlier. It's been a quiet night evidently, and I haven't taken a day off for months."

"Good. Let's see if we can find some stuff in the fridge and pack a picnic lunch."

Ed left his jacket and guns in the house, and I gave him one of Chris's T-shirts and a pair of shorts. With sunglasses and a baseball cap, it would be difficult to recognize him.

After a swim and our picnic lunch, we docked the boat and headed back to the house. JP fell asleep in his crib as soon as he put his head on his little pillow.

My bed was still unmade. Ed and I lay down next to each other on the rumpled sheets. My shorts were tight, so I took them off. Ed looked at me curiously and removing the rest of my clothes, he pulled me toward him. His body was warm, his embrace firm. We had another passionate encounter. Ed was again surprisingly gentle—a wonderful partner. We stayed in bed until JP woke up.

Afterward, Ed turned his radio and cell phone back on. Trouble had broken out everywhere it seemed, not surprisingly up here since it was going toward Saturday night, so Ed had to leave. Truly, dating a law enforcement officer was far from dating an accountant.

"I'll call tomorrow sometime," he said simply and left.

I dreaded the long Saturday night and Sunday ahead. Ed clearly cared for me, but he had never said he loved me. I realized I needed to be realistic and not expect too much.

30

TRIP TO SANTA MONICA

E d called Sunday night to say he was going to Tucson, Arizona, the coming week. He sounded tired.

"Have you been at the station all weekend?" I asked sympathetically.

"Yeah, pretty much, but I'll be on my way home shortly. Tomorrow, I'll drive out really early for a conference at a hotel out there. I'll call you after I have checked in."

"I'll miss you," I said.

"I'll miss you too."

"Is it always this hectic in your line of work?" I asked.

"No, not at all. But right now there's a lot of chatter among different groups out there that for some reason want to harm us—in addition to our own drug busts, armed robberies, petty thefts, domestic violence, and other local crimes. Actually, that's what the conference is all about. How does everyone handle it all?" He hesitated. "I wish you could come with me, but there's nothing for you to do out there. I'll be back Friday night, I promise."

"It's okay, Ed. I'll be busy."

"That's good."

"But then, when you return, you'll be able to take some time off?" I said hopefully.

"Yeah, for sure. Maybe we'll go out on another date, as you call it."

"Looking forward to it. But it's still going to be a long week," I said teasingly.

Maria spent less time with us now, and I took JP to his playgroup at least two times a week myself. During my alone time, I worked on my novel. The Aldo Bandini case was also smoldering in my mind. Where had that van gone in Santa Monica?

The next day I decided to call Carrie Jensen, the FBI agent from Minnesota I had connected with. I reminded her that I was still deputized by the sheriff and asked if they had learned the final destination of the moving van from the pale yellow house, but she said no further progress had been made. "We have a lot of open cases, and we are understaffed, but we'll get to it," she said apologetically.

"I'm going down to Santa Monica tomorrow to meet someone," I said untruthfully. "If I hear or see something, I'll let you know."

I asked Maria if she could take care of JP for a couple of days because I had something to take care of in Los Angeles.

"No hay problema," she replied with a smile.

"Thank you, Maria. Gracias."

I wasn't sure exactly where and how to start my investigation, but I had a little idea. Despite my dislike for Vee, I called her to ask if she knew of a good realtor in Santa Monica.

"Are you looking for beach property?" she asked innocently.

"Maybe," I said slowly. "Something to rent first with an option to buy."

"Give me a few minutes, and I'll call you back."

It was a good half hour later when she called back with the name of an associate at Berkshire of Santa Monica.

"Her name is Crystal Cheng," Vee said. "I told her you were interested in renting a beach property. She's expecting your call."

"Thank you, Vee," I said in as friendly a voice as I could muster. After all, she was doing me a big favor, although she was probably already thinking of her referral commission.

"Oh, by the way," she said hurriedly. "You know Ed is in Arizona this week, right?"

"Yes, I know," I said curtly. "He'll be gone for a few days."

"I'm thinking of joining him for one or two days."

"Really? Is the real estate market that slow around here now?" I said sarcastically, but I suddenly felt a sting in my stomach. Was Ed two-timing me?

"No, I'm doing well, honey. But I need to take some time off and spend some of my well-earned commission money. I also want to look at some properties out there."

"Well, have a good trip, Vee. I'll call Ms. Cheng right away."

Which I did, and we made an appointment for the next day before noon.

Instead of waiting for Ed to call that evening, I called him. He picked up right away.

"Is everything okay?" he asked immediately. When someone called, he probably expected disaster.

"Yes, everything is fine. How are you doing out there? Is it very hot?"

"Yes, over 100 degrees."

"How was the drive?"

"Good. I was well on my way before rush-hour traffic and checked in at a Best Western before noon."

"That was smart." I hesitated before I continued, "I'm going down to Los Angeles to take care of some business for a couple of days," I said. "Maria is taking care of JP."

"I see. And I take it you'll check in with your doctor friend. Is that what you wanna tell me?"

"No, but I might, although I doubt it." I took a deep breath. "I talked to Vee, and she told me that she was going out to Tucson to see you for a day or two."

"Really?" he said dryly. "She called you to tell you that?"

"No, not really. I called to talk to her about something else, but it seemed important to her that I should know that she was going to see you out there."

"Actually, she told me that she was coming out to look at a couple of properties," he continued sheepishly.

"And you'll take her out on a date, I assume," I said sarcastically.

"I told her we might have dinner one night, but I don't think so. I won't have time. I need to network with as many law enforcement people as possible while I'm here. I want to see what other states and counties are doing."

"That sounds like a good idea."

I sighed and remained silent for a few moments. This conversation wasn't going the way I wanted it to.

"Megan, listen. If you think I have any particular interest in Vee, you're mistaken," he said firmly.

"The same interest as I have in my doctor friend, as you call him?"

"Did you call to pick a fight?" he asked accusingly.

"No, but I have to admit that I found it strange to hear that Vee was going out to see you for a couple of days, especially after our great date on Friday and Saturday."

"Okay, I see now, but that's not how she put it to me. She was coming out to look at real estate. She's a local girl. I've known her for a long time, and she said she might need some help. That's all."

"I'm sorry I brought it up, Ed. You have to figure out what you want to do yourself. Have a good time and learn as much as you can. I'll be waiting for you on Friday night."

"Can't wait, Megan. Be careful."

———

Chrystal Cheng met me in her real estate office the next morning. She was a petite Chinese woman who appeared to be in her thirties or forties, although it was hard to tell. Like many Asian women, she might have been older than she looked. She had small, brown, intelligent eyes and a shrewd expression on her face. She was professionally dressed in a turquoise pantsuit and high heels. The elegant office was newly refurbished with dark cherrywood desks and shelves.

I told her that I was a private investigator looking for a middle-aged couple with a small white poodle and terrier mutt who had just moved into a place, probably a rental, near the beach. "I know it's a long shot, but I've been told that you are a master at keeping updated on properties in this area."

"Thank you," she said politely.

"A white moving van drove in last week. I lost sight of it on Santa Monica Boulevard when all the lanes but one were closed, and I was stopped. I'll pay you the usual commission, the same as the commission on a rental if you'll help me locate them. How's that?"

"Well, we can look at the local listings and see what's been on the market recently, and what has leased or rented the last few weeks," she suggested. "I also have friends at the electric and gas companies as well as the water company, who for a fee can check who has switched on utilities lately."

"That sounds wonderful," I said, truly impressed with how quickly she caught on. Vee had come through with a sharp woman here.

We sat down at her computer and poured over the listings that Crystal pulled up on the screen. We soon found several good prospects.

"We could check these out and look up the renters' credit ratings," Crystal continued.

"Good idea, but this couple may have applied under false names. They've used Leo Smith before, and they may have paid for six months or a year in cash."

"Cash? Are you kidding?" Crystal said and laughed. "Do you know how much rent is around here, especially near the beach?"

"I thought Santa Monica had rent control," I said.

"Some areas do, but the rent is still high. No one would invest in apartment buildings here if the rent was not close to market value."

"Good point. But these people probably operate in cash anyway. At least I think so."

"Are they American?" Crystal asked.

"Yes, I believe so," I said.

"Because there are many Asians and Iranians who come here with a lot of cash but they usually go farther up the coast to Malibu and even Santa Barbara."

"What about this one?" I said, pointing at the screen. "Deborah and Ron Smith."

"Yes," Crystal agreed. "That's a nice place, as are all these buildings along 1st Avenue." She quickly made up a list of possibilities.

I invited her to lunch at the Marriott Hotel nearby, and she accepted.

"I'll drive," she said generously. "Afterwards, we can stop at some of these places."

"Are you sure you can take the time?"

"It's okay. Today is a slow day, and I'd rather be out with a potential client than sit in the office. Tomorrow will be busy, when all the realtors go on a tour of the new listings in the area."

Crystal knew all the streets and turned out to be a good driver, so after lunch we drove to the addresses on her list. I hadn't been out here since my days in graduate school at UCLA, when I often went with friends to Santa Monica Beach. And before we married and left for Africa, Robert and I had gone swimming here on warm days.

At each stop, Crystal rang the doorbell, and, carrying a small basket with all kinds of goodies, she introduced herself as the Welcome-Wagon lady. I stood around the corner to see if I recognized the new occupants. But no luck.

"You're a clever one, Crystal," I said admiringly.

"Actually, I do volunteer for the Welcome Wagon," she said and laughed. "So it wasn't entirely fake."

"I see."

"Well, it's good for business."

"That's very clever."

We returned to her office. I would continue on my own tomorrow.

I checked into the Marriott for the night, and in the early evening, I decided to take a stroll along the boardwalk. Right before sunset, I spotted the same white poodle-terrier mutt coming toward me, but I didn't recognize the woman at the other end of the leash. She had dark, almost black hair, but she was the same height as the woman I had seen in the mountains. The woman and the dog were still far away, and I quickly walked out into the sand toward the water. When I looked back again, they had turned around and were headed back in the other direction. I noticed she had the same gait as the woman I had seen before. I often recognize people by their gait. She could have dyed her hair.

I followed slowly at a distance and saw her turn into an elegant apartment complex overlooking the ocean. I didn't dare go near the building to check the address, so I sat down on a bench to wait for darkness, using my phone to take pictures of the beautiful cloud formations as the sun began to set, just like an ordinary tourist. Then I called Chrystal to tell her what I'd seen.

"I'll get the address after dark," I said. "Can I come over tomorrow to check it against your files?"

"Sure, but can you make it early? I'll meet the other brokers and agents at ten to check out new listings, as I mentioned."

"Absolutely. Is 8:30 too early?"

"No, that's fine. See you then."

An hour later, I ventured forth, crossing to the back side of the elegant complex. As soon as I saw the address, I walked quickly back to the hotel.

The next morning, Crystal checked the address on her computer and confirmed that two apartments at that address had rented two weeks earlier. Number 600 had been leased by a family from Germany in the name of Heinz Bauman. However, the occupants in number 304 were Mr. and Mrs. Dave Perez, and, yes, they had a small pet and had paid cash. I gave Chrystal my address and told her to send me a bill for her hours as I knew she was in a hurry to meet her co-workers and competitors. Then I went back to the hotel and booked the room for another night, all the while debating with myself what to do next. I called Maria to make sure she could handle JP for another day. I didn't want to call Ed again, and in any case, he was probably in the middle of a presentation. I realized I had to call my contacts in the FBI, and I needed to contemplate exactly how to lay it out to them.

31

DISCOVERY

After a long lunch and several cups of coffee, I went up to my room to retrieve my big hat and change into a T-shirt, shorts and walking sandals. I strolled leisurely down to the beach and walked a couple of miles along the bike path in the opposite direction of the apartment building in question before I found an isolated bench from which to call Agent Jensen, with whom I had by now developed a rapport. She picked up the phone right away.

"Is this a convenient time to talk?" I inquired politely.

"It's okay. We're out in the field, but I can step aside for a few minutes. What's happening?"

"Well," I said hesitatingly. "I think I discovered the final destination of the white moving van that you followed from our mountain lake to Santa Monica." I paused to catch my breath. "I was out with my realtor looking at beach properties when I saw the little white poodle-terrier mix with what looked like the same woman I met at her house one time. She had dyed her hair dark brown, almost black, but she was the same height and had the same distinctive gait. I saw her entering an elegant apartment complex overlooking the ocean, and my realtor said that an apartment in the building had just been rented to a middle-aged couple in the name of Dave Perez. They had a small pet and had paid rent in cash for six months in advance. Perez is most likely a pseudonym, of course, since the realtors do not necessarily run credit checks when people pay cash in advance."

"Okay, good work. I'll see if we can have someone there to keep an eye on the place. What's the address?"

I gave her the address. "And the apartment is number 304. I have not seen the husband, but the apartment is evidently rented in his name."

"Good. Maybe we can finally nab him. He's been on the run long enough. That he has eluded us as long as he has is a sore point with our chief. Got to go."

I took my time walking back to the hotel. I could have gone back up the mountain that afternoon, but the rush-hour traffic out of Los Angeles is horrendous, and anyway, I had booked the room for another night.

The next morning the traffic was light, and the drive back up took less than two hours. I told Maria that I would take care of everything for the rest of the week, and she was probably pleased to have some time to herself, although she also went down the hill to clean and cook for Joe. I'm sure he paid her handsomely for all of us. I kept busy with shopping, reading to JP, and plotting out the next chapter of my novel.

As I was getting ready for bed, Ed called. "Sorry I haven't called you earlier, but I didn't know if you were back home yet and I have hardly had a moment free."

"Yeah, right! A likely story," I said teasingly. "I came home this morning, and I was actually about to call you to wish you goodnight before I went to bed. How has the conference been?"

"Great. There's so much going on around the country that people and the media are unaware of, or if some media outlets are aware of some of it, they're keeping quiet about it, and that's probably best. But I do know we have to be more proactive." He cleared his throat. "And how was your trip down the mountain?"

"Okay. I saw some friends and took care of some business," I said vaguely. "And all is well." It was true in a general sense. Chrystal had sort of become a friend, and I had taken care of some important business. I would explain it all to him later. "I gave Maria the rest of the week off, and I think she appreciated that," I continued. "She doesn't exactly have a helpful husband in my view, and she has spoiled her sons."

"That's probably true," Ed agreed. "She's there for everyone. She has a good heart."

"And she's been like a mother to you and Chris, hasn't she?"

"Yes, she's been loyal to our family." He sighed audibly. "But then my father pays her well too."

"Do you think she's a little bit in love with your father?"

"Who knows?" He hesitated. "But I don't think so."

"Are you planning to return tomorrow?"

"Yes, that's my plan."

"Do you have an idea when you'll leave?"

"The conference is over after lunch, and I'll be packed up and ready to go after that."

"Do you want to come over here for dinner?" I said invitingly.

"That sounds like a good idea," he replied rather flatly.

"You don't sound too enthusiastic."

"Oh, I am, but I'll probably be tired."

"Do you want to cancel our date then?"

"Oh, well okay. I don't know." He sounded uncertain.

"What's wrong, Ed?"

"Okay, I guess I'd better tell you since Vee will probably call you anyway."

"Vee?"

"You probably won't believe me but I didn't initiate any of this."

My heart sank, and I felt faint for a moment.

"Ed, what's happened?" I asked unsteadily. "Tell me. I'll believe you."

"Well, Vee flew out here yesterday. I didn't have time to see her, and she told me she was busy with her real estate anyway." He hesitated. "But then she called again and asked for a ride back home because she had purchased a one-way ticket only. I told you she's not as worldly and independent as you are, and she needed help, so I agreed to pick her up."

"I see," I said finally. "So I won't see you this weekend then?"

"Why not? I should be back by early evening. I'll drop Vee off at her house, stop by the station for a few minutes, and then head on over to your place. How's that?" He seemed to try to sound cheerful.

"Okay, Ed. I understand your dilemma, but can we have a serious talk about all of this sometime?"

"Fine, but surely you know that Vee means nothing to me, and I don't believe she's interested in me either, although you seem to think so."

"Maybe it's a woman's intuition, but never mind. We'll have a nice dinner, take it easy, and forget all of this nonsense." I reflected for a moment. "And I may also have some news about the Aldo Bandini case."

"Megan, let the FBI handle that now."

"I am, but I'm also an incurably nosy person, and an unsolved case bothers me." I paused. "Drive carefully. And see you when you get here."

At lunchtime the next day, I took a break from writing, and later in the afternoon, Ed called from his car.

"Where exactly are you?" I asked.

"I'm two hours away according to the GPS, but it depends on the traffic."

"Are you on the speakerphone?" I asked.

"No, but I can turn it on." He paused. "Say hi to Megan, Vee."

"Hi, honey," she said annoyingly.

"Hi, Vee," I said. "How are you?"

"I'm fine, honey. Ed and I are having a great time. Are you having problems?"

"No problems, Vee." Then I said to Ed, "When can I expect you, Ed?"

"I'll drop Vee off first and stop by the station for a few minutes. Probably between two-and-a-half to three hours from now. Can you wait for me that long?" he added playfully.

"Of course, sweetheart. I'll be waiting in my new see-through negligee. How do you like that?"

"That sounds exciting. I can't wait."

"Good."

Surely, this exchange would send a loud and clear message to Vee. She actually appeared at a loss for words, but who could figure out how much went through that bird brain of hers? She probably thought we were just bantering.

JP returned from a play date with a little friend after playgroup. He was brought to the door by a cute young mother, no more than eighteen or nineteen years old, with a blonde ponytail and a blue tank top, shorts, and flip-flops.

"The boys had a lot of fun," she said, just as the two boys ran past her and straight out to the deck where JP's toys were. She ran after them and picked up her little charge and was out the door like a whirlwind.

"Thank you," I called after her.

I had just been seasoning two T-bone steaks that we would grill when Ed arrived. They would be served with baked potatoes, sour cream and chives, and a small salad.

I heard Ed's car door slam before he entered through the unlocked front door. JP came running in from the deck, and I was coming out from the kitchen in my usual T-shirt and shorts and my hair pulled back in a bun.

"Where's that see-through negligee?" Ed asked teasingly. He looked a little rumpled in his civilian clothes.

"That's for later," I said laughingly.

He reached inside his jacket and took out a shiny miniature sheriff's patrol car that he gave to JP, who quickly trotted off with it.

"Actually, the negligee was for Vee's benefit," I said. "I hope she got the hint. She's awfully slow to catch on."

"Yeah, I'm sorry. I'll get one of my deputies to take over as the object of her nurturing instinct."

He reached into his pants pocket and pulled out a small box.

"This is for you," he said simply. "I hope you like it."

It was a silver bracelet set with large turquoise stones.

"It's lovely," I said and put it around my left wrist.

"It's made by the Native Americans in Arizona with local stones. At least that's what they told me."

"Thank you, Ed. That's so sweet of you."

I hugged him. He embraced me and held me tight until I pushed myself away and led him into the kitchen.

"We're going to have T-bone steaks on the grill," I said. "The grill is already lit. And since it's such a beautiful evening, I thought we could have our dinner on the deck. I haven't picked out the wine yet, but maybe you could look in Chris's wine cabinet and choose something."

He removed his sports coat and gun and hung them on a hook by the kitchen door before going over to the wine cabinet, where he picked out a Merlot. We enjoyed a quiet dinner together. Afterward, Ed cleaned up while I put JP to bed. We returned to the deck with another glass of wine, and he told me about the conference. Then he asked suddenly, "What's new with the Aldo Bandini case?"

"Well, a realtor friend in Santa Monica discovered the destination of the white moving van that the FBI agents lost sight of on Santa Monica Boulevard. An apartment in a luxury complex by the beach had apparently been rented to a middle-aged couple fitting the description of the people who lived in the pale yellow house. They have a small white dog and had paid cash for six months' rent in advance in addition to the security deposit." I had to catch my breath before I continued., "Agent Jensen and I have a good relationship, so I called her. She's placing an agent outside the apartment to observe and determine if these are the people they're looking for."

Ed looked at me seriously, and I smiled innocently.

"Why do I get the impression that this is not the whole story," he said. "Your trip down the mountain while I was gone included Santa Monica, didn't it?"

"Well, I wanted to look at some beach properties there. Wouldn't it be nice to have a beach house next to the ocean? We have money that ought to be invested in property, don't you think?"

"You're impossible," he said sternly. "Didn't you tell me that curiosity killed the cat?" He shook his head.

"Don't be upset with me, Ed. I won't do anything foolish. I just did not believe it could be that difficult to figure out where that van had gone." I sighed. "Maybe I shouldn't have told you."

"Yes, I want to know what you're up to, and you appear to have the nose of a detective. But I think I'll have to have a talk with your friend Agent Jensen."

"She's not my friend, but I do like her a lot." I looked at him searchingly.

We sat in silence for a while, sipping our drinks and watching the dark lake in front of us, the pinpricks of lights from the cabins and mansions that surrounded the lake, and the twinkling stars above.

"What made you want to choose a career in law enforcement, Ed?" I asked after a while.

"Okay, well, I think I may have told you that I took drafting in high school and knew I didn't want to sit at a desk all day, and being in law enforcement had always interested me. As you know, I got my master's degree in criminal justice at USC. The rest seemed to just fall into place."

"Yes, that's how we all fall into our careers, isn't it?" I said thoughtfully.

We finished our drinks.

"Do you want me to spend the night?" he asked simply and shot me a quick glance.

"I was hoping you were planning to," I said.

He rose, took my hand, and led me into the bedroom.

32

CAPTURE

It was mid-week when I turned on the television and saw the tail end of the breaking news that John (Little Johnny) Frazzano Junior, the son of notorious New York gangster John Frazzano, had been arrested in Santa Monica. I turned on the computer to read the entire report:

SANTA MONICA, Calif. — John (Little Johnny) Frazzano Jr., the son of New York mobster John Frazzano, was arrested by federal authorities in Santa Monica Tuesday evening on charges of murder, narcotics distribution, extortion, and money laundering. The arrest ended a nationwide manhunt that had gone on since Mr. Frazzano had disappeared seven years ago, the FBI announced.

Mr. Frazzano was apprehended without incident at his beachfront apartment, where he lived with his wife, Grace, at the time of the arrest, the FBI said.

The arrest came following a tip from a neighbor who recognized the couple's dog, a white poodle and terrier mix, and positively identified both Mr. and Mrs. Frazzano from FBI file photos she previously had had access to. Using a ruse, FBI agents and other task force members lured Mr. Frazzano down to the garage, where they rushed him, guns drawn.

"I asked the landlord to call apartment 304 and notify the occupant that his storage locker had been flooded by a broken water main and to come down to see what had been damaged," said Andrew Wells, the

*officer in charge. "His wife said that her husband would be right down.
As he came out of the elevator, we identified ourselves and asked him to
put his hands up. He turned toward us, and his hands went up right away.
I asked him to identify himself, but this was a man who was used to being
in control, and he asked me to f-ing identify myself. 'You know who I am,'
I said and then asked him if he was John Frazzano. He said, 'Yes.' And I
said, 'You're under arrest on narcotics charges and the murder of Aldo
Bandini.' He swore he hadn't killed anyone and didn't know anything
about Aldo Bandini. I told him Mr. Bandini was a New York lawyer
working for the mob. 'I know who Aldo is,' he said, 'but I don't know
anything about any murder.'"*

*Agent Wells said they had found over 800,000 dollars in cash in the
couple's two-bedroom luxury apartment, along with several forms of
false identification and over two dozen loaded firearms, including a
MAC-10 machine pistol and an AR 15 assault rifle.*

*Mr. Frazzano's wife was arrested for harboring a fugitive. The couple
is now held in the Metropolitan Detention Center in Los Angeles. The
FBI would not identify the tipster at this time for fear of retaliation.*

The next day, I called Carrie Jensen. "I heard the news," I said. "Good
job!"

"Thank you, although I guess we should thank you instead for being
observant. Of course, we don't want to release your name before we see
how all this plays out."

"Thank you, and I really have to give the credit to our local sheriff
who understood early on the importance of this case," I said and slowly
added, "Strangely though, he didn't admit to the murder of Aldo
Bandini."

"You mean Mr. Frazzano?"

"Yes, it's strange that he so readily acknowledged who he was, even
though he was living under a different name, but then denied he had killed
Aldo Bandini."

"Yes, we wondered about that. But who knows what motives people
like him have?"

"True," I agreed. "The television report also added that his wife had
told neighbors in the building that her husband suffered from the
beginning stages of Alzheimer's. One neighbor who came down to do her
laundry while the agents were there introduced herself and said the man
they were trying to arrest suffered from delusions. A thought flashed

through the agents' minds that they were arresting the wrong man, a man who lived under the delusion that he was John Frazzano. But then Mr. Frazzano shot right back, 'She's f-ing nuts. I am John Frazzano.' Yet he insisted he knew nothing about the death of Aldo Bandini."

"Yes. And it sounds eerily believable," Ms. Jensen said reluctantly.

"But who then killed Aldo Bandini?" I said in bewilderment.

"That's a good question."

"Well, I may have a little idea," I said slowly.

"If you do, let us know. We'd like to wrap this case up."

At lunchtime, I stopped by the local coffee shop to pick up two cups of coffee and a couple of sandwiches to take to Ed's office to surprise him. On my way into the station, a deputy passed by and told me Ed was in. His door was open, and he was leaning back in his chair behind his big wooden desk, talking on the phone. He hung up as I walked in.

"I thought I'd bring you a snack," I said cheerfully, "now that Vee no longer brings you lunch."

"Oh, she still comes by."

"But I'm sure you dispatch her over to one of your deputies. Of course, on the pretense that you have to attend an important meeting. Right?"

He grumbled something, and I left it at that.

"So what's going on today?" I asked.

"Oh, a couple of thefts. Someone stole power tools from an unlocked shed, and then someone took tools from an uncovered bed of a truck. I wish people would lock their doors."

"Oops. I don't think I locked the door before I left today."

"Lock it. Felons out on parole know they'll go straight back to jail if they break into a locked building, but if they just walk in and help themselves, they'll not be prosecuted."

"Yes, I do know that, of course, from my research. I'll be more careful from now on." I paused and cleared my throat. "Are you planning to come over for dinner tonight? I'm going grocery shopping and wondered if you'd like something special."

"No, whatever you want to fix is fine with me. Then tomorrow will be my treat. How about Settlers Inn again? I don't know of any conventions or conferences at the resort this weekend."

"Great. Maybe we can finally have a normal date."

He looked at me and smiled benevolently.

For a few minutes, we munched on our sandwiches and sipped our coffee.

"I wish I had more free time to spend with you," he said softly, "but this is a resort town, and a lot of tourists arrive from everywhere. Every weekend I expect a drowning from raucous parties. People go out on the lake in their boats, drunk as a skunk. We have at least a couple boating accidents every summer. And some people come up here from Hollywood, Beverly Hills, and who knows where, driving around in fancy sports cars, flaunting expensive jewelry, and spreading cash."

"That's good for business, though," I interjected. "And shouldn't people be able to flaunt whatever they want? After all, isn't it the job of law enforcement to keep them safe, no matter what kind of cars they drive or what they wear?"

"Yeah, you're right."

"You sound tired," I said.

"I am, but I'll be fine. I'll come over a little later. We'll have a meeting this afternoon to prepare for our 'coffee with a cop' tomorrow morning at the market in Coldwater, and then I'll take off."

"Sounds good. I may have something to share with you."

"Oh, yeah? What?"

"It's a long story," I said. "But everything is good. See you later."

I took the wrappers from our lunch out with me and deposited it all in the bin outside.

He arrived early evening with the usual chirp of his siren. I had picked up JP since Maria had gone down to Joe's place to take care of Joe and Sandy.

Ed was still in full summer uniform, beige shirt and black tie. He was hot and removed his tie and holster before picking up JP and embracing me.

"So, what were you going to tell me?" he inquired without introduction.

"Let's wait until after dinner and after I've put JP to bed. It's sort of complicated. It's going to take a while."

"Have you gotten involved in another case?" he asked, his eyebrows drawn together in disapproval.

"No, no," I assured him. "Don't worry."

He looked at me searchingly and sighed.

For supper, I had made gazpacho soup to be served cold with what the

French call Croque-Monsieur sandwiches, grilled cheese and ham. By now we had a routine that Ed cleaned up while I got JP ready for bed.

"So," I said finally, "I talked to Carrie Jensen, the FBI agent today, and she told me that they had arrested the couple from the pale yellow house at their apartment near the beach in Santa Monica. I printed out the Internet article for you. The husband was arrested first without incident and readily admitted he was John Frazzano Jr., the son of the notorious New York Mafia boss and a fugitive from Federal law enforcement, but he denied he had killed Aldo Bandini, and the FBI believe that he may have spoken the truth."

I gave Ed the article, and we walked into the living room and sat down on the couch so he could relax and read the whole piece.

"So, who is the 'neighbor' that tipped off the FBI?"

"Agent Jensen said my name would not be released, so there's no problem." I reached out for his hand, but he withdrew it and put his arms around my shoulders instead.

"What am I gonna do with you?" he said lovingly but in an avuncular way and pulled me toward him. "And now I guess you'll continue to search for the killer of Aldo Bandini." He hesitated. "I take it that in your mind the gangster didn't do it, and, of course, he may not have done it himself but rather had one of his goons do it."

"Maybe, but I actually have another idea."

"Oh, yeah? And what's that?"

"I don't know exactly, but I'd like to go down to the Los Angeles Detention Center and talk to the gangster's wife. I feel that she may know something."

"Megan, why is this so important to you?" he asked almost pleadingly.

"I don't know. I just don't like loose ends, that's all."

"I don't have time to go with you, and I absolutely forbid you to go alone."

"Ed, first of all, you can't do that," I said indignantly. "But, in any case, I'll go with Ms. Jensen."

"When?"

"As soon as possible," I said but quickly corrected myself. "As soon as Ms. Jensen can fit the trip into her schedule. But it has to be before their court appearance and before the marshals escort the couple back to New York."

"Is there nothing I can say or do to get this out of your mind? These people are part of an unscrupulous gang."

"I know. After this affair is resolved, I'll stay home and prepare for our trip to Europe to see your son."

"You're impossible," he said with a fake sigh for the umpteenth time.

I looked at him triumphantly, put my arm around his neck and kissed him on the cheek. "Let's go upstairs and see if there's anything about it on the news."

However, either we missed it, or the case was not big enough out here amidst murders, shootings, and controversial arrests to make even the local news channel. I shrugged my shoulders, and we both walked back downstairs again. Even though it was a weekday, Ed decided to spend the night.

33

WHO KILLED ALDO BANDINI?

Having secured Maria to come over Friday afternoon to take care of JP, Ed picked me up early, elegantly casual in a sports coat over a golf shirt and slacks.

"You look nice, Ed," I said as I welcomed him with a hug. "Strong and sporty and nice," I added laughingly.

"Thank you. I have a hot date tonight," he replied mischievously.

"Okay, what are you up to?" I said.

"Oh, just dinner and a quiet evening at home, unless you want to do something else."

"No, I love an early dinner at Settlers Inn. Do I look all right? Different? Sporty?" I had put on the same dress I wore on our previous date.

"You look great," he said. He took my hand and led me out to the car.

Al, the maître d', met us at the door and after drinks led us to the same table at the window overlooking the lake. This time we were left alone. I treasured our evening together because Ed left Saturday morning and worked the rest of the weekend.

By Wednesday, Agent Jensen had not called, and I feared that the Frazzanos might be arraigned and escorted back to New York any day. I decided if Ms. Jensen did not call by the next day, I would go to the detention center by myself. I would force my way into the facility somehow to get my answer. However, later that same evening, Carrie

Jensen finally called. We agreed to go to LA together the next day after we met at her house in Long Beach.

The Los Angeles Metropolitan Detention Center, a huge concrete building with a multitude of small windows, is located in the middle of downtown Los Angeles, where parking is near impossible. But after showing her ID, Carrie was able to park in the visitors' lot for free. Despite its sleek architecture and ample lighting, the MDC is a gloomy place, like an asylum, with bars and code locks everywhere, not an easy place to sneak into or out of. We went through security where I showed my permit to carry a concealed weapon and checked my little Chic Lady. Carrie did the same.

We were both dressed in white shirts; Carrie wore her customary dark Dockers and I a straight black skirt. The black security guard looked us over carefully, but Carrie's ID afforded us quick access to the visitors' area, which was even more forbidding. Prisoners—actually more like patients—shuffled along, chained and shouting the F-word, indicating they wanted out of there.

I had pulled my hair back rather severely and put on heavy make-up, in the hope that Mrs. Frazzano would not recognize me. She finally appeared in her prison overall, led by a grim-faced female guard. She looked older without her styled hair and expensive clothing. I didn't recognize her until she started speaking. Agent Jensen introduced herself as an FBI agent and me as a deputized private citizen. We sat down on light aluminum tube chairs.

"When is your arraignment, Mrs. Frazzano?" I asked for lack of a better way to start our conversation. I wondered if she recognized my voice as I recognized hers.

"Tomorrow," she said without looking up at me.

"And then you'll be flown back to New York, right?"

"I think that's the plan."

"And how have you been so far?" I asked soothingly. "Are you comfortable? Do you need anything?"

"Oh, I haven't seen Johnny," she said unhappily.

"He's all right," I said in a comforting tone, although naturally I didn't have the slightest idea how he was. "Maybe I could arrange for you to see him."

She looked up at me with hope in her eyes.

"You must feel relieved that it's over, that you, and especially Johnny, no longer have to look over your shoulder all the time."

"In a way, yes, but not really." She paused. "I was told my little dog, Whitey, is well taken care of." She smiled as if mentioning her dog brought her joy.

"Oh, yes, of course," I said, again without the slightest idea where her dog was. "Mrs. Frazzano," I said, finally getting to the point of our visit. "Grace, isn't it? May I call you Grace?"

"Yes, of course," she said and smiled.

"Grace, if Johnny didn't kill Aldo Bandini, who did?"

"I did," she said simply.

"You did, Grace?" I stayed calm, although I was about to fall off the chair. "How did you do that, Grace?"

"Aldo Bandini was breaking the code of silence and wanted out. I knew Johnny wouldn't like that, but Johnny wasn't there, and I thought, 'What would Johnny do?' And immediately I knew and hired one of Johnny's associates, and we killed him and dumped the body in the lake in the middle of the night."

"That was a clever thing to do, Grace. Aldo Bandini was a no-good guy, wasn't he?"

She hesitated for a moment. "How did you know he was dead?"

"I guess a sleepless tourist saw the body being pushed out of the boat."

"But it was in the middle of the night and dark."

"The moon was out, and someone was out wandering around."

"I bet it was that nosy neighbor. I shot at her once to try to scare her away. Dumb gal."

I shrank. The couple had better be convicted and put away, or I would be in deep yogurt. Ed was right. This was no game. My heart sank. I realized that I had put not only myself but also my son in danger. But of course they would be convicted. She had confessed to the murder outright, and agent Jensen was taking notes.

"Maybe, Grace. But I heard it was one of those pesky tourists," I said helplessly. "In any case, it was smart of you to confess. Aldo Bandini got what he deserved, right?"

"Yes, you don't screw around with Johnny. You know I never told him. It's true what he told the officers. He doesn't know what happened to Aldo."

"It will clear Mr. Frazzano of this murder charge," Carrie said sharply. "Unfortunately, you will now be charged with the murder of Aldo

Bandini." She took charge of the situation from then on while I kept up my friendly attitude and said I would try to help out.

"And who did you call to help you with all of this, Grace?" Carrie asked a little more softly.

"I called Biaggio, and he took care of it. I think the guy came out from Colorado," Grace answered without hesitation.

I felt sorry for Grace. She seemed so trusting. I offered to send her some nice toiletries and asked her to give me a list, which she did. Then, we left Mrs. Frazzano to the guard.

Outside, Carrie called her supervisor and told him that the arraignment the next day would have to be postponed in order to have time to put together the case against Grace Frazzano, which turned out not to be her legal name because she was not legally married to Mr. Frazzano. Carrie complimented me on my soft approach that this time led to results, and she divulged that she had recorded the entire interview, I knew, however, that the evidence might not be foolproof since she had not been read her rights.

"She was read her rights when she was initially arrested," Carrie countered.

"But that was for a different crime."

"True, it's not a clear-cut case. But officers do not read the rights to everyone they think might have some information. She was not a suspect. Her confession came as a surprise to me and was completely voluntary. There was no coercion."

"I agree. And hopefully a good prosecutor can convince a jury of that. Grace will no doubt have expert defense lawyers."

"Right. But, no matter what, she'll serve time for aiding and abetting."

"Yes," I said slowly. But despite Carrie's assurances I had a sinking feeling that the whole affair might l not be over.

On my way up the mountain, after saying good-bye to Carrie, I called Ed and left a message that I was on my way home and had some good news. No sooner had I sat down at the kitchen table with a glass of water than Ed announced his arrival.

"What happened," he said sternly as he strode through the living room to the kitchen.

I rose and walked toward him. "We discovered who killed Aldo Bandini," I said as calmly as possible.

"Who?"

"Mrs. Frazzano. Grace Frazzano, or actually Grace Marino."

His eyebrows rose.

"The woman I met at the pale yellow house," I continued. "But she didn't recognize me." I told him the whole story as he kept shaking his head in disbelief.

"I know what you're thinking," I said. "But they'll be convicted."

"Yeah, but they have friends, 'associates' that Johnny Frazzano controls."

"I know, and I wish I had listened to you, Ed, but it's too late now, and I promise this is the last time I will meddle."

He sighed and remained silent. Then he embraced me, ruffled my hair, and kissed me. He finally let me go and sat down. I brought him a glass of ice water and sat down opposite him.

"To tell you the truth, I'm not happy with the FBI," he said. "They have not been straight with me, but mostly I'm upset that they involved you in all of this and put you at risk. But this case has been a sore point for them."

"Why is that?" I said and rose again to take out the casserole Maria had prepared. I put it in the microwave on reheat. Then I refilled our glasses with more ice water.

"It appears that Johnny Frazzano had been an informant for the Bureau, and the agent he worked with, who is now retired, tipped Mr. Frazzano off when agents were about to arrest him. That was seven years ago. That's evidently when he moved west and lived under various aliases, and one of his places of refuge was our resort town. Who knew?"

"So, the FBI had actively been after him all this time," I said incredulously.

"It appears so, yes. And they had no idea he was in the Los Angeles area."

I was beginning to comprehend the magnitude of this whole affair but amazed at the slow pace of this famous government agency.

"So, you're telling me that I came along and, on a hunch, suspected something nefarious in the pale yellow house. How was I to know that this was not just a simple murder case?" I paused to catch my breath. "Mrs. Frazzano also told me she had taken some pot-shots at a nosy neighbor to try to scare her off. 'A dumb gal,' she said."

He laughed.

"When I went to see her, I wore my hair differently. I had put on a lot of make-up, and wore a uniform-like white shirt and a straight skirt."

"But they still know where you live."

"I suppose so, but I told her that a sleepless tourist had spotted the body being dumped out of the boat. She's a simple woman."

"I'll demand that the agency stations an agent outside your house, at least for a while, since they got you involved in the first place. I shouldn't have to use my own deputies. Of course, I will if I have to."

I sighed and looked down at my hands, my ruby ring, my fingernails, trimmed short in order to handle JP and play the piano.

"I've had guards outside my door before," I said at last. "But that was in Africa. I never expected to need that here."

"I know, and it may come to nothing. Don't worry, honey. I'll do my best to take care of you."

I looked up at him. "Thank you, Ed. I'm sorry to cause you trouble."

"It's okay," he said reassuringly. "Maybe I'm overreacting. I'll call Maria and tell her to pick up JP and bring him home. Then we'll have a nice, quiet family evening and forget about crime and criminals. I'm not going back to the station tonight."

34

SCHOOL SHOOTING

When I came out on the deck with my laptop a few days later, a patrol boat appeared to be heading straight for the pale yellow house. I put my laptop down and leaned over the railing to confirm that it steered into the underground slip. I quickly got my hiking boots, hat, and sunscreen and made my way up the trail to the house that I had avoided for quite a while now. Two sheriff's cars were parked outside, and although I wanted to join the deputies inside, I thought it best not to interfere. Instead, I hiked down to the water. Sure enough, two or three deputies in a boat were exploring the dark cave. No one paid any attention to me, and I decided to return to my deck and watch from afar. Ed would update me later.

The operation took no more than a few hours. There couldn't be many clues left, other than some fingerprints and perhaps some DNA material. In any case, the two previous occupants of the house had confessed, and there was not much more to be done.

I called Ed in the evening, and he assured me that there was still plenty of evidence that the Frazzanos had lived in the house. And in the tunnel under the house, the deputies had found one bag of black tar heroin and another bag of white heroin as well as various paraphernalia in a box left hidden and overlooked in the machinery that hoisted their boat out of the water. The drugs appeared to be ready for distribution.

"That figures," I said righteously. "I knew that the tunnel had to be a hiding place for something nefarious."

"Yeah, I guess you were right," he said and sighed.

"I thought it was the FBI's case now," I said.

"It is, and they obtained the search warrant. My deputies just went along to assist."

"Are you coming over this evening?"

"I'll be working late tonight. I'll come over sometime tomorrow, probably in the afternoon or evening. Is that okay?"

"Yes, of course, that's fine." I may have sounded a little disappointed, but I had a lot to do anyway. "I'm starting to check into renting a plane for our big trip to Europe to see James," I continued. "Do you think you can take a week off in late August?"

"I believe so, but let's try to make it simple. And I don't mind taking a commercial flight."

"I'll check it out."

However, the next day all hell broke out in our little resort town. Ed called a little after noon to say there had been a shooting at the high school. "Go and pick up JP immediately," he said in his professional authoritative voice. "I'm instructing all the schools in the area to shelter in place and close as soon as possible in case there are more shooters out there."

I put my laptop away and turned on the local news channel. "Breaking News" flashed across the screen. It was Maria's day off, so I drove over to pick up JP. Other parents had already received the message, and Mrs. Kurtz, the office secretary said that on the sheriff's advice they would close the facility as soon as all the children had been picked up.

I had left the television on, and the local news channels were already on the spot. Pictures showed firefighters and law enforcement officers from San Bernardino who had come up to assist the local first responders. One firefighter who was interviewed said that he had never seen so many firetrucks and cop cars in one place.

One of the teachers, a former Marine and the football coach who also taught English part-time, had thrown a ball at the lone shooter and tackled him. He kept a basketball at his desk, he said, and threw it to students whose turn it was to answer a question. He had been shot in the arm and shoulder but was not in critical condition. He was being treated at the local hospital. If it hadn't been for his heroic action, the reporter said, it could have been much worse.

Two students had been killed, one a female who reportedly had been the love interest of the seventeen-year-old shooter, which was cited as a possible motive. Apparently, he had been scorned. Visibly shaken survivors also said that the shooter, the son of Eastern European immigrants, had been bullied. The shooter's name was not released because of his age.

Several students were injured and had been taken to the bigger hospital down the hill in Colton. Ed made a brief statement and praised all the first responders for their quick response and valor. I thought he carried himself well. His hands would be full all day, and, no doubt all hands were on deck at the station, but I knew they were well prepared. No one seemed surprised. It was no longer a question of *if* something like this would happen but *when*, although most people may not have expected a school shooting during the summer break. However, many students, maybe most, took summer school up here.

I emailed James with the names of the victims and also the name of the coach as he might know some of them, and he would certainly know the coach. Because of the time difference, he wouldn't receive the news until the next day.

Ed came by late in the day and flung himself down on the couch. Although he must have been shaken, he didn't show it. JP came and climbed onto his lap, and that brought a smile to his face. How wonderful kids are in stressful situations, I thought.

Ed didn't provide any more details than what I had heard and seen on television, except that he knew the coach and the parents of all the victims.

"I saw it all on TV…and you too," I said. "And you handled yourself well."

"Thank you. We knew that it would happen here too, but perhaps not at the height of summer," Ed said reflectively. "The kid was carrying his father's shotgun and a pistol. It could have been worse. Coach Gary is a hero."

I agreed and looked at him.

"We can't track every kid who's been rejected by his girlfriend," he said solemnly.

I watched him quietly for a few moments. "I'll heat up some leftovers so you can have something to eat," I said and walked into the kitchen. He followed.

"Okay, thank you. Then I'll go down to the hospital and see the injured kids and their parents. After that comes the terrible task of trying to comfort the grieving parents of the children who were killed. As you know, it's a parent's worst nightmare. I'll stop by the hospital to see Coach Gary too."

"Is there anything I can do?" I asked softly.

"No. You take care of your son and yourself. Later we'll all go to the memorial services. That's gonna be a tough one, but the whole community will be out in support."

"I'm sorry, Ed. I never realized how tough a police officer's job can be." I paused. "Thank God, it was a homegrown shooter and not an international terrorist group. I know it doesn't make any difference to the bereaved parents, but can you imagine the rage around here if this had been in any way related to ISIS or the so-called Islamist state?"

Ed just sat there motionless.

"I can see why you want to retire early and become an educator," I said. "You'll be a terrific teacher."

"Thank you," he said quietly.

We ate the rest of the spaghetti sauce and pasta, and JP made such a royal mess that we both had to smile, at least a little. Then Ed rose and gave both JP and me warm hugs.

"Don't get yourself involved in anything," he said seriously. And then he left.

It's strange how everything works out, I thought. The shooting overshadowed every other news item in our resort town. The search of the pale yellow house received no news coverage, just a small notice next to other drug busts listed in the local paper's Sheriff's Log. No mention of who the occupants of the pale yellow house were, and no mention of where the drugs were discovered. The hiding place in the underground tunnel was no more spectacular than other places where bags of heroin had been found. According to the Log, several bags had also turned up in furniture stored in a U-Haul truck. Two nightstands and a dresser were stuffed with illicit drugs with street values in the millions. What a shame that dealers refused to use their creativity for more productive pursuits!

As usual, politicians constantly appeared on television with their empty rhetoric. Even the president made an appearance with a few platitudes. I did not see much of Ed, and thankfully no reports appeared to criticize him or his deputies for failing to foil the attack altogether. People seemed to realize that there's simply no defense against lone wolves who are bent on causing havoc.

After I had digested it all, I emailed James, and he emailed me back the next day. He knew most of the victims, although they were not close friends. He said he would email Coach Gary and wish him a speedy recovery. From his email it seemed that the school shooting had received just as much coverage in Europe as it had received in the United States, and he said people in Oslo wondered what we were doing over here with all kinds of people running around with guns. Of course, people around the world do not understand the gun culture we live in here, I thought. The Wild West is still with us.

One day I spent looking into booking a small jet for late August and learned that for eight people it would not cost that much more than flying first class on a commercial plane. We could fly out of San Bernardino International Airport, only half an hour down the highway, which was now set up for international travel with customs and immigration. SBI has convenient parking and very little traffic. An agent would meet us at the entrance there and take us to the gate, and we wouldn't have to be there more than fifteen minutes before departure. The Gulfstream jet would probably stop in Bangor, Maine, or some place on the East Coast to refuel, the sales representative informed me, and we had a choice of airports around London if that was our destination. In France, we would fly into Le Bourget Airport near Paris, where another agent would meet us and take us to our hotel. It would be so much more convenient.

"When is the latest we can book the plane for late August?" I asked.

"Just a few days or a week ahead of departure, so not to worry," the representative replied.

James emailed me to say that after the summer course was over, he and a couple of American friends were planning to take a train down to Copenhagen, through Germany, the Netherlands, and Belgium to Paris, and so we decided to meet up in Paris.

And how would you like to take another train through the Chunnel to London and sign up for the fall semester at a small college located in a gorgeous park in that city? If I can persuade Thomas's parents, Thomas could also come with us. How's that? I wrote.

James was all for it but seriously doubted Thomas would want to come, and that was okay. However, when I called Thomas and he handed the phone to his parents, they were all really excited. Daniel, Thomas's father, was a local businessman who owned a couple of buildings in our resort town and ran a clothing and shoe store.

Both he and his wife, Linda, came over the next day to discuss the details. He was reportedly a veteran and like most ex-military men up here had short military-style hair. As usual he was neatly dressed, but today his pale eyes looked weary.

"I guess it will be expensive," he said thoughtfully. "But so is going to college here."

"If we leave seven or eight people, we'll charter a private jet out of San Bernardino Airport. Otherwise we'll take Air France or another commercial airline. You could pay for Thomas's airfare and tuition, room and board at the school in London. We'll take care of the hotel in Paris where we'll meet James, if the two boys are okay with sharing a room."

Thomas's mother, Linda, a plain woman of medium height with light brown hair and deep-set dark brown eyes, was so excited that she gave me a big hug. "I know it's a big responsibility," she conceded. "But you're a teacher and know what to do. I always wish I had gotten out more before I married and settled down."

"Thomas is a good boy," I said reassuringly. "And it will be good for him to get away. The world has changed. People today seldom continue to live in the same place they were born." We left it at that. "I'll be in touch," I said as I walked them out to their car.

35

AFTERMATH

The high school shooting and its aftermath took a toll on our small community. It felt as if a pall had been draped over the entire mountain. Nearly everyone knew the coach and at least one of the victims. The injured were soon released from the hospital, and all recovered physically, although some might be mentally scarred for life. But most young people are remarkably resilient. The whole community attended both funerals, and the services were heart-wrenching. I'm sure everyone thought about their own children and wondered how and why they had been spared.

Even Vee appeared more subdued. For both occasions, she wore nondescript beige outfits. Her face was pale, and her usually flaming red hair appeared less fiery. Her teenage daughter had known the victims, the deceased as well as the injured. One mother whom I barely knew came up to me and threw her arms around my neck and would not let me go. I had no idea what to say, so I just stood there, holding her and letting her cry.

"I can't bear it," she kept repeating. "My son. I feel I'm going to faint."

I thought she might be suffering from shock. Eventually I took her arm and led her over to a chair and sat her down. I just stood by her side and held her hand. She told me she had lost her son. She was the mother of the second victim and a friend of the shooter's love interest.

Ed was everywhere and paid little attention to anyone other than those who had suffered losses. The principal spoke movingly about the deceased children and praised the heroic coach and his quick thinking.

In the days following the funerals, many students protested in front of the school in solidarity with students at other schools that had experienced senseless violence and loss. However, there was little mention of stricter gun control. This was gun country, and most were vocal supporters of the Second Amendment. I had often reminded my young college students to also focus on the opening phrase of the Second Amendment: "A well-regulated militia being necessary to the security of a free state…" and not only the last part of the sentence, "…the right to keep and bear arms shall not be infringed." It would be hard to form a militia that could go up against the US Airforce, even with military-style assault weapons. Of course, such talk fell on deaf ears up here.

I seemed to have become numb to death and all the grieving. In fact, I was reluctant to go out because I didn't know what to say to people. I had experienced loss as well. I was in shock after news reached me that Robert had been killed in Africa. Then Elizabeth, Ed's wife and James's mother, passed away, and finally there was Chris's accident followed by his death. However, I also knew that staying away was worse for the inconsolable parents, so I went out of my way to seek them out to see if there was anything I could do.

As the weeks went by, however, people started to return to their daily routines. "The dead are soon forgotten," as Norwegian playwright Henrik Ibsen said in one of his plays that I used to teach in my literature classes. My teaching career suddenly seemed so long ago. Soon I would probably have to think about returning to work, or perhaps I'd complete my degree first.

Ed seemed a little more distant, although he came by often and sometimes spent the night.

"James's summer course is almost over, Ed," I said casually one afternoon in early August. I was standing by the door to the kitchen, and Ed was sitting on the couch. I looked at him searchingly. He had lost weight, his face was paler, and his eyes had lost some of their glitter.

He looked up at me. "I guess so," he said quietly. "But I don't think he's ready to come home yet."

"He and a couple of friends are planning to take a train trip down to Copenhagen and from there through Germany, the Netherlands, and Belgium to France. Do you still want to go over to Europe to meet him there?"

"Yeah, that sounds like a good idea," he said a little doubtfully. "When?"

"Soon." I went over to the couch and sat down next to him. He put his arm around my shoulder. "I've looked into hiring a private plane and leaving from San Bernardino Airport. It's really convenient, and if we fly with seven or eight people, it's no more expensive than traveling first class on a commercial flight."

"Really?" he said slowly with an air of surprise.

"Really. We'll stop in Bangor, Maine, or another airport on the East Coast to refuel and then fly through the night directly into Le Bourget, an airport near Paris. A representative from the charter company will meet us there and take us to our hotel." I paused. "What do you think?"

"Who would come with us?"

"Joe and Sandy, Maria and JP. And then Thomas, and maybe even Cheryl and Jonathan."

"That's quite a crowd."

"Well, maybe not Cheryl and Jonathan." I looked at him. His brows were drawn together. "Let's try to wipe that gloom off your face." I pinched his cheek. "Or, if it's just you and me and Thomas, we could take a nonstop flight out of LAX. Maybe fly business class on Air France or another airline."

"That sounds good. I think I prefer the second option. Maria could take care of JP for a week, and Joe and Sandy would be available in case of an emergency."

"Yes, that would work. You'll have to leave your guns at home. Bringing guns into France would be too much of a hassle."

"I know, and that's okay."

"The question then is, can you take a week off, maybe toward the end of August?"

"I think so." His voice sounded weary.

"You don't sound too enthusiastic," I said accusingly.

"I am. It's just that I'm tired and need a good night's sleep. I have good people who can take over, and they'll not begrudge me some time off with my girlfriend." He looked at me with a faint grin.

"Girlfriend?"

"Well, aren't you my girlfriend?"

"I'd like to be." I smiled and gave him a hug and a kiss on the cheek.

He pulled me close and kissed me more seriously.

"I have an idea," I said cheerfully. "Why don't you call the station and tell them that you won't be back tonight. When Maria brings JP back, I'll make something for dinner. And afterwards I'll put JP to bed. Then you and I can go to sleep in each other's arms." I laughed at my imagined scenario, and Ed started laughing too.

"And will you tell me some more stories from *Arabian Nights*? What was the name of that princess again?" he said teasingly.

"Scheherazade."

He called the station. Then we both worked in the kitchen to put together a creative casserole of random leftovers in the fridge. Everything was ready when Maria returned with JP, and we all sat down to dinner. Maria took the rest of our creative dish home as I didn't want to have leftovers of leftovers. After JP went to sleep, Ed and I also went to bed, and instead of telling stories from Arabia, I talked about Paris and all its romantic spots, how we would walk hand-in-hand and listen to nimble Parisian accordion players in their black berets and mustaches while bicyclists passed by with baguettes strapped to their backs until his eyes closed and I heard heavy breathing.

36

PARIS

We pulled into the long-term parking lot at Los Angeles Airport in the afternoon, more than three hours before departure. Ed drove. Thomas's parents had brought their son over to my house, and we all left from there.

Getting through LAX was less of a hassle than I had expected. Since we were early, we passed through security quickly and had time for Starbucks special drinks before takeoff. Ed and I had premium tickets and were allowed to board early, but we waited for Thomas whose seat was at the front of the economy section.

Soon we were on our way, and because we were traveling against time, it turned dark quickly, and after drinks, meals, movies, and sleep we landed at Charles de Gaulle Airport near Paris. I had ordered a car to pick us up to take us to the hotel, and we were met by a jovial French driver, looking every bit the part in a chauffeur's hat and a black mustache.

"Welcome to France," he said in English as he helped us with our luggage. "I have a limousine waiting outside. To the Monna Lisa, right? Near Champs Élysées?"

"That's right," I said as we followed him out to the street. Less than an hour later we arrived at an old but elegant hotel with ornate, paneled walls and 18th century furniture.

"It's different from the hotel chains back home," I said. "But I thought it would be more interesting. The location is great, and breakfast is included. What do you think, Thomas?"

"It's awesome, Mrs. Cronin."

"Megan," I said. "You and James will share one of the rooms," I said as we followed the porter upstairs and waited as he opened the doors to our two rooms. "How do you think you'll like it?"

"Thank you, Mrs....I mean Megan."

Our two hotel rooms were adjacent. Thomas took his suitcase and tested the bed in the one closest to the stairs. Each room had two big beds with headboards in shiny dark wood. A large ornate dresser occupied one wall. On the other walls were prints of French landscapes. I went into the other room and sat down in one of the Queen Anne-style armchairs by the window and looked out at a busy tree-lined street below.

I looked at Ed who had followed me. "I guess you and I will share this room, Ed," I said.

Ed smiled. "I guess you have it all arranged," he said indulgently and sat down on the bed near the door.

"I thought you'd want to sleep with your 'girlfriend'...in Paris of all places."

"No objection there," he said.

"Since we rested on the plane, and if you're not overly tired, may I suggest a walk up to L'Arc de Triomphe, only a short distance up the famous avenue of Champs Élysées," I said.

Once Ed agreed, I went into Thomas's room to invite him to come along as well.

The temperature was perfect but traffic was horrendous, with a cacophony of screeching brakes, honking horns, and taxi drivers hollering out of their windows. With our sensible sports shoes and I with my fanny pack, we were screaming "tourists," of course, but that was, after all, what we were. The Parisians wore dress shoes, the women high heels, and both men and women carried some kind of a handbag.

"This is one city where I would not recommend driving," I said to Thomas. "It's fortunate that the sidewalks are so nice and wide. Otherwise, it wouldn't even be safe to walk around here."

To reach the monument, we had to go through an underpass, which brought us directly to the ticket booth.

"We can take the *ascenseur* or climb the steps to the top," I said.

Ed decided on the elevator, while Thomas and I climbed the stairs.

"Wow!" Ed exclaimed as he stepped onto the roomy terrace on top of the monument. "What a great panoramic view of the city. It's stunning."

"Yes," I agreed. "And see how the streets branch out in all directions like a star. That's why it was originally called Place de l'Étoile, which means star. Now it has been renamed Place Charles de Gaulle." I pointed over to the right. "There is the Eiffel Tower. We'll walk over there tomorrow."

I took out my phone to take pictures and emailed a couple to James with directions on how to get to our hotel.

"This place is even more diverse than Los Angeles," Ed commented as he looked around at the people. "And what's with all these Japanese? It's a wonder there are any Japanese left in Japan."

I smiled. "Yes, they truly are traveling people. And they spend lots of money wherever they go."

"Amazing!" Ed exclaimed as we looked over the wall down on Champs Élysées, which stretched all the way down to the famous Louvre Museum. I don't think I had seen Ed this enthusiastic for quite a while.

"What do you think, Thomas?" I said as Thomas passed us, snapping pictures in all directions.

"It's awesome," he said. "Thank you for taking me, Mrs. Cronin... sorry, Megan."

"I first came here with Robert what now seems like a very long time ago," I said to Ed. "What impressed him the most was that after one of the wars, I think it was World War I, someone flew a bi-plane right through the Arc."

"Well, that was quite a feat, wasn't it?" Ed said and put his arm around me.

"What's your favorite, then?"

"I'm probably most impressed by the view and beautiful sculptures of mythical figures that decorate all the walls and archways."

"You and Elizabeth didn't take much time off to travel, did you?" I said.

"No, there didn't seem to be time, but I'd like to make up for it now. How about going to Ireland and Italy someday? As you probably know, Cronin is an Irish name, but my mother's family came from Italy."

"Yes, I'd love to go there with you," I said encouragingly.

He pulled me a little closer but remained quiet.

On the way back to the hotel we stopped at a little corner restaurant.

"May I recommend an omelette as something typically French?" I suggested. "It's also light and easier to digest since our meal schedule is out of whack because of the change in time."

Ed and Thomas both agreed, and here I was able to show off my French and was duly praised. Otherwise, people spoke perfect English everywhere.

We were only a short distance from the hotel but decided to walk through the shopping area among a myriad of women from the Arabian Peninsula, dressed in their black *abayas* and veils.

"This ranks among the most exclusive shopping districts in the world," I said to no one in particular. "Aren't the window displays magnificent?"

"The prices are sure high," Ed mumbled with a frown as he looked at some exquisite jewelry.

"Don't worry, Ed," I said reassuringly. "I don't need any of this. I have all the jewelry I want."

But he kept looking, trying to make quick conversions from Euros to dollars.

James had just arrived when we returned to the hotel. The two boys greeted each other a little awkwardly.

Ed was not in the habit of showing emotions, but he momentarily lost his composure when he saw James. "I think you've grown taller. You look different," he said a little unsteadily as he embraced him.

"Where are your friends?" I asked after I, too, had embraced him.

"They're going on to Provence and the Mediterranean," he said nonchalantly.

"Are you hungry?"

"No, I just ate with the guys before they left."

"We should go to bed early then."

Both Ed and the boys agreed. James did not look surprised that Ed and I shared a bedroom. Or at least he didn't show it. I hadn't wanted to tell him about his father's and my relationship until he was well ensconced at the school in London. But our relationship may have been apparent to him anyway. He may even have found it to be a natural progression. After all, I was part of the family.

"I hope you don't mind my bossing everyone around, Ed," I said when we were alone in our room. "I know you're used to taking control, but this is my old stomping ground."

"I know, and I love it, Megan. You could always get a job as a tour operator if times get tough."

A FINAL QUESTION UNDER THE LINDEN TREE

In the next few days, we trudged through the Louvre, the Georges Pompidou Centre, and the Musée d'Orsay, but when we arrived at the ancient cathedral of Notre Dame, it was closed. A crowd had gathered outside, and several small Peugeot police cars were parked over to the side.

"*Qu'est-ce qui s'est passé?*" I asked an officer, and he told me that someone had been killed inside in the sanctuary.

Ed perked up when I told him.

"Ed," I said sternly. "We're on vacation, and we are in France. The French police are perfectly capable of handling their own affairs."

Ed didn't say anything but looked at me and nodded in agreement.

I told James and Thomas to stand back, which they already did.

One woman had bared her breasts and was screaming, while two officers led a man to one of their cars. Two other officers tried to restrain the screaming woman by throwing a blanket over her, hiding her nakedness. They eventually led her away as well.

"I bet they put on that show so you'd feel right at home, Ed," I said jokingly.

"Megan, you just said that someone had been killed. That's no laughing matter, honey."

"You're right, and I'm sorry," I said apologetically.

"But I have to say the officers handled it well. Everything calm. No shots fired. The killer must not have been armed."

"People don't run around with guns around here, Ed."

"I'm aware of that, and as you know, I am for common sense gun control at home too."

In a few minutes, the crowd dispersed. The massive doors to the church opened, and we were able to admire the Gothic architecture, the beautiful stained-glass windows, and the priceless artwork everywhere.

"It's bigger than I thought," Ed commented as we made our way outside again. "And to think this was built over 800 years ago by hand, brick by brick, without power tools and other modern equipment. All the carved biblical figures everywhere are amazing."

"And people still go to church here."

I turned to James and Thomas. "Maybe you guys want to check out the girls," I suggested. "You can't get lost if you stay close to the river."

"That's the river Seine, right Megan?" Thomas said.

"Yes, that's right," I said.

Ed gave them some money, and they were off.

"What do you want to do, Ed?" I said. "Are you tired?"

"No," he said definitively. "How about a walk along the river too?"

"Good idea. Let's buy a couple of crepes from a street vendor and watch the riverboat traffic."

We ate our crepes standing up. Then we found a bench in a cozy grove of linden trees from where we could watch the boats and barges. Because of the drought, the leaves were already red and gold and starting to fall, decorating the ground in autumn colors. A French accordion player, a short man in a black beret, came out from the shadows and started to sing and play for us.

"*Oh, je voudrais tant que tu te souviennes…*" he sang as his accordion wailed the tune "Autumn Leaves."

Ed took my hand and looked at me. His eyes had regained their glitter.

"This is a great trip, Megan, and this is a beautiful spot." He kissed me on the cheek. "But, of course, not as beautiful as the woman sitting beside me."

"Oh, Ed, come on," I said and laughed. "But truly, the French know how to create inspiring spots for lovers, don't they?"

"They sure do." He took a moment before continuing. "And now I want to ask you a question. I've thought about it for a long time, but this seems to be the perfect moment."

My eyebrows went up, and I looked at him. "What's on your mind?"

"Do you want to marry me?" he said simply.

My jaw dropped, and I remained speechless for a few moments.

"You're full of surprises, Ed," I said truthfully. "You've never really said you loved me."

The accordion player had come closer and started to sing the song in English with a most charming French accent. "The falling leaves drift by my window…"

"Well, what's your answer?" Ed said.

"Yes, Ed. I want to marry you. You just took me by surprise. I thought you said I was too independent."

"I can handle that, and I do love you. I didn't think I'd ever say that again after I lost Elizabeth. But there you are." He cleared his throat. "But I wanted to make sure, and now I am sure. Do you think you can put up with me?"

"I don't know, but I'll give it a try," I said teasingly.

"Oh, you squarehead you," he said and pursed his lips as he pinched my cheek.

"But maybe we should keep our engagement under the hat for now," I said cautiously.

"What for?"

"It might be better for James to hear about it when he returns from London in December. I have it all arranged, for both him and Thomas as I told you. I thought we'd take them there by train the day after tomorrow. School has just started, but the admissions officer said she'd hold a room for them. They can add classes the first week of school with no problem."

The accordion player now stood right in front of us, singing and playing and probably hoping for a good tip. Ed gave him a wad of Euros, probably unaware how much it was.

"*Merci et félicitation*," he said and bowed gallantly, removing his beret. Then he sauntered jauntily over to another couple. We watched him and laughed. We rose and ambled hand in hand up toward the museum again.

"I didn't buy you a ring yet, but we could pick one out together at one of the jewelers near our hotel if you want."

"That would be awesome, Ed, but I'm okay with waiting too."

We walked on in silence.

"I thought Elizabeth's ring should go to James when he finds the right girl. Don't you think?"

"Yes."

"You seem distant. Do you have second thoughts already?"

"No, of course not. I'm just overwhelmed. I knew you wanted a 'girlfriend.' I didn't know you wanted a wife."

"But I do."

I looked up at him and smiled. Then we walked more briskly to one of the jewelers we had seen on our first day. I had no problem picking out a diamond solitaire with smaller diamonds artistically arranged around it. Ed took it from the sales clerk and put it on my right ring finger since I still wore Chris's ruby ring on my left hand. Then, he kissed me long and passionately to the applause and shouts of *félicitations* from everyone in the store.

The next day I made reservations on the Eurostar, the high-speed train that goes through the Chunnel from Gare du Nord in Paris to St. Pancreas in London. I called my friend Caroline to see if she could meet us for lunch.

"So, you're still in Paris then?" she asked.

"Yes. We'll take the early morning train from Paris tomorrow and go straight to the school."

"Splendid. How about lunch at the Wallace Collection at 2 o'clock? That's just a short walk from the college. Maybe your nephew and his friend would like to see the old armor, shield, and weapons collection."

"Wonderful. And I'll be bringing a new beau."

"What? Already a new one?"

"Well, it's Chris's brother, the sheriff of our town who I told you about."

"Oh, yes, I remember, and that's brilliant, although I've hardly had time to get used to you with Chris. What's the brother's name again? I forgot."

"Ed. And he's a really nice guy too. You'll like him."

"Oh, I'm sure I will, but I miss Robert and deep down you probably still do too."

"Yes, of course. But I'm very glad to have had Chris and also my son naturally. Life goes on as you know. Ed has been a wonderful help in this terrible time too."

"Yes, and I'm so sorry, Megan. Ed sounds great. Being a sheriff and all, he may be more stable, not such a risk taker as Robert was…and Chris too, right?"

"Yes, you are spot on about that."

Static on the line interrupted our conversation for a few moments before Caroline could continue. "Richard is going to a meeting at the Temple Church again tomorrow but he should be able to join us too. We're really spending the fall in the country, but luckily, we're in town this week. We'd both love to see you. We'd love to meet Ed, of course, and also to talk about the good old days."

"Okay, we'll catch up then."

We left for London on our last day in Paris. The trip took just a little over two hours.

"We'll hop on a double-decker bus that takes us straight to Regent's Park," I said.

"So you really want to stay here a whole semester, then," Ed said to James and Thomas.

"Yes, Dad," James said with a sigh.

"But then it's on to USC to do some serious studying, James."

"Why USC?"

"Well, not necessarily USC, but a serious university and some serious studying, so you can get a job someday."

"Okay, Dad," he replied with another demonstrative sigh, and we walked up toward the old school, Ed and I pulling the biggest suitcases and the two boys the lighter ones.

"It's just like an ivy-league school," Thomas exclaimed with excitement as soon as he saw the ivy-covered brick buildings of the college.

They both skipped along.

"Yes," I thought. "It is definitely a good idea for these two boys to take a year off before starting more serious studies."

The woman at the front desk of the admissions office, an efficient-looking woman of about forty, with very short brown hair, rimless glasses, and uneven teeth, remembered me from our phone conversations and was expecting us.

"David, darling, can you show these new students from California the campus and take them to their room, please?" she said in the Queen's best English.

David, a young man of about twenty with black, bushy hair and a friendly smile, was introduced as a student worker from Israel. He showed us around and got James and Thomas situated in the dorm.

It was a little after one o'clock when we arrived at the Wallace Museum.

"It's a good thing admission is free," I commented laughingly. "We've already spent a bundle on this trip."

A guide took us downstairs to see the weapons and armor collection before we went upstairs to admire the art exhibit. We were just about museum-ed out, however, and soon made our way to the restaurant, where Caroline and Richard were waiting for us.

Caroline looked as cool and elegant as ever in a blue shirt-dress that matched her beautiful eyes, the focal point of her delicate face. Richard looked the same as always—tall, thin, and formal in a gray suit and tie.

I introduced Ed as my new partner, and he and Richard seemed to hit it off. Caroline looked approvingly at Ed.

Then I introduced James and Thomas, who shook hands with both Caroline and Richard before they sat down at a small table next to us.

"Where's the little one?" Caroline asked.

"At home in California with his nanny and grandfather. We're going right back to Paris on the evening train, and tomorrow we have to get ready to return to California. But I really wanted to say hello. I can't imagine coming to London without seeing you."

"Yes, I would have wondered if you hadn't at least called. We'll keep an eye on your nephew while he's here. Did you give him my number?"

"Not yet, but I will."

"His last name is Cronin as well, I presume."

"Yes, James Cronin. Thomas will be his roommate. He's from our town, but I hope they'll make lots of other friends."

"Brilliant. I'm sure they will."

As usual we reminisced about Africa and the people we knew out there.

A little later, we had to leave our friends to walk James and Thomas back to the school. Ed was unusually quiet and kept clearing his throat. He was struggling to say good-bye to his son, but James and Thomas were hurrying ahead, paying little attention to us.

"It will be just a little over three months until he's back, Ed. And now you'll have me to take care of, remember?" I held up my right hand with my new sparkling ring. He put his arm around my shoulder and gave me a hug.

"We'll have a lot to do," I said, "preparing for a spring wedding, maybe a big wedding even. I never had one before. The town sheriff getting married is a big deal in a small town. We should invite everybody. James will be happy when we finally tell him, but I don't think we should take his attention away from school right now. Actually, he's old enough to be your best man. Susie will be my maid of honor. Caroline and Richard will come over from London. It'll be a lot of fun."

"How about we keep it simple? I hear they do some great weddings in Las Vegas. Quick and painless. Then we could invite everyone for a party afterwards. I already went through a big wedding, and from what I remember, it wasn't that great."

I looked at him and smiled. I realized we still had some negotiating to do.

"Stay out of trouble, Son," were Ed's only words to James as he embraced him before he walked into the venerable building. "And take care of each other," he said to Thomas as he shook Thomas's hand. "We'll see you both in December."

We took a taxi back to the train station.

"Tomorrow we'll leave this whirlwind adventure behind," Ed said with a sigh as we sat in our comfortable seats.

"And may we find all well when we return," I said poetically.

"What kind of gloomy statement is that?" Ed complained.

"I just paraphrased a line from a story by Nathaniel Hawthorne," I said.

As the highspeed Eurostar pulled out of the station, we leaned back and fell asleep.

THE END

———

Don't miss out on your next favorite book!

Join the Satin Romance mailing list
www.satinromance.com/mail.html

THANK YOU FOR READING

———

Did you enjoy this book?

We invite you to leave a review at your favorite book site, such as Goodreads, Amazon, Barnes & Noble, etc.

DID YOU KNOW THAT LEAVING A REVIEW…

- Helps other readers find books they may enjoy.
- Gives you a chance to let your voice be heard.
- Gives authors recognition for their hard work.
- Doesn't have to be long. A sentence or two about why you liked the book will do.

ACKNOWLEDGMENTS

I wish to thank colleagues and friends who have encouraged me, made suggestions, and checked facts during the process of writing this novel. I would especially like to thank Dr. Montague Blundon III, MD, Joan Cashion, Dr. Duncan Earle, Dana Graham, Sharon Johnson, Antoinette and John Lane, Dr. Greg Levonian, Matthew Nadelson, Bruce Schwartz, and Dr. Charles Spurgeon.

ABOUT THE AUTHOR

Kari Sayers graduated from California State University, Long Beach, with a BA in English and an MA in linguistics. She went on two tours with her husband to Saudi Arabia, where she first worked as a music teacher at Riyadh International Community School and then as a journalist for an English newspaper over there, writing under censorship. After returning to the States, she taught ESL (English as a Second Language) at various colleges in the Los Angeles area and finally composition and literature at Marymount California University while also freelancing as a theater, concert and opera reviewer for local newspapers and magazines. She has traveled in 70 foreign countries and 40 states in the United States, including Alaska, Hawaii, and Puerto Rico. She has three grown children and three young grandchildren and lives in Los Angeles with her cat.

https://kari-sayers.com/author/karihsayers/

ALSO BY KARI H. SAYERS

AVAILABLE FROM SATIN ROMANCE

Roses Where Thorns Grow